Cat Dragons

JoAnn Parsley

2025, TWB Press
https://www.twbpress.com

CatDragons – Book 3 – The Hafling Saga
Copyright © 2025 by JoAnn Parsley

Edited by Terry Wright

Cover Art by Terry Wright

ISBN: 978-1-959768-79-1

Dedication

"To all the cats who indulge the humans in their kingdoms."

PART ONE

The Kingdom

CHAPTER 1

The Hafling stared at the Faerie. Due to his stay in Halvarrarde, he had seen as many of the faeries in the garden, between the Healer's Hall and the Scribe's Library, as there were bees among the flowers. Some faeries were small enough to ride the bees, the dragonflies, and the butterflies, which also visited the garden. Considering his size and theirs, he had little to do with them, save idly watching for a moment.

Besides, he was not considered a Magical. Faeries were Magicals. As were Humans with magical abilities like the Sorceress he lived with and loved. And who loved him, despite his being considered a mistake: part human, part hillcat.

An over-grown, golden-furred mistake. Yet, a Badged Ranger with a green tunic that said he had already spent many years walking the roads of the Kingdom. While a broad-shouldered and lithe body in that tunic said that he worked chopping firewood, hunting, whatever was to hand, until he stopped, usually to over-winter or to aid the villagers.

However, the Faerie who faced him now was barely four-foot tall and hovered at his eye-level on delicate translucent wings. She wore a pastel blue gown, pearl shoes, and a glittering band in her long purple hair. Folding her wings down her back, she settled to the wooden porch. "Hello, Harrel. The Wizard wants you at the Keep." Her flawless yellow-green complexion beamed.

By this time, the Sorceress had joined Harrel at the door. "Both of us," Vallezza said. "Right?" She was as dark as Harrel was light. Black hair with blue highlights. Beautiful, to some. To others, she was a Magical to be avoided. The Wizards had said she had no real magic, meaning she had a natural magic, not learned in their Halls, their books, their lectures and apprenticeships. Worse, she smiled. Laughed. And teased the Ranger who, being half hillcat, had only a cat's sense of humor.

He had yet to learn, too, that being enspelled by a Sorceress meant that her magic engulfed him as well as herself. He would live many extra years because of her healing magic.

"Only him," the Faerie replied. "The Ranger."

"And the Sorceress. Or neither."

Now the Faerie stared at the Hafling. "The Wizard's problem. Not mine. Come along."

"Come along? It'll take months to get there. Boats. Horses. Hiking. Climbing. Unless the Wizard can cast a Transport Spell, which no wizard can."

"He wants The Ranger at the Keep. Today." The Faerie managed to be smug. "Packs. Cloaks. Heavy. It's still cold at the Keep. And sword."

Harrel sighed at that last. He drilled every day with his newest sword, sometimes with the King's Guards, but he did not like to wear a sword. Or actually use it. He only had both a pack and a cloak ready because they were new. Like most Rangers, he had lost the old ones.

Val had the same packs, both ready. He left her and the Faerie in the doorway to fetch the packs. And a supply of journey cakes for his belt pouch. Those he would need long after he lost the sword.

Both of them faced the impatient Faerie. Faeries were notorious for sparking when they became impatient or annoyed, and they could leave burn marks or holes in just about anything, including people."

"Come along." She lifted her wings.

"To where?" the Sorceress asked.

The Ranger kept quiet. He had spent many seasons waiting for instructions and kept the habit.

"Step off," she said and stepped off the porch, into the air...and vanished.

"I wonder if that opening has been there all along," the Sorceress grumbled. She stared at the spot, and reaching back, took Harrel's hand in hers. "Well... Here goes..."

***

It was like walking through dry water. Both of them could feel an edge, then something of an all-over tingling, and the Sorceress fell through to the other side. Harrel was more balanced, on guard, although his hands were full.

He immediately dropped the pack and Val's hand, snarling. The room—he knew he was in a room—was full of people, but he saw only one: a Barbarian.

Not quite as dark, hairy and red streaked as before, but a Barbarian nonetheless. And in armor with one hand on a sword. Harrel touched his own and bared his fangs.

"Hold," a voice ordered, and both men froze. Totally unable to move, not from obedience but enspelled.

Harrel could still growl. The Barbarian matched him.

"Songlest, you must learn how to warn people..." the Wizard began, only to end with a shrug.

A Faerie did whatever it chose, no matter what size or how willing and able it was to be a messenger. This one could sense the magical transporting doors and went, instantly, from place to place. It was too much to ask she be pleasant or warn others where they were going and who they were to meet.

"Hands off the swords, sirs. You are in no danger." An old man, a traditional-looking Wizard, stepped between them. "Ah, M'Lady. Good of you to join us."

"Andruss." Vallezza acknowledged the Wizard. She raised a

hand, and smiling, wiggled fingers as if unknotting them.

Harrel moved, freed from the Hold Spell. The Barbarian did the same. The two no longer glared, suspicious of each other, yet they were on guard.

Now that he could see the entire room, Harrel was no more at ease. It was a large stone room with a very open window on one side to view forest-covered mountains, green-shaded with new spring growth. A narrow valley and a Road led into more distant mountains and forests.

The rest of the room, not open to the beginnings of a stone stairwell, was covered with things. Candles. Holders. Jars small and large. Small skeletons that moved on their own. Goblets. Boxes. Wooden and stone. And in the remains of a tree: an owl. Large. With what looked like ears above his wide-open gold-rimmed eyes.

A very large and carved wooden table dominated the center, along with book-filled chairs. Some almost plain. Others suited to a throne room.

And, of course, a large stone fireplace with kettles hanging over a low fire. Logs and pine cones burned in a controlled manner. On the mantle, looking back at him, sat the largest tabby cat he had ever seen. It blinked, slowly. Harrel returned the greeting with his own blue eyes before looking at the others. Especially the Barbarian.

A second glance and he looked less like his kin. The same size as Harrel but shorn. Or mayhap the stripes above his ears were meant to conceal the shaved marking instead of highlighting them.

Most reassuring of all was the ordinary leather and worked iron of a common guardsman's armor. Plus, on his left breast: a Badge. Dark blue so he was badged to a Magical, but with a flower or, more likely, a silver snowflake in the center. Harrel's own badge was an easily recognized green tree on a field of blue surmounted by the gold sword of justice: A King's Ranger. Hard to say what either a flower or snowflake meant.

He turned away to look at the others. An impatient Lady slapped one gloved hand with a leather-covered stick. Her badge was gold-cloth with, perhaps, a jeweled sun over a stone-wrought white flower. A second Lady was as richly clothed, but her embroidery was merely gold-colored and white. M'Lady and her companion.

The Faerie and two stone-still guards were at the stairwell's opening. The guards were young and therefore given the simple task of guarding an entrance.

Why? Harrel asked himself. He turned his attention to the Wizard. Before he could speak, the Lady began.

"I am, in your rankings, the Lady Orwren. From the far North. Premontii. We're not unknown here in the Kingdom because we're trading partners with a few of your distant villages. And the Northern Horsemen. But mostly with the Northmen. Not usually with those on the Coast. The ones which raid your Northerly sailing boats. But they are kin so, of course, they trade with each other. Of late there has been...something wrong. Our wizards, so to speak, went North. They have not returned, and I doubt that they will. Also, the Trolls are gone."

"Not necessarily a bad thing," the Wizard said.

"Our Trolls are not as...maligned as yours." She was careful with her words, but clearly annoyed. "Our Trolls build bridges. Wondrous. Amazing stone bridges. Over the riffs and chasms where no one else can build such strong and yet beautiful stone bridges. Their best is in Bridgedale. But they're gone. At least it seems so." She paused for a breath. "I am sent here...to the nearest Wizard for help. Magical help, perhaps, but more likely help from your vaunted Rangers. You, Sir. Or so he says."

It was clear from her expression she did not believe a Hafling, Badged Ranger or no, was going to be of much help. Harrel took a moment to at least look like he was thinking. Were he to be honest, he had no idea what he could do to help her. He was not even sure of the problem.

"What Rangers do first," he said, "is go there. On horseback. Or is there one of those *Transporting* doors?" Now he looked at the Faerie.

"None I know of," she answered.

"Then it's horses. One for everyone going and at least two pack animals. Tents, if available. Shelter covers otherwise. Pots. Fire Starters. Fingers are faster. More reliable, but..." He snapped his, and a small flame flickered from one. He went on, dousing the tiny flame. "Fish hooks. Line. Rope." He would have continued with the list, but the Barbarian waved a hand.

"StableMaster has all that. And the pick of the horses. He'll want to know how well everyone can ride. That can be done this afternoon."

The Lady looked warily convinced because of the lists both men were reciting. Without further words or complaints, she and her companion obeyed the Wizard's silent suggestion that they go down the stairs. To the stables. To the Hall for a meal. Even to a bath, the last bath with hot water undoubtedly. Or to a bed.

He did give the Sorceress a knowing smile, expecting that both of them knew the onslaught of words quieted the Lady for only a brief moment. Horses would be next, and again both knew she was not going to expect the shaggy mountain ponies they would take on a long journey.

The Wizard sighed over their loss, however. The wonderfully sturdy and sure-footed "ponies" would be hard to replace. And he would have to listen to the StableMaster's complaints until they were.

CHAPTER 2

The rest of the day and most of the night was, if Lady Orwren was asked, wasted on choosing horses, ponies they were called, and the larger horses Harrel and the Barbarian would ride, and finding supplies. Then pack them. And packing them again on the pack horses, well before the riders were ready to leave.

There was also what seemed a Farewell meal, and by then, the travelers were tired and, for the most part, went to bed. Some slept. Some did not.

However they spent the remainder of the night, they were awake before dawn and dressed. A quick meal, whatever was to hand, and they came down the stairs to a foggy courtyard full of horses, stablelads and noisy dogs.

And one hillcat.

Harrel stopped. Vallezza, behind him on the stairs and pulling on her riding gloves, bumped into his shoulder. She said nothing, knowing his thoughts from one long night when he told her about the one hillcat he had seen, bloody and screaming in pain and fury until the Barbarians had skinned it. He had later sat alone before a fire while the cat's hide burned, wondering how just a piece of amazingly soft fur could enspell him or anyone else who touched it. It had deserved a destroying fire, not to be made into a piece of clothing or hung on a wall.

This hillcat was alive. Winter-thick golden fur covered a well-muscled sleek body while a dark blue harness—not a collar—said this cat was a guard. A powerful, respected and trained guard. One who could stand on hind legs and stare, eyes to eyes, with him.

Sky-blue eyes stared back at Hafling's own blue eyes until they seemed to be the only two in the swirling mists and noise. One very big cat and one very big Hafling. Neither had ever seen the likes of the other.

Harrel knew she was a female who regarded him for a moment. All hillcats could speak. If they cared to do so. This one did not. She flipped her whiskers at him before padding away. Silently.

"She'll scratch herself bare because there are two of us now," a voice said, and the Barbarian came down the stairs.

"Scratch?" Harrel was instantly alert and curious. His hand went to the piece of leather he wore beneath his belt to keep him from scratching himself when magic was near. And usually threatening.

"Like a cat when confronted by a situation that makes her uneasy, she'll scratch herself raw."

"She's coming with us?" Vallezza asked. She was polite and curious. Harrel was still too aware of the cat's gesture to say more than one word. He had often made his own whiskers flip forward and back—dismissively. Insultingly so.

"And not at all happy about it," the man replied. "Slash is one of the Keep's Guard, not some wandering cat. That's what she's called, by the way. Prefers it to how Humans mangle her name. As I do. Mine own is my rank. Captain." His tone was cold, not just polite, and demanding.

"But you *are* a Barbarian."

He paused in thought before answering her. "Was. But to hear M'Sire tell the Tale, the day M'Mother arrived at the Dragon's Keep, he crossed us over the river and left. I remember some of the journey. That was long and tiring. Near to winter when we arrived here."

Vallezza doubted the small family had been welcomed.

"That spring I became an apprentice."

"Yet you still wear *scars*?"

There was a code of politeness to obey, a long trip ahead, and the size and training of the Sorceress's companion to heed. "They are what was intended," he said quietly. "A reminder of who I was and where I came from. But they also remind me of M'Sire. They also remind me of the reasons he left the Keep. No one, he said, was ever going to scar his son again. The Wizard healed the infection, but the scars remain. Along with the knowledge of what M'Sire wanted me to become."

"I'd say he would be proud of you...Captain."

He bowed slightly and went to his horse.

"I've been flipped at by a cat and reminded that I am a maligned Hafling...and just an ordinary Ranger."

"Not a Dragon Rider?" Val teased.

"Hopefully no one knows the words to that *damned* Song," he growled out, and then went after his own horse. Not hers. He was not being disrespectful; he simply knew she was sensible and with enough training to get on a horse and travel without any patronizing help from him.

Harrel took the lead rope for the pack horses. He had spent some time with the StableMaster learning which horses worked well with each other and looking at the Road maps where they would be traveling. During the first day of travel, there were farms, a stopping place for mid-meal, places to walk the horses, and at the end of the day, a well-kept Traveler's Hut and stables. The kitchen provisions would be sufficient for three meals, then they would trade at the fewer farms, find the nut trees that still held a stubborn crop on their branches...or last season's crop uneaten on the ground. After that, Harrel especially, would be expected to hunt, usually for rabbits. Even here, in the higher mountains, there was an abundance of rabbits.

According to the StableMaster's information, the Wizard expected them to stop in a handful of days at the nearby village.

This was in trade for the horses because the Keep had a few problems with the villagers. They had arrived—en masse—several seasons back and were both thriving and discontented. They were convinced that the FaerFolk's rules were prejudiced against them and wanted to 'go home.'

Since no one in the Keep knew where they came from, and the FaerFolk did not care, this was impossible. No one had enough magic to send them 'home.'

Songlest could fly back to the Keep, report, and fly back to rejoin the travelers before they had gone much farther. She, the StableMaster said, could fly over the hills and valleys they had to walk.

All of this meant that Harrel, his two charges, and Vallezza were last through the Keep's gates. If Lady Orwren was convinced the Ranger should be leading them; he would take the lead in a day or two.

This day was for enjoying the mountains.

Some of the lower hills were covered with flowering trees: winter resistant apple trees for the most part. Nut trees of every size. Freshly turned fields sprouting a haze of greenery. The streams and rivers were also spring-full, so there were waterfalls to admire.

For mid-meal there was a view usually seen through palace windows, and the Traveler's Hut was as promised—well stocked. And it was left even more so since there were two men willing to chop firewood for the next travelers.

The next day was less interesting for both riders and horses. And there was rain. Farmer's Rain some called it. It was constant rain. More than mist, yet not a bothersome downpour. In season, it would slowly produce new spring crops in already plowed fields...and mud in any season. The road was a good one, but it had ruts, puddles and, therefore, mud.

This made the promised inn more than welcome. It was small,

only the lower half stone, one large room with a second wooden floor balanced above. Up the wooden staircase, there were private rooms and a few dormers for servants, single travelers and guards. If there were two rooms and a number of guests, then the smaller on one side was for women, with men on the other. A kitchen, bathing room, and stables were attached to the rear.

All of this was empty.

Captain, being a more experienced guard than the Ranger, walked his horse to the main door, dismounted and waited—sword in hand—for someone to come out, giving Harrel time to walk his horse around to the stables. When there was still no one, Captain entered, trusting that the noise he made would tell the Hafling to enter through the back.

The main room was empty. The fireplace was cold.

There were wooden tables, chairs and benches where guests ate, drank and even slept. Some were intact, but some were broken and heaped into a pile near the large stone fireplace. The room was still morning-cold and damp. Empty. And it had been this way for some time. Yet as Captain walked from table to table, he saw plates, cutlery, jars full of the usual syrups, jams and spices. Plus, wax-laden candle holders and various bowls, cups and tankards. Most encrusted. Others were broken and shoved away from what had to have been generously called place settings.

There was a brief dimming of light before Lady Orwren and Vallezza entered.

"It's empty," the Lady said in tones that relayed she could see this for herself; she did not need either of them—or a sword—to protect her from the obvious. She disdainfully looked around and moved to the fireplace. Perhaps she awaited her companion's return or she had decided that now she had, in other travelers, servants to build fires and cook meals for her. Since she said nothing about the horses, the others were left to assume she had sent the horses with the Faerie and her companion to the stables.

Not to care for them—to be available to Harrel and Captain to stable, feed and groom.

Vallezza was simply following her.

The Sorceress stopped suddenly and, with all the caution of a cat, walked slowly into the shadows beyond the fireplace and the light from the doorway. "Hello," she said softly, yet firm and certain.

The shadows coalesced, then separated, as a vague shape formed into a grey swirl. A shivering. Then a shape. "Hello." The shape breathed in a whisper softer than Harrel's. "Magical?" it asked.

"Vallezza. Sorceress. And you?"

Harrel moved carefully behind her. His middle itched, but no more than usual. If the shape before him was magical, it was no more so than the rest of the inn.

"I can't remember," it said. "Too long. Been here too long." The whispers were a little stronger. More certain despite the halting words.

"Val?" Harrel whispered.

"A Wraith," she replied. "And gone..."

Before there were questions or answers, the Faerie and the companion burst through the kitchen entrance. "Men!" Elleha, the Lady's companion, cried. "Surrounding us."

"What?"

"Who?"

"Humans," Songlest answered. "All around us. Coming closer."

Captain swore.

Harrel asked, "Who?"

The Wraith moaned. "Robbers. People...thrown out of the village. Terrible men."

It was Vallezza's turn to swear. "A Nullifier," she hissed. "No wonder I sensed nothing. He...He's dampened the magic. But they're right. There are men. All around us. A handful in back. And in front," she reported to the Ranger. "More than you can handle."

Captain had his sword at the ready, but as usual, Harrel had left his with his horse. He had his own defense and his dangerously runed belt knife, but neither were defenses against two handfuls of robbers—or more.

Vallezza raised her hands.

"No! No," the Wraith cried. "No magic. You will wake them."

"Who?"

"The ones they left. Below. They're confused. And angry. Very angry."

"The people who were here?" Harrel asked. "In the inn?"

"Yes. Yes. The...welcoming ones. All below now. Angry."

"The robbers killed them all," Harrel reasoned and explained. "They'll do the same to us. After... Magic anyway?" he asked of Vallezza.

"No." The Wraith moaned.

"It's magic or death," Harrel said, touching his knife. "We can't escape otherwise. Can we?"

"His magic...fights mine. I can use it, but it will be bloody."

"Escape," the Wraith repeated. "Escape. They built..." As it remembered, the Wraith became more solidified and vocal. Yet it slid into the floorboards. Half in, half out. "Down here. Not with the others. Here. No one remembers."

"We can't slide through the floor," Vallezza said.

"Oh, yes. Yes. Solid." It waded through the floor to a place beside the fire. "Here. Move it." The Wraith uselessly pushed against a bin barely containing logs and kindling.

Harrel glanced at Captain. He sheathed his sword and joined the Ranger. The bin and logs were heavy, less so had the bin been full. Still, no one had moved it in many Seasons—and it should have been full. Both pushed. It moved. Not easily, but it moved away from the unused floorboards and debris. Harrel bent and brushed this away. There was a dent in one of the boards. Not a handle or repaired hole—a dent. With a layer of packed sawdust at one end.

The Hafling pushed this aside, hooked his claws into the wood and yanked. Twice. The entire section rose. Captain grabbed a board and lifted.

There was a dark hole and the remains of a ladder on the dirt floor. The Wraith slid into the darkness. "See. See."

"Candles," Vallezza ordered. "You." She pointed at Lady Orwren. "You first. They can drop you down."

She looked as if she might protest, then accepted Captain's outstretched hand. He caught both, swinging her around so she was backwards and pushed. She dropped into the dark hole, and he let go. She landed upright on the floor.

"You," a male voice shouted from outside. "In there. Come out. Or we be comin' in."

"Hurry." Captain caught Elleha's hands. He repeated the drop and quickly followed her.

"Val?" Harrel held out a hand.

"You first. Catch me."

He nodded and dropped into the hole.

"Where are they? Under the floor?" Vallezza hissed. "Exactly."

The Wraith came out of the floor to hover. It moved nearer to the kitchen, and Vallezza followed.

The male voice yelled orders. Men and horses moved nearer. Their ponies whinnied.

"Come and get us." She opened her arms, then pushed downward on nothing but air.

A man's wordless noise echoed, loudly, from beneath the floor.

"Ain't in here." Another voice came from the kitchen. "Be

eight horses."

"Ladies." Someone chortled.

Vallezza pushed at both the wards. Moans came from beneath the floor as they were being released from their magical prison.

"Val," Harrel shouted from below.

The two men from the kitchen came rushing in, swords drawn—only to fall, face down. Their swords plunged into the floor and stuck. They started swearing, yanking on the swords as they tried to stand. Vallezza ran to the floor opening. One man tried to grab her. He reached out and caught a handful of...not quite nothing. He screamed and Vallezza turned and dropped into the darkness and Harrel's waiting arms.

"Here," Captain said, gesturing with a lit candle. Harrel had snapped his fingers at the candles, lighting them, while waiting for the Sorceress. And while growling.

Captain was gesturing at another darkness, this time in a ripped open wall of very old boards. The others were already inside, candle light flickering in the darkness. He extended his candle and ducked into the hole.

Vallezza pushed Harrel to go first. He growled but obeyed. She followed to the edge of the wall, turned and pulled down her hands. Boards and dirt followed the magic, and the old exit was closed.

The slide of debris and magic closed off the screams, as well. Some of the screams were men's voices, while others were faint and the wordless anger of both men and women.

"Come on." Harrel caught her hand. He could see, easily, in just the dim light of the two candles.

Everyone had to trust that the old shoring was made by masters of their trade, while busily ignoring spider webs, mud, and things that either yielded softly to hurrying feet or crunched beneath their boots.

"Here. Help," Captain called in a low voice. "There's a door.

But I can see green. Dirt and growing things. Old. And stuck."

Harrel came forward, while the two women and their candle joined the Sorceress back behind them and out of his way. It took two tries with both pushing at the old boards. The builders had fortunately realized that the tunnel might not be used for many growing seasons—if at all—and built the exit sideways instead of above—like the flooring. Otherwise, there would have been many layers of dirt, leaves and probably tree roots piled on the doors.

They crept out cautiously, into a forest of young trees. They could have been moved, but Vallezza did not want to use any magic—even theirs. So, all of them pushed carefully past the trees and clinging branches.

The nervous whinny of a horse told them where they were. Neither man wanted to leave the women, while they went after the horses, but neither spoke. There were too many horses to find and lead away from the stables. Fortunately, no one had stabled their horses. They were all outside the building, none too patiently waiting, along with four more. All four tired and worn looking.

"Catch them anyway," Harrel said while catching his two and another. They all wanted to be stubborn, relieved of their burdens, fed and watered—but they trotted after the familiar Hafling without too much noise. The rest did the same.

Only Vallezza and her mount halted. "Wraith? You want to come with us? Or stay?"

"Um. Go with you. That lot..." A swirl of gray indicated the inn. There was now silence within.

"Can't leave them to do harm," Vallezza said thoughtfully and raised her arms. Her horse stood absolutely still although she moved. Her arm circled, enveloping and gathering...something. Harrel watched, but saw nothing for a moment, then smelled smoke. Whifs of smoke, then a low fire burned toward the inn and the stables.

"Fire?" he asked. "But the..." He stopped, because he did not know who to name. There were robbers...had been robbers and the people under the floor they had killed.

"The robbers are already as dead as the ones they killed," Vallezza said. If she had been just a magical, cleaning away debris, Harrel would not have remained silent or agreeable. Instead, there was a sadness in her voice.

She pulled on her horse's reins, and the animal—as well as the Wraith—followed to where Harrel stood waiting.

CHAPTER 3

The next day, the nearly forgotten hillcat was waiting for them. Between the comments on why Slash did not want to travel with them, someone had said that she was hunting. Taking out her temper on deer.

This proved to be the truth, for she waited with a freshly killed young buck. The kill was hers, but the dressing, then the cooking was a chore for the others—those with hands and knives.

Harrel made quick work of cutting out the best pieces for eating, then more for drying and smoking while they ate. Captain used the same expertise for a fire, sticks for spitting and the drying rack. Having the two of them was a convenience Harrel missed as a solitary Ranger, and though he had welcomed Captain's help in hunting rabbits, he would like to pair with Slash for deer. The hillcat could find and chase deer to where Harrel waited with the unused bow he had claimed at the Keep. He had kept in practice with his own bow, as well as the knife, so he would make a quick, clean kill if Slash would give him a chance. He planned to ask her to hunt with him, or ask to hunt with her, more likely, after they left the village.

During the time before they were supposed to arrive, he had other pursuits and questions—for the Sorceress. All he had to do before he asked was get enough privacy. To get that, he convinced the two horses to dawdle, just a little, then Vallezza joined him.

"Back there," he began, "what...what can Wraiths do? To humans."

"I don't exactly know." Whenever she could, Val answered

him honestly. "But there's some reason why they're called Wraiths instead of some...harmless word."

Both of them looked to see the whereabouts of their own Wraith. There was a shimmer in the air next to the Lady, which was all they could see.

"From the screams," he began again, "they must have been doing something fatal. Unlike MistMen. They just...surround people in fog. Disorient them. They aren't too frightening," he added from experience.

"That's something all of them could do...but these Wraiths were dangerous. Angry. So, they do more than envelop people. Terrorize, them, I suspect. So... they couldn't breathe. Worse... They probably have enough magic, foul magics, I'm sure, left in them to pull them through the floor."

"You mean—"

"Exactly what I said. Bit by bit they would pull their killers down below. With them. They'd be dead by the time they went through. And the Wraiths would need all the magic remaining to them. Then they wouldn't be dangerous to others. Travelers. Villagers. But I burned down the inn to be certain."

Harrel loved this woman, but sometimes, what the Sorceress could do—and be so complacent about it—made his fur rise.

A half-day's ride from the village—according to the maps—the travelers began to feel nervous. It was spring, and the fields should have been plowed, or worked in some fashion. They were not. The winter-killed weeds were still tall, ready to fall when the new shoots sprouted. Nor had any of the fields been burned to provide clean ashes and kill the weed seeds.

Meadows were empty of sheep, goats or cows.

Only one dog came out, barked, and duty done, retreated back to houses with weed-filled yards, though some flowers struggled to rise above the fences and bloom.

"I thought this was a prosperous village." Lady Orwren

sneered. She had been complaining about stopping to check on a prosperous village when the trip to hers, even with horses, was going to take a moon cycle.

"T'was," Captain replied. "Or it was the last time I was here."

They followed a road which seemed intent on growing mud. The solitary dog barked again. Briefly.

"Someone quieted that dog," Harrel said. Only Slash's hearing matched his.

"M'Lady," Elleha called. "Come on out. Here be a Ranger to help yers."

"There's some sort of meeting house...down the way a bit." Captain started to walk his horse forward when a woman opened a door.

Someone behind her protested. "Leave 'em pass."

"Rober. We need help," the woman insisted. "Yers be from the Keep?" she asked them.

"Aye, lady. The Wizard wants to know...wants to help."

A tall, thin man joined her in the doorway. "Down the road apiece."

She waved them forward. "We... We'll join you there."

There was a little hesitation by everyone before they all went 'down the road apiece' to what Captain labeled The Meeting House. As usual, it was a stone building. Four walls with windows on either side of an ordinary door, protected from rain and snow by a small wooden porch built up off the muddy ground. There was nothing else: no furniture, lamps, just a box for firewood or muddy boots. There were rails on either side of the stairs, and enclosed stables sat on the side of the building. There was a well with a horse trough, but no feed or bedding. Harrel and Captain looked for stalls to use after they unpacked and took whatever necessary inside. The horses were tired and willing to just stand with their reins loosely tied to posts that might have held hitching rails some time ago.

Harrel was deliberately slow. He had seen Slash enter the stables and wanted to be near if the hillcat found something inside.

Slash came out suddenly, chasing after a small black and white cat that was running full-out in front of her then vanished. Slash skidded to a halt. "You...see that?"

"Yes. But what happened?"

Both of them stared at the empty spot where the cat had last been seen.

Harrel hissed. "What did you do?"

"Nothing." She then looked embarrassed. "I was looking at a line of tails."

"Tails?"

"Mouse tails. A line of 'em. Side by side. Mouse tails. When something... I saw something move and swiped at it. Not hard, just to knock it off its feet. It went rolling and then, it ran. I chased it out here. It disappeared." Her scorn dared him to say otherwise.

"I saw it. A small cat. Or mayhap just a kitten."

"Humph. I don't hurt kittens. Or even small barn cats."

Harrel shrugged. He had seen it only briefly, a small black and white cat that was running before it vanished. "I'll tell the Sorceress."

The hillcat made a noise and did what cats do when confronted with a problem; she sat and licked a forepaw.

Harrel finished with the horses, although he did not stable them for the night. He went inside the stables, uneasy, wondering what sort of magic they might hold—besides a small magical cat.

There was a line of tails on the floor where no human could miss them. "Mouse tails, alright," he said when he returned.

The hillcat made a noise. "Annoying things. Kittens. Barn cats. But it's gone, so we may as well go in and see what these humans want help with."

Harrel followed her. In part because he agreed with what they needed to do, but also curious as to how a hillcat opened a door.

Easily, he discovered. Claws hooked latches, paws as dexterous as hands twisted and pulled, and the door swung open.

Inside, there were more women, most of them crying, but fell silent when the Hillcat and Hafling entered. The few small children and babies were pulled closer and quieted.

"There've always been people sayin' they wanted to go back home," the first woman continued. "Wasn't 'til...oh, a year or two ago, Martin said we couldn't celebrate Mid-Winter. We did anyway. But last winter he tried to dissuade us again. Said we didn't know the right date. I never paid him too much mind. The Healer that was here for a bit taught me a lot. Nuts. Mushrooms. Flowers 'n' roots. I was doin' well, but Martin said..."

She paused to look over her audience, then: "Martin said we couldn't eat the nuts. Damned fool. We near live off 'em. Cooked. Raw. Flour. Couldn't serve 'em lookin' like themselves, so they was ground for flour. For cakes. And porridge. With fruits and berries. Only them. No nuts. An' then he tells me to watch what I be sayin'...to him an' others. Meaning the men. The ones always with him. I was only a woman. Too young to know much of anything. Not properly ed-u-cated. Then he said there'd be no feasting this last year. An' I wasn't to do naught by m'self. Or be so dis-re-spectful...to him 'an'..."

Slash made that noise again, which earned him a harsh glance from the woman before she went on.

"What made me start thinking about leaving was when those friends of his...Thom, Reggie, and the rest took horses and left. And no one from the inn came as they promised. Nobody came. Since then, someone's come visitin' with deer. Skins. Extras. People from the Keep. Other places. We started talking... Well, I never got quiet, and the others came to me. Quiet like and said they didn't want to go home neither. Weren't that much here for some of us."

She waved a hand at the others. "But there was less back

there. I be a whore back home. Bar maid. Be decent here, but Martin...he says I ain't. He *gave* me to Reggie 'cause a man can't use a decent woman if he's gotta...you know. So, I run off. We all started running off when they started packing. Said they was goin' home. Martin says they was."

"They got some of us," another spoke. "This be Marla's boy. She had to go back 'n' they caught her."

When it looked like each one wanted to speak—all at the same time—Lady Orwren held up a silencing hand. "What do you want now?"

"Not to be here...not if Thom an' the others be staying' at the inn. Martin and them others may have gone home, but them's at the inn."

"No one's staying at the inn," Vallezza said quietly. "They killed the innkeepers. Were killed themselves. The inn burned."

"It seems to me, that all of you need to go to the Keep." Lady Orwren spoke as if she alone had the reasons and the authority to decide for everyone.

"What'll happen there?" "More of the same?" Questions came from the disbelievers.

"Food," Harrel said. There may have been many more questions, but few were as important as his single word answers. "Safety. Shelter."

Captain spoke next. "If you're worried about the men, don't be. They're used to women. There are a number of them in the Keep itself and more on the Farms."

"The choice is yours," Harrel added. "You just need to know what you want. And what you will allow."

"And rules and laws," one of the men muttered this time.

Harrel shrugged. "And Rangers. Ladies. Lords. Even a Wizard instead of someone deadening the magic around him. Deadening it for you too.

"Stand tall and say what's wrong. Or needed."

"Learn how to kick 'em in the balls," Slash proclaimed.

Once the surprise was dealt with, most laughed. Nervously, but they laughed.

"Goes for men too." Slash yawned.

The more reasonable folks noted her long fangs and decided her advice did not apply to hillcats.

Of course, Lady Orwren had the last word. "There are four of your horses brought back, so some of you, and the little ones, can ride. The rest of you pack what you need. And only what you can carry. You will leave on the morrow. Early."

CHAPTER 4

Harrel said, "That is a white and black cat. Not black and white."

"Clearly." Vallezza was also adept at stating the obvious. The small cat in her arms, purring loudly, was sleek, muscular and white—except for the tail. That was black. "And enough of a Magical to recognize the magic around me. So, it spared you a chase and came to me. He's also very good at visually pointing out flaws in human reasoning. No one here believes that cats, especially barn cats, can talk, so he won't talk to them. Instead, he leaves mouse tails to remind that 'Martin' person why there's a good reason to keep cats. They catch mice."

"Kill off the cats, and there are more mice. And mouse tails."

"Seems so. He forbids anyone to take them home. And I'm sorry to say, he had most of the others killed. Those that survived escaped into the forest. We'll need a basket. To carry this one."

"He's coming with us?" Harrel was willing to make a basket as long as he did not have to talk about it as well.

There had been discussions, almost arguments, as to which people went where. No one had talked about cats. Just people. It had taken most of the night before it was settled: all the villagers were to go to the Keep. Those who disliked or distrusted the Wizard and his guards, went as well. Then they were free to go wherever they chose. Songlest was to return to the Keep, anyway, so she could take the Villagers home, along the Road, and fly back.

She was not enthusiastic. She was the Wizard's messenger, she'd said, not a herder of people. Not one of whom she wanted in the Keep. It did not help her disposition that the Villagers added others to those who wanted to go...somewhere else. There was another small village, off to the North or Northeast that needed help. None of these villagers had ever walked to this distant village or knew its exact direction—but Songlest could fly there and back in a day if there were no transporting doors nearby.

Harrel *let* Vallezza tell her, for the Faerie not only sparked when she was annoyed, she was dangerously sharp. All faeries were. They had sharply pointed ears, fingers and toes. If ever drawn, the lines would all come to points and perhaps burn holes in the paper.

She left, grumbling, and the Villagers swore they would leave at dawning—or near to—and simply follow the Road back to the Wizard's Keep. Songlest could follow them and the Road and tell the Head Woman if and when the new Villagers would follow.

Lady Orwren's own words now came from her companion. Elleha had not been any freer than the Villagers to choose her life, and now she wanted a choice. She wanted to go back to the Keep, not travel home just to continue being a Companion. She had been polite enough to call herself that, but she meant Servant. She wanted to be free to choose, like the others who listened to Lady Orwren. The Lady herself had to accept, gracefully, the results of her own words.

However, she did not have to accept what the Villagers termed *early*.

By dawning, the village was alive with busy people, crying people and a number—mostly with babes and small children—preparing or eating a meal. Harrel and Captain had already chosen horses, saddled and packed, something of an easier task now that there was only one pack animal. All the extras, whether horses or equipment, had been given to the Head Woman to pack or throw away.

The Hafling and the Guardsman were the only ones with

tracking experience in their small party, but they could have been novices and still found the trail of the villagers following 'Martin'. None of those left behind knew if the Head Man, Martin, had gone to the inn and was not returning, not ever, or if he was leading his villagers. All of them were headed in a westerly direction where there were none of the magical Roads. Instead, there was a recently made dirt and crushed stone path. A path made by humans.

Well before the last tracks overlaid the first, the path and the beaten ground beside it became mud. Experience was necessary to know that the last were going to be very slow. Whoever had charge of all of them should have had the wagons in front where there was solid ground, even if it was uphill and barely grazed pasture. Instead, the thick wheels of the heavily laden farm wagons sank into the churned and softened ground, tiring the horses.

Long before Harrel and the other three were ready to stop following, there were odd, usually heavy, items thrown from packs and wagons off to the sides.

This was where Harrel slowed his horses to a walk. The ground was solid beside the villager's path and the discards easy to avoid—as long as no one wanted to stop and inspect something that might have been valuable. Harrel had immediately decided that whatever was thrown away was not necessarily unwanted, just not of any real value. A worn pot. Bedding. A poorly carved box that was not worth opening.

They were all poor things. Valued by someone, but as he told Vallezza, not by those who had the same, but of much better quality.

"Small wonder some of them didn't want to go back...home," she said softly, sadly, then smiled. "How is our smallest rescue?"

Harrel turned in his saddle although all he could see was the basket he had woven and securely fastened to his pack and cloak.

"He seems to be asleep."

"Meyow," a voice replied and nothing more.

"Care to explain?" Harrel asked, and as he expected, she laughed.

"He's very magical. Black and white when he's being chased by a cat monster and white and black when he's a cat himself. Or as much a cat as he can ever be. He didn't mean for you to see him levitate. It's something not even Wizards can manage, yet most cats can go from one place to another. If wizards studied cats, they might learn how, but cats try not to be seen when they jump. You scared him."

Harrel made a noise at the gentle teasing. He owed her that. Making a basket out of the materials the villagers left had been easy compared to finding and catching the small agile cat.

His attention was mostly on Lady Orwren and Captain. Even Slash was behaving oddly, crisscrossing the wide swath of a trail, ignoring the almost empty meadows before them. Well into the distance, there was a small herd of deer of some sort. Brown mostly but with a black stripe, and all of them had small, oddly curved horns. Hooks instead of antlers.

"What's wrong?" he called out to Slash, urging his horse nearer. Vallezza followed.

"They've stopped," Lady Orwren answered.

"Not stopped," Slash said. "Gone. All of 'em. No more people tracks. Not much left of the road. Stones. Dirt. Not tracks."

"Impossible?" Harrel muttered, knowing the question had an answer, but the Sorceress remained silent. Like him, she wanted to see for herself.

First the Sorceress, then the others—save Slash—crossed the muddy ground, going back and forth until the four were on untrampled grass. At the end of the wide trail, there was mud and trampled grass. Where the mud suddenly ended, there was now spring growth. No tracks.

"Where did they go?" Lady Orwren's question was more of a demand.

"Back. Maybe..." Vallezza said. "I once found one of those magical books. The ones that wander in and out of book shops and libraries. It explained what it called *Fairy Tales*. It said there was an old *fairy tale* about a village that vanished. No one tells the tale anymore, but I read a newer version. The explanation. It says the villagers returned. In the middle of a war against the same enemies they'd escaped. And that's the only reason anyone pays attention to the newer tale. The outspoken leaders died immediately, while the others...dispersed. All over the country. After their enemies were defeated."

"Not a very pleasant *fairy tale*," Harrel said.

"None of them were. The book said the endings were moral, but dark. This one...I guess it says you can't escape your fate."

Harrel sniffed in disagreement. "There's always a choice. You may not like any of them, but there's always a choice."

"Oh, I agree, but there's a problem. *When* did they go back?"

"What do you mean *when*? Now. Only a few mornings ago."

"That's when they left. But *when* is it now? Is it still today? Or season upon season ago? Time, as we know it, means nothing to the FaerFolk. It's all one continuous...time." She had neither magic nor an explanation about time from the FaerFolk. It just *was*. "In all the Tales, a person, or an entire village, can go through what we think of as a doorway and return *home* seasons later.

"And be much older. They lived here...how long? Perhaps long enough to be forgotten by those they left? That may be better than terrifying their grandchildren with impossible Tales."

She let them think on this for a moment, before adding, "There is nothing we can do. Some have been rescued. Some have not."

"We go on," Harrel put in. "Like Rangers always do. We go on. And never know what happened. Captain, what do you know about this grassland?" He waved at the grassland. More animals were now grazing on the fresh grass, and a number of birds flew overhead. Better than that bit of normalcy, there were rabbits. They would all eat this night. And perhaps sleep in something of a hut. Like them, the road continued, and where there was a road, old or new, there was water and shelter.

"If I remember the Keep's old maps," Captain began, "last used when the Villagers arrived. The grassland extends..." He hesitated to consult his memory. "Maybe to where the Cave Dwellers lived. The grasslands would be...above them. Away from them. They hunted some distance away from their Cave and the river, so, no one really knew about their cave. Or where they hunted."

"Wondered about that," Harrel murmured. "And the road?"

"Turns. There's a true Road going Northward. Naught but forest and grass for days, however."

"Good." Reading the Reports from the Keep was as close as Harrel wanted to get to the Barbarian's Cave. He was getting used to having one for company, but it helped that Captain did not look like his brethren.

It did not help that Val knew what he was thinking. He would have to ask if she thought prejudice was something almost normal. It was definitely something to fight, but was it ordinary? Something to fight against rather than act upon.

But later was not now. The grasslands held his attention. He had been told that the real Grasslands stretched from horizon to horizon, and while these were large, they were more like a string of wide pastures bounded by forest.

And now that most of the villagers were gone, the herds had returned to graze. There were more of the black-streaked deer, small clusters of ordinary deer who eyed the small party—or just the hillcat—nervously. They were everyone's prey, as evidenced by the small pack of wolves that stayed, half-concealed, at the edge of the forest.

Between the herds, there were solitary animals—foxes,

badgers and cats. Small short-tailed cats for the most part.

Plus, the innumerable rabbits and something furry that dug holes and whistled and clicked when Slash and horses came near their holes.

Flocks of birds. Small songbirds, chicken-sized runners who wove through the old grasses on clearly marked trails, which made Harrel think of snares while wondering if the birds were edible, but not the hawks and vultures.

And creeks. And small ponds full of greenery, frogs and shellbacks that plopped loudly into the safe, fish-filled waters.

There were even a few horses that wanted nothing to do with humans anymore. If they ever had.

Finally, once the Ranger's followers were deep within the forests, and the promised Road was found, there was the ruins of a small hut and a stable full of mice. When let out of his basket, the little cat performed his proper chores, then caught two mice. Like him, Harrel and Captain wanted to go hunting but were too busy. There were horses to care for, fires to be made, and along with the gathered firewood, they needed material for snares. Slash dispensed with snares and caught a fresh rabbit for her meal. The others ate what was left in the packs, then the same on the morrow.

The rabbits they snared overnight—a handful—were dressed and hung on the pack horse. They would be mid-meal.

Now too, the Road changed. It turned as foretold by the maps, went into the open woods at first before becoming a magical dirt and rock passage between walls of grass and thick trees.

There was even a small stone bridge.

Occupied.

"What...is that?"

Before them stood a very large lump of brownish-black fur, big enough to block the entire bridge.

"Is it dangerous?" Lady Orwren inquired.

Her horse snorted, but this was more a reaction to her than to the beast.

"There are claws on the ends of those paws," Harrel said. "So, yes. I'd say it's wise for us to keep off the bridge."

The horses were becoming nervous, whinnying and snorting, but a horse's instinct when confronting a new and strange animal was to run. Some of them ran from small animals, and this one was not small. It had a muzzled head and massive shoulders; its hind quarters said it could run. Probably as fast as a horse.

Then it reared up on its hind legs, now taller, more muscular than Harrel, and covered in long dark fur. It stared at them as if deciding to warn them it could be very big and very dangerous if it wanted to be.

And it was clear it wanted to be.

It opened a gigantic mouth filled with sharp teeth and made a loud warning noise, something between a deep growl and a grunt.

"There was one like this in the Red Cave," Harrel said, remembering. "But bigger. Its skull huge. And body smaller. This size. Captain?"

"Don't remember any red caves." He was having trouble controlling his skittish horse.

The creature waved the claw-tipped paws, and if the others did not know about the power of claws, Harrel and Slash did.

"Run," she ordered.

Harrel swung his horse around to come face to face with the pack horse. He was yanking on the lead rope and snorting. Harrel dropped it, and seeing Vallezza turn, he let his horse go forward. When level with Val's mount, the pair ran.

The creature roared, came down to all four paws and bounced. The bridge groaned, and a number of stones fell into the running water. Then it lunged forward, leaped off the bridge, and chased after them. The horses had only the slightest lead, but they became a fast herd and out distanced the creature. It roared and ran faster. That made them all race to take the lead.

The slowest could become a meal.

Not one was intelligent enough to think about that, but their riders could, and they did what they could to win the race. Mostly, hanging on to saddles and manes as best they could. They all knew how to ride, but the horses knew how to run, how fast and where. The Lady and Captain's horses out distanced the others very quickly.

Slash was left to their defense. She paused near a large tree—large enough to hold a climbing hillcat—and screamed. If she had never seen whatever this menace was, then it had never heard a hillcat.

The horses knew what was screaming. They plunged and bucked and yanked on the confining reins as they ran. Harrel let go of the bucking pack horse and raced after Val. He was on a bigger, faster horse, but her pony only carried her light weight He managed to keep sight of her, stay aware of her.

Finally, she pulled firmly on the reins, and the horse plowed to a stop. Harrel's mount did the same, and although it thought about prancing, it obediently stood fast and breathed.

Val patted her horse's neck and dismounted. "Lost the pack horse already, Ranger?"

He made a grumbling noise as he dismounted, but any excuse for the old jest was lost in a loud, demanding scream, a minor version of Slash's, but hair-raising just the same. He unhooked the latch on the basket, and the cat flowed out—without any magical help—and scrambled up a tree. There, he complained, loudly screeching, about his treatment. How he had been bounced about until his fur went every which way. Even when he settled on a branch and prepared to thoroughly wash, he muttered little grumbles.

"I saw the pack horse run past," Val reported to the Ranger. "He'd lost the pack. Anything in it worth a hunt?"

"Tents. Cookware. Blankets we might need after a while." He

shrugged. In her, he had all he needed or cared for, far less than the loose horse and lost pack.

"And the others?"

He shuddered. "I don't even know where *we* are."

"So. What does a Ranger do now?"

"He finds a place to shelter. Safe from that...animal."

His sharper ears caught the sound of a branch cracking underfoot, and he reached for the sword, which was now gone. He still had the belt knife and carefully took it out of its sheath. There was a swear word and Slash came out of the forest.

"Hate trees," she growled.

"You found us."

"Hard not to. You've got a noisy cat."

The cat growled something as insulting as her swearing.

"You'd make a nice, quick bite." Slash growled at him. "But there's no danger. Whatever that thing was, it's gone. Went south, I suppose."

"South?" Harrel asked, looking through the trees for the sun.

"South. North." She spit. "People directions. About as useful as smelly old maps."

"Then we go...that way. Mayhap it's North. Mayhap, not. It's more important to find water. Without bridges."

CHAPTER 5

With two Magicals and four animals, finding water was simple. And not only was it available within a half-day's walk, but it was also in a pond stocked with frogs, shellbacks and fish. As soon as Harrel let the horses drink, he hobbled them in the small surrounding meadow and then went fishing. Experience had taught him to always carry a fishhook and string.

The small cat had the chore of finding worms, once he understood what and why they were needed, while Slash went with Val. She gathered firewood and whatever edibles she could find in the forest. The very northern forests were notoriously empty of life, except competing pines and hemlocks. Even in a valley, next to a pond, there were no nut trees.

"What do we do next?" Val asked after they had finished eating. The fire and the pond were still welcomed. It was going to be a cool night, and the pines were not useful for shelters or safety.

"Use those air bubbles you talk about to make a shelter. On the morrow, we go on." Harrel wanted to watch her make bubbles large enough to shelter four sleepers.

As he knew, it was interesting to watch the bubbles form with them inside. When she was finished, and he was convinced he had more than enough air to breathe, they lay together on a bed of pine boughs. He became less convinced that he just wanted shelter and company, but even Slash was curled inside the bubble. That made it too crowded for anything besides sleeping.

Above them, there were stars. With an occasional rainbow wandering over the bubble. The two cats fell asleep immediately, since they had no interest in stars or rainbows, while Harrel and Vallezza spoke, drowsily, about what they saw or thought. Yet they were soon asleep. All of them were confident that one of them, or one of the grazing horses, would wake them if necessary.

What woke them, on the morrow, was the first light through the clear bubble wall. Once again there was fire and fresh fish, both of which delayed the real start to the day. There was simply no sign of the other two. Oh, three. While the Wraith need not fear much of anything since nothing could harm him, he was easily forgotten.

Finally, at mid-morning, Harrel said, "We need to go on...this way until we find the Northerly Road."

"Will it be the right one?"

"No matter. A Road always goes somewhere, and there's usually someone on it."

"Like a large, furry brown...whatever beast." She saddled and mounted her pony.

On the second day, they found a waterfall and bathed. Unlike the springs and creeks in the Kingdom, which were at least warm, this far into the mountains, the falling water was cold. Val could have used a Cleaning Spell on them, but both preferred water and soap weed.

The two cats and the horses just watched. Water, as far as all of them were concerned, was for drinking. Slash tried to catch a fish with her paw, before Harrel provided a fish for each of them, then a fire and shelter was readied for the night.

Vallezza was hesitant instead of willing, even eager, to make love to Harrel when he held her, suggestively, in his arms. Then she was saddened by her own refusal.

"What's wrong?" he asked, making her more comfortable against his shoulder. This was his method of encouraging her to talk to him if she was not going to sleep.

"Nothing." She cuddled against him. "I would not like

to...disappoint you."

"Never."

"It's possible. Remember what I said? That I'd not even make a good whore. That I laugh too much."

"I remember." He remembered every confidence, loving them and her.

"I did so. Once. I had what little I didn't already know explained to me by a Healer. Because, you know, I'd just turned fifteen. Of age. So, I had to talk to someone. What surprised me was the...honor. He was honoring me because I was just an apprentice. Yet I was honoring him with my first time. I hadn't expected so much...fuss being made for such a *natural* activity." She paused, then whispered, "It was the...WizardMaster."

Harrel could not help but growl. From their first meeting, he and the Wizard were at odds, and this only added to his dislike of the man.

"Behave." She chuckled. "It was some time ago and...a disaster. I was very naïve for my age. I knew all the facts. Hard not to with randy fairies and animals all around. But I was very nervous, probably because I was not at all interested in having him..." There was a slight giggle in her tone. "But he was very ready. I couldn't help it. I laughed. He went all red. And furious. I stopped laughing when I thought he was...I don't know what I thought, but I was scared. I was well trained by then, but he was a Master. If I had to, I could scream. I knew there were others pretending not to listen. Others who added to his fury when he left. From then on, I was no one. And still am. There were no more lessons. No special treatment. Nothing. So, I left on the day I met you. The day you smiled at me. The first smile I'd been given in some time. And it makes me sad, sometimes, to know that a lot of all this," she waved at the bubble and the forest, "is due to his pettiness. You gave me enough confidence to go on. Learn whatever I could. And return, later, only to be told I had to go into the great wide world without any magic. To be a companion. Supposedly to do nothing." In her voice there was more laughter along with love...for him.

Yet Harrel could not help but ask, "But that...first time?"

"Oh, that went to a very nice boy who did his best. Considering it was his first time, as well. It was over and done, and both of us were grateful."

She managed to wiggle closer. "But something was always lacking."

"Which was?"

"Love, Sir Ranger, and you well know it. So go to sleep and disappoint our audience."

He did so, holding her close until the morning sun came through the trees. Then, she was The Sorceress again. Smiling and competent enough to cook fresh fish, then saddle her own pony. He loved her for that, too.

They rode silently under the hemlocks and tall pines, circling the clusters of ground-hugging young pines and found a road. Not the old Road built with stones and magic, but a dirt track with weeds and winter damage that spoke of horses and hunters and a nearby village.

And a pasture enclosed in a stone-laid fence. Nothing grazed inside, but there had been a herd. In the next pasture, there were barking dogs and uninterested sheep. Freshly shorn. No shepherd. Not even a small boy.

Yet they had passed wolves a while back. Slash and the pack leader had exchanged insults. The wolf had started it, otherwise, they would have asked for directions.

Dogs knew more about their villages but were usually too defensive to be of aid.

Aid was not needed. The dirt road joined The Old Road. It swung around the pasture, widening as if the travelers and wagons were interested and awed by the sudden view below them, where an entire valley spread out: the crisscrossing Road, a village of houses clustered on one side of an immense and uncrossable ravine—at least by people and wagons—but they had built a stone bridge arching into the air and crossing between the high cliffs. Beyond that, the Road continued over and around another grassland, slowly enveloped by trees.

On either side, there were waterfalls, which would be immense if viewed from the river at the bottom of the stony cliffs.

Harrel had found several maps in the Keep, but none mentioned the river or this village. "Have you ever heard of this village? Or the river?" he asked both Val and Slash.

Neither was paying attention. Slash was sniffing for rabbits, and Val was busily smoothing her hands down her sides. Behind them, the dark blue of her long tunic swirled into a worn light blue. The dragon she wore as a badge had already turned into a blue square with white stones in flower patterns. The badge was rimmed in gold-colored thread, denoting her rank of Master Witch.

"A Witch?" he asked. He had to let the cat out of his basket. He peed in the dirt, covered the small puddle, and joined Slash to search for mice.

"I am," Val answered. "A Master of my trade. Anything I witch can do, I can do as well. And if anyone does ask, a Witch's badge will put them at ease. And, no, I've never heard of this place."

"Because..?"

"Something. Mayhap Lady Orwren's warning that something is wrong. Best not to find out as a Magical."

The cat jumped and floated back onto the basket.

"Avoid doing that from now on," the Sorceress said. "No magics. Or very little."

"No-ow," the cat replied, settling himself to watch from the basket instead of sleeping inside.

Harrel started his horse down the narrower Road. Val and

Slash followed.

The Road was wide enough for a wagon—if the driver was an expert. It wove in and out of carefully terraced gardens. Water trickled down narrow gullies, sometimes going carefully under the Road. Sometimes being a water fall, turning small water wheels to irrigate a garden.

There was late afternoon sunshine on the plants, and it would be full-on them before the sun set beyond the distant grasslands and hills. At first, the crops were mostly wild—sunflowers and weeds—but received more attention the lower they rode. Almost down to the well-tended stones of the Road through the houses, and just above a line of slate roofs, a sign pointed to a second road. It was, both decided, a symbol of a kettle over a fire, the sign for an inn.

The inn itself was a curiosity. The cliffs dictated its structure. The narrow road ended at a turn-around and the inn's front door. The building itself went upwards, with walkways over the road and a balcony over the door. The rest of the inn was built on top of the lower houses. Somewhere, there would be a kitchen and the stables.

Wherever they were, the front door and skinny alleys disgorged stablelads and innkeepers.

"Welcome. Welco..." The innkeeper nearly choked at the sight of his customers. The Ranger and the Witch were perhaps welcome, but a hillcat? And a black and white cat riding behind the Ranger? "Welcome," he managed again, waving at the leader of the pack of stablelads. The lad hesitated for a moment, before deciding that the Witch's pony was the more docile. As was she.

The Ranger was big. And now that they were all closer...He was clearly a Hafling. As much a hillcat as the one that padded beside his large horse.

A second in charge had to take the reins of Harrel's mount, and it was clear he did not want to. Most of them, including the innkeeper, did not want to be close when the Hafling dismounted. He wanted to growl at them but merely smiled with a flash of his long fangs. It wasn't enough, but Val's expression as he helped her dismount, said it was too much. She could have said a word or two more but dismissed the incident.

The innkeeper managed to bow. "Sir Ranger. M'Lady," he said, waving them in the door. It was now crowded with an older woman and two maids. "Uh?"

"Yes?" Val inquired.

"Ah. The...ah, cats? M'Lady? Where—"

"Usually, where ever they want. The stables most of the time."

"Yes, M'Lady." He bowed again, clearly hoping any insults were dismissed with the liberal use of the honorifics. "Sir," he added, twice being better than once. He also waved at his lady.

It was her turn to add honorifics and wave them inside.

There were steps up to the doors, making it even easier for Harrel to see the commotion of stabling two horses and a hillcat. Double doors swung open almost beside the front doors. Wide enough for horses, boys and cats. Wide enough for wagons, as well, although Harrel had to wonder where a wagon would go—or even back out. The cliff wall was lined with stables and storage. Little room for wagons or the deliveries of hay and straw he could see hanging from an overhead loft.

There must have been another door because he also saw one of the stablelads look around, to see who was watching, before racing toward the shadowy back wall and vanishing.

A rat-faced boy, he thought, ignored the woman's greeting. He had to wonder how and why there were so many rat-faced humans. He had a cat's face, but then he was half cat. That boy was not half rat; just rat faced. Something he had done to himself.

Why? he wondered, then tucked the thought away to enter the inn. Not so much why the boy had the face of a rat, but where he was scuttling to so fast.

Val smiled at him. She had paused when she heard no response to the woman and turned.

"What?" he asked, and her smile managed to become more intimate.

"You are being a confident Ranger."

"Humph. I'm being observant."

"Confident. And handsome."

That silenced him for a while.

The inn was like every other inn. The main common-room was dug into the cliffs and large enough for a handful of tables and mostly benches. A huge fireplace had room for two kettles and a rabbit or two—plus a chicken. There were two brown-clad patrons of medium age playing a counting game. Or were. The newcomers were more of an interest than their game. The two maids were now standing near the fireplace while the woman—Mistress Carra, she'd named herself—was trying to usher Vallezza toward the stairs. One staircase went up while a wider one went down— probably into the baths. Most travelers would need them before a meal. Vallezza was no exception. She followed the woman down the stairs.

The baths were at the foot of the stairs, below a shelf of rock that forced Harrel to bend. Even Vallezza was too tall for the low opening. A lady's bath was to the right, men to the left. In the Kingdom, there was usually only one very large tub for both.

Vallezza smiled, but Harrel felt like growling. There was something annoying him. Not magic or he would have been scratching at the wide leather band around his middle. It was there for exactly that reason—to prevent him from really scratching at any itchy magic. He would have forgone the bath if his middle itched, but as it did not, and since something just annoyed him, he stripped and climbed into the hot water.

Another boy appeared when he was almost comfortably

immersed, and after bowing a few times, he made off with Harrel's clothing. Another was working on his boots and belt. He would be clean, but still annoyed. By the time he was washed—with real soap—the boy returned with his clothes. This meant Val had used a common 'Wash and Dry' spell on them.

Now he was hungry, and he returned to the Common Room for whatever was simmering in the kettles. A nervous maid waved him toward a fireside table while another brought water in one of the expensive glass mugs. Ordinarily, people were served beer in horns or ceramic mugs, but again this was Val's doing. Harrel only drank water or fresh pressed cider. Anything else made him sneeze.

She joined him as two bowls full of soft vegetables and meat were placed on the table. Along with fresh bread, butter and jars of jams and jellies. The spoons and knives were pewter, as were the candlesticks. Harrel had already touched a finger to the candle and lit it with magic. Common magic, and it was well known—at least in the Kingdom—that Rangers had the power of three spells. Fire. Release or loosen. And minor healing.

A Witch would know even more spells. And powerful ones.

She came from the bath, dressed, perfumed and with her hair braided and crowned on her head. She looked pleased, although she usually wore a long braid down her back or in what she called a pony's tail. Harrel preferred the braids.

"Well?" she asked, smiling.

"You look like a respectable witch."

"I meant the stew."

"It's good."

"It better be." Slash growled, suddenly laying her head on the table top. "There're mice in the stables. More'n enough to feed that cat. Cats do not eat dog food."

Laughing, Vallezza ordered a bowl of stew. "With no vegetables. And please, another from the kitchen with only fresh, raw meat. No bones."

While one maid ladled stew into a bowl, the others ran for the kitchen. It made no matter whether they knew Slash was a hillcat. She was a big cat, with long sharp fangs she showed as she yawned. Carefully, although her hands shook, the maid sensibly put the bowl of stew onto the floor near the cat. Slash looked at her, and she ran.

For a while, there was only the sound of eating, then loud, frightened voices came from the kitchen. Instead of a maid, the innkeeper's spouse—if that was what she was—rushed into the room. She was yanking off her apron. "M'Lady! M'Lady! Yers be a true Witch?" She was so worried and hopeful she bent eye to eye with Vallezza.

Vallezza tapped her badge in answer.

"Oh, M'Lady. 'Tis Sommie. She be early. Ain' her time yet, but the babe's comin'. Now! Yers can see the foot."

"Oh, my..." Vallezza turned pale and stood.

Harrel touched her arm. "What is it?"

"A baby. Early and breech from the sounds."

The woman moaned agreement. "Can you do anything?"

She took a deep breath and shook her head. "Mayhap. But I've nothing..." She patted her belt pouch. For a birthing, a Witch usually carried a basket or bag. A pouch contained only a few items for common ailments or emergencies. "A breech. And early. I must...try."

The woman had already signaled for her own cloak and now for Vallezza's.

"Slash?" Harrel asked.

"N'much good, but...I'll see where they go. Be back."

The three of them hurried out the front doors while the maids fluttered in the doorway. One had the sense to close the doors, freeing them all to rush noisily into the kitchen.

Harrel was left alone.

CHAPTER 6

Harrel wandered out to the stables to supposedly check on the horses and Blacktail. Slash had returned to say that there was a lot of screaming in the house where Vallezza had gone. Not worrisome screaming, just noise to be avoided by cats with sensitive ears. Birthing, she said, was no place for cats.

Then she curled up on a rug and went to sleep.

The horses had been fed, watered and groomed by the herd of stablelads. They were now gone on business of their own. The horses were drowsy, almost asleep, and the rest of the stalls were empty. Apparently, the men who arrived a while ago were only interested in their beer and had come afoot. There was a small wagon outside, but the horse was still with it if not the driver.

Blacktail was up in the lofts, playing with a mouse before eating it. Or leaving it for one of the barn cats. There were a handful watching both the little cat and Harrel.

He was admittedly bored. All he knew about human birthing was that it took time. Horses, he knew from stable duty, took less time once the process was started.

There was a shadow at the far end of the stalls. Nothing of any real interest, just enough to make a cat curious. There was also a door, and it was open a crack, admitting a flicker of light inside. Now, Harrel was interested. Flickering lights meant candles—or worse, fires. There should not be flickering lights or fires in a hay-filled stable.

He walked forward, senses alert.

The door slammed open, and something swung out of a bright

light, blinding him before it hit his head. Shadows jumped on him, binding his arms, and although he snarled, exposing his fangs and claws, he went to the floor.

And the darkness enclosed him.

Blacktail left his mouse for the nearest barn cat and went to the edge of the lofts. Well below him, men were twisting ropes around the Hafling. One of the younger barn cats moved closer to them, curious, and was kicked away. Had the man's boots connected with more than a glancing blow, the cat would have been killed. Blacktail thought this was a good warning and stayed hidden. He was too small to help, and the men were between him and Slash. The best he could do was watch.

The men carried the unconscious Ranger out the door, and the cat dropped down into a shadow. He was already black and white, so he stayed that way and slid out the open door.

The men threw the Hafling into a wagon with none of the gentleness used when Blacktail went into his travel basket. Then covered him with a blanket and left.

Blacktail followed, carefully moving from one shadow to another. He had enough experience with roads to understand how he could cut from one loop to another while the wagon had to follow the road down the hills. He even splashed through a mud puddle to darken his white paws, but no one was looking for a cat. Sometimes, he followed, and sometimes he was in front of them.

Yet he almost missed them when they turned away, onto another road and up a second solitary and highly banked road. Even just pretending to be an ordinary cat, he had to slink along those banks rather than be exposed on the cleaned road above him. Then he had to wait as the men and the wagon climbed to a stone castle. It was perched on the side of a hill. Yet there were stone walls and low trees and bushes for a cat's cover when the wagon crept its way across a crack in the cliff and through an open door. Still, he waited a bit longer before running through shadows and flying across deep creek beds.

He did not need the now-closed doors because there were a number of openings in the stone walls, all with bars of iron. All with too wide spaces to stop a small cat. Or rats.

He snorted with distaste, but went in the nearest, down a length of tunnel and out yet another broadly barred opening. This time it was a people-walkway with doors and alcoves and shadows. Now too, he could smell Harrel. Not the unpleasant smell of some humans, but distinctive. A cat who was not a cat.

He crept carefully forward—quickly backed into a shadow as a human walked past. Taking a chance, he tried again. Around a corner, in a large dark room lit with candles and torches, the men were throwing the Hafling into a large iron-barred cage. One of them quickly cut the ropes off him and was himself yanked by the others as Harrel came awake, snarling and slashing.

He caught the man's tunic in his claws and yanked. The cloth ripped, and the man fell forward, yelling. The others grabbed him, pulling him out before slamming the cage door shut. Harrel hit the bars with his shoulder, but they had the latch and bar secure. Then locked.

Harrel almost screamed. Instead, he moved away.

"Ah, good. You're being sensible." A tall thin man in a plain gold tunic with no badge—just a large sparkling stone wrapped in gold wire, came out of the shadows. He reminded Harrel of the rat-faced stable lad. This one had managed to become an adult. Or at least he had managed to grow to a modest size. He still looked like a rat. "Stay that way and you'll be freed. Eventually."

Harrel growled, but softly. "Why?"

"That Witch you are with has magic."

"Not very much," Harrel muttered.

"Hah! You should choose your friends more carefully. The Lady Orwren has a mouth on her. And a swollen head to go with it. A Lady and a Hafling Ranger. Impossible to miss. Especially along with a hillcat. In a light blue harness." He laughed.

Harrel had to agree with him about Lady Orwren. She talked too much and carelessly. To convince others of her superiority, as well as herself.

"Your Witch is a Magical. She'll share."

"No. She won't."

"Hah! She will if I threaten you. Laws say we can't kill off Hafling babies, but you... Who'll know?"

"She won't come here."

The listening cat did not understand all of what the two were saying. He was still young and not used to humans. Even half humans, but he began to think that the Ranger knew he was nearby. He guessed—hoped—that the Ranger meant that the Lady—The Sorceress—should not come to this place. No one should, he thought. Especially himself.

Turning on his all-black tail, he slipped back into the passageway, into the tunnel and then out. For a cat who was careless with his flying, the return to the inn was an easy trip, but tiring. Both the energy and magic became depleted. He hoped the Sorceress had returned, and thought about him, for he was slowing and doubted he had enough magic to open doors.

Vallezza had indeed returned and found the inn empty. Slash had awakened, but she had been locked inside, behind closed doors with no one about to open them.

"Harrel?" the Sorceress called and was answered only by the hillcat.

"He is not here, M'Lady. No one is."

Tired though she was, Vallezza turned and went to the stable doors. They opened easily but only their own two horses greeted her.

"He's been here, but...no longer." Slash padded to the back doors. These opened easily. "Curious. He was here. But not walking. In a wagon. With other men."

Vallezza swore. Not because Harrel was gone, but for the manner of his going. Too many wanted to be rid of a Hafling. "Where's Blacktail?"

"Not here." Slash sniffed. "Gone out the doors. After the wagon."

"Don't see why." Vallezza turned, patted a horse's nose and strode back to the inn, Slash following. The hillcat scampered straight to the simmering stew. The Sorceress strode into the kitchen. There was no one there either. A kettle bubbled over a lowering fire, filling the air with the smell of scorched porridge. Someone had planned to be awake before the guests—herself and Harrel—were up and demanding a meal.

She hurried back into the common-room.

A grayed black and white cat bounded through the doors she had left open. "M'Lady!" The exhausted little cat fell to his belly, paws outstretched. "They've got him!"

"Damn," Vallezza said, carefully, in English. "Stay where you are," she ordered the little cat and went for a bowl of stew. It was mostly warm liquid with a few soft pieces of meat. Perfect for both cats. She needed some herself but was too frustrated to eat.

Blacktail and Slash dug in.

"Now. Slowly. Tell me. Where's the Ranger?"

"Gone with those men. They...rolled him up. Took him to a castle. In a wagon. Put him in a cage. A big iron cage," he cried, indignant. "That Rat-man wants your magic."

"This rat? Another kind of hafling?"

"Uh, no. He just looks like a rat. He smells like one. Stinky magic." Blacktail had finished the stew and lay flat on the cool stones, a welcome relief.

"This rat has magic? But he wants more? From me? And will keep Harrel caged until he gets it? Can I get inside?"

"Ah. No. I don't think so. There are men. Lots of men. An' the Ranger's in a cage. Bars and locks. Lots of bars and locks."

despite his yawns, he told her about the long, empty roadway, the doors, the stone walls, and rooms, and then he suddenly fell asleep.

"His report was very good," Slash said. "Doesn't sound like we could get inside." Slash evaluated the little cat's report as if she was a trained guard.

"And I can't use magic. He—whoever he is—might be able to use it against me. He'll certainly kill Harrel long before we get to him."

"So, eat, M'Lady. Always wise to eat when you can."

"The Ranger agrees." She managed to smile and filled her own bowl of stew.

Slash settled near, her forepaws tucked under her white ruff. "M'Lady? That...ah, baby?"

"Survived. Both of them." She swore again. "And with no help from anyone else. I'd swear, Slash, someone used magic to force that labor. It wasn't time for either of them." She nearly bit her spoon she was so angry. "How could anyone do that? Be so careless with lives?"

She managed a few more mouthfuls.

"That...rat-monster must've used magic. He has some but wants more, just doesn't want to work for it."

CHAPTER 7

T he Sorceress worked through her anger and frustration by gathering anything she thought she might need from the inn. She found chopped meat on the carving table, so she fed the cats an extra meal. Being cats, they were happy to eat it.

Filled a pouch full of what resembled journey cakes and were palatable. Water. Hardened honey. Even a bar of sweet soap.

Then she went to the stables, and the curious cats followed.

She saddled both horses, strapped on the packs and the cat's basket then left. Blacktail, his tail matching his name since he turned white, led her out of the back doors. Slash followed, guarding the rear.

Their progress was only a little faster than that of the wagon and slower than Blacktail's since they remained on the looping road. A few people looked out windows or came onto the road, only to run away or close windows and curtains. No one thought about stopping them, but Vallezza was certain they sent word on ahead.

When the ever-nervous innkeeper told the wizard, his master, what Lady Orwren had said—that a real Witch and a Hafling Ranger were following her to Premontii, the wizard had soothed the innkeeper's fears. He had ordered him to welcome the pair, because, he said, dragons and dragon slayers were a Ranger's Tale. Lies. Told by the King's Rangers to keep the Lords subjugated and paying their taxes.

There were no dragons. No dragon slayers, because there were no dragons. He was a lesser wizard, another lie that irked him, and when he insisted on the honorific of Wizard Master, he told the same tale every day. There were no dragons nor dragon slayers oathed to the King. The Rangers told that Tale to keep everyone paying their taxes, as if they needed the King's help to kill dragons. There were no dragons. Just the King's unfair taxes. The innkeeper believed him. The officers believed him. His people believed him. Besides, if the Ranger had slain the beast, there was nothing to fear. If there were any in the village who did not believe him, they kept quiet.

On his orders, all of them watched the Road for this powerful Witch.

They reported a cloaked and quiet woman who rode out on one small horse and trailed another. Larger. A pack horse, most like. She rode out of the village, noisily because of the hooves on stones, and across to the other side of the deep ravine. Like most travelers, she paused, investigated the depths at the distant river and shivered. Then, like most others, she went on. Grateful for the safety of the sturdy bridge.

Surprise would be to their advantage. It was not something the Sorceress expected.

She expected the help of two cats. She had asked for it and they immediately agreed, not even knowing what she wanted. Except to help the Ranger.

Now they stood on the other side of the bridge, and she understood what Blacktail had described—the new road was a causeway. A well cared for high road that looked to have a guard at every turning. And there was no other way to the castle.

Unless they flew.

"I need flyers," she said. "Completely unexpected flyers. Yet known to Harrel. I need dragons. Both of you. Most like."

Being cats, they did not look surprised. They were astounded, but only looked interested. Ears forward. Paws together. Cat statues.

"The only way to enter that castle is by flying over it. I thought so before and know it now. Do either of you have any questions?"

"Ho-oww?" Blacktail asked.

"Magic, of course. A Change Spell. To make you CatDragons. Inside, a cat. Outside a dragon. Wings. And fire. It is a bit more difficult than that with no time to practice. But it's not impossible. I've already done an inside-outside dragon. A *kite*. So most of that's easy. It's the outside part... You have to think of the changes. Larger claws. No fur. Snakes. No, lizards. Bat wings. And honesty. You must *believe* in magic. Want to be a dragon. To fly over that castle and burn the *damned* thing down. With dragon-fire."

"But not before we rescue the Ranger," Slash put in.

Vallezza laughed. "No. Not before. I'm sure he'd appreciate that."

"How do we begin?"

The Sorceress looked at Blacktail.

"Wings, hum?" He licked his nose. "Pigeons. Pigeon pie."

Both cats smiled.

"Think of wings. You haven't seen that many bats, but you've watched those pigeons fly off. Birds at feeders. Flocks of 'em. Hawks chasing rabbits."

Both cats flexed their shoulders.

"Lizards. Claws. Long tails." Now the Sorceress was smoothing her hands over the two cats. The silvery marks on her left hand were glowing. "Wings. Fire. Dragons."

Blacktail's wings opened. He arched his neck, making them flap. His tail swished. Curled. It was as black as a leather belt, a snake's tail. His white hide itched. Glowed.

Now Slash's wings opened. She was golden. With under wings a light blue-sky color. Her skin was leather armor. Small metal knobs traced along her wings and legs. Her harness had been fastened with metal. Her claws lengthened as her lizard fingers stretched. She lifted up on strong hind legs, tail lashing.

Blacktail followed. He was lighter in weight and easily floated off the ground.

Eyes glowed. Ears lengthened. Flattened. Ruffs and fur became leathery frills.

Both dragons beat wings, rose higher into the air.

Slash screamed...a terrifying hillcat scream.

Blacktail meowed.

"Try fire," Vallezza said.

The new dragons flew higher into the night sky, and she did not know if they had heard her. Their attention was on flying and the castle.

The castle's attention was on things other than what had to have been birds.

The two dragons circled the castle, riding almost expertly on warm air currents, before Slash dropped suddenly. She flew onto an open balcony, prepared to land if she could go no farther.

The balcony doors were open.

She flew into a large room with only furniture and tapestries. No people. A good place, she decided after seeing another open door, to practice breathing fire.

Blacktail entered the room just as Slash managed fire on the first try, scorching a tapestry. The little dragon tried...and failed.

"There. That door," Slash cried. "And down. Find. The Ranger."

Blacktail zipped through the doorway and flew, immediately, to a stairwell. Being larger, Slash had to judge the extent of her wing tips and fly slightly sideways. On one stairwell, she simply folded her wings and plummeted down. Blacktail followed.

"Don't..." Slash warned, breathless from the last aerobatics," ...burn the place down. We must get out."

"Ah-roww," Blacktail yelled, seeing a man open a door, much to both their surprise. Blacktail's fire was less than a torch's, but it was fire and it burned. The man slammed the door shut, and the little dragon flew on, his brief fire finished.

Slash screamed, as well, and this time she had an answer. There were doors; they were open. Guards and servants behind them were hearing screams, smelling smoke, and yelling about dragons. Some were beginning to panic and run away, spreading the worst of the tales.

"Tunnel. Behind the cloth. The doors," Blacktail yelled.

Slash spread her wings to zoom into a wide old tunnel. There were tapestries and wooden doors at the end—where she had heard the hillcat's scream.

Gathering courage and foolhardiness, she blasted the tapestries with fire, hoping the solid wood doors were open. Then she slammed into the burning fabric.

The doors behind them were open.

Screaming, the two dragons dived into the room. Slash breathing fire. Blacktail aiming for Harrel's cage. He added to the din and the terror with his own furious scream and slammed into the cage door.

It was locked and stayed locked.

A guard unsheathed his sword, and Slash hit him with her outstretched wing. Wings and metal knobs knocked him across the floor, and the sword clattered uselessly away. The guard lay still.

"There are no dragons." The Wizard was yelling. "These are not dragons."

The guards were used to listening to their master, but Blacktail was flying in circles around the iron cage. Slash was swooping in the freer air space and spitting gusts of flame—until she could not. Then she flew to the top of the cage, hooked all four clawed feet into the bars and screamed.

"Not dragons," the Wizard managed.

Blacktail came sideways around the cage to fly past the inept Wizard. He raked across the Wizard's back with his claws, tearing off pieces of his tunic. Then flesh.

A dip and a swirl around and he faced the Wizard. His fire was only a small blast, but the ripped tunic caught. The Wizard shrieked.

"Enough," Harrel yelled. "Keys. Pouch."

Blacktail managed to turn under his tail while chasing after the Wizard. He came at him, forepaws outstretched. A quick swirl and he was at the man's side. He grabbed for the pouch belt. Pouch and belt loosened, fell to the floor, and the Wizard hesitated. Blacktail slammed into him, knocking him off balance. He tripped and righted, and the small CatDragon made another under-tail turn to grab the pouch. The heavy belt came with it and he faltered, landing.

Slash dived off the cage, and with wings spread, caught up the pouch and belt in his forefeet, knocking the Wizard away. He rolled on the floor, and Blacktail raced over him, gathering enough speed to fly.

"Pouch. Here," Harrel shouted.

Slash flew to the cage and dropped the pouch between the bars. Harrel yanked it up and dumped the contents onto the floor. A striker. A spoon. A stone, maybe gold or an uncut gem to go along with the three cut stones. Blue. And a ring of keys, one iron and larger than the others. Harrel took up all three and slipped his hand out between the bars. Slash flew down to sit in front of the door. Someone, she reasoned, would have to lift the latch.

With her help on the latches, Harrel had the door open. He slipped out, took a deep, cleansing breath and growled.

He hated cages. And the people who put him in them.

The evil Wizard had scrambled to all fours, and even with Blacktail following, he had escaped. His guards had all run away.

"Sword," Slash said.

The Ranger grabbed the one on the floor, and he knew he was angry enough to use his training on anyone in his way.

"Outside," he yelled. "Run."

First one, then the other dragon arrowed through the burning tapestry. An officer on the other side had ordered a few swordsmen to hold the stairs. Harrel screamed at them and waved his sword. This was not part of his training, but they had even less. Those in the rear broke and ran away. Slash went flying over the rest, and they ran. Two of them even ran down the stairs and through the burning tapestry. The officer yelled and faced Harrel.

The Hafling snarled, showing his fangs. When the man held his ground, Harrel returned to his training routine. This had not been taught to these guards either.

Swords clashed, ringing. Harrel turned as if he was going to foolishly turn his back—only to swing back, sword ready.

A backswing, honed by training and a Hafling's well-used, ordinary muscles, relieved the officer of his sword and his courage. He turned and, although he wanted to run somewhere else—anywhere, ran up the stairs.

Blacktail followed, hissing.

Slash was already chasing guards up the stairs. One tried to shut a door, and she hit it with all four feet, slamming it open and the guard onto the floor. Harrel ran over him, not even bothering with his sword. Slash paused, taking time to regain her energy and her fire.

The hall was aflame. Tapestries. Furniture. Doors. Most were alight. There was more wood in the stone castle than anyone ever thought.

And when Slash regained her fire, stones burned. The thick, oily dragon fire—as anyone in the Kingdom knew—burned stones. It would not burn down the entire castle—Slash was a small, tiring dragon—but whatever the flames touched, burned.

Blacktail had learned to swipe any guardsman in his path. He was a cat, and he knew how to use his claws—especially new and long claws. Flying just gave him more opportunity.

Small fires were turning into big fires. Whole walls seemed aflame as the old tapestries burned. There were people fighting the fires, pulling down draperies and flags. Most were taking whatever they could carry and running for safety.

"Ran-ger," a small voice cried, and Harrel returned to his humanity in time to see Blacktail land on the floor. Cat or dragon, he was exhausted. Harrel turned back and caught up the small creature.

"Up," he said and wrapped the dragon around his neck, head on one shoulder, tail over the other. Like any cat, he hooked his claws into Harrel's tunic. Harrel did not even feel them.

All around him there were people running, screaming. All of them concerned with their own safety. One was screaming something that made Harrel's belly itch. He paused, looking for the source of the magic and found the Wizard lurking off to the side. He had a sword in hand and was waving it. Cursing.

Anyone in the Kingdom could have told him that there was one way to truly rule a castle or an entire Kingdom—everyone, from the King himself to the lowest barncat, had to know his or her duties; they had to be thoroughly trained.

No one in this castle seemed to be trained in much of anything, especially this greedy Wizard.

Whatever he was yelling was not a properly worded spell. Nor was it natural magic. Harrel would have felt either. And to work a spell's gestures, the Wizard would have used his dominant, or magical, hand. The same hand he had to use for his sword.

A well-trained apprentice could best him with a sword, and Harrel's apprentice days were long behind him. He advanced up the stairs, sword at the ready. Despite the small dragon he carried.

The Wizard's sword was down, since Harrel was below him and he would have to lift his. Harrel did so, easily hitting the Wizard's sword with the unnerving sound of metal on metal, then lifting higher. A quick, powerful movement, and the other sword was knocked away.

Harrel's sword sliced.

The incantations ceased immediately, replaced by the rip of material, then flesh. How deeply, Harrel neither knew nor cared.

"Fire," the small CatDragon hissed in his ear.

The Wizard was backlit by flames, shadowing the hand he held against his stomach. He lost balance and fell, suddenly, backwards into the flames.

Harrel swore, and stepping away, began to run up the stairs and out, hampered by his sword and the noisy crowd. They were all running. Some screaming. The rest saving their breath.

The Ranger caught up a small crying child, and with it in his arms, followed Slash's directions. Once again, there was a snarl at the gate as too many people tried to leave as the guards tried to keep them inside. Slash managed to fly over everyone's head. Some turned back, but most slammed into the walls. The guards vanished.

Harrel pushed his way through. He tried his best not to knock anyone down, especially any of the fleeing women, but all of them—knowing or not—were preventing his escape out of the castle.

"This way," Slash yelled. She had flown through the gate, creating something of a pathway, and now rose higher. Above the walls, she had a bird's view of the causeway road, then the village. The road had been built for the castle's convenience, and it led straight to the bridge across the ravine.

Harrel shoved the child into a woman's arms and ran after Slash. He had sense enough to know he could not race to the bridge, for he had only a cat's endurance. He dropped his speed to a ground-covering trot. If he had to run, he wanted to be able to do so.

"Bridge. Go Over." Slash shouted when he was on the last loop of the road bordered by houses.

A turn and he was on a new road. One that looked as if its builders had sheared through the existing houses and roadside buildings. On one side there were curiously fronted houses: on the other, a verge of grass and low shrubs. It required confidence in the builders not to pause and look over the edge into the ravine. And stop.

Beyond the curve, the bridge arched through the air, solidly resting on two strong pylons on either side of the river. Solid. And yet...

Harrel ran toward it, following Slash. She flew overhead in circles. And as if she was the cause, a rock fell off the low retaining wall.

CHAPTER 8

The bridge was the largest Harrel had ever seen. Larger than any in the Kingdom. As he swung on the flat roadway, it seemed to have grown larger. "Hang on, cat."

He ran, full speed. Boots pounding on the stone. Breath coming in gasps, choking his throat.

Slash was flying circles on the far side.

Blacktail's ridged tail was choking Harrel's neck.

As he hit the middle, he realized the footfalls were stones crashing into the water far below. He did not know how, but he managed to increase his pace. Behind him, like a wave he could sense, but not see, the bridge stones fell apart and into the river.

Blacktail's wings lifted as if to aid him by lessening his weight.

There was a spot of grass...on the Road. Weeds. Grown this last spring...

He hit the edge of the bridge and road when, he swore, the entire bridge behind him collapsed into the river.

More steps. Impossible, but...

His legs gave out and he too collapsed, somehow cradling Blacktail as he hit the grass, but the little CatDragon was free to jump and slide off his shoulder. He skidded and lay full length. Exhausted. Breathing in loud gasps.

He wanted to keep lying in the grass. Breathing. But he crawled up. Sitting. Looking back.

Where the bridge had been there was a cloud of dust slowly falling to finish splashing into the river. He could not see if the stones were now a dam, but he did not care. He was alive, his breath slowing and the aches in his body growing. If he did not move, his muscles would freeze. Painfully.

He did not move. He leaned his arms on his knees and breathed. Slowly, he began to realize there were people on the far side, looking at the ruins of their only access to his side. They were possibly leaderless, if the slice from his sword had been deep enough to end the evil Wizard's life. He thought so, but did not know for certain. He would probably never know.

And that was another thing he did not care to know.

If the Wizard was alive, someone would have to go back to the Wizard's Keep and inform the real Wizard. Then it would be his problem, not a Ranger's. As would Bridgedale's lost source of supply or help.

And for rebuilding the bridge.

The people on the far side were waving, yelling at him. He could not understand them. He could not decide if they wanted help or explanations, or if they just wanted to throw him into the river.

It occurred to him then that there was silence on his side of the river. There were two CatDragons breathing and the distant sound of water, but there was too much silence.

"Val?" he cried, standing.

It was an all-too-common truth and a jest that Rangers lost everything they had, but if he lost Val... He could not imagine what he would do if he lost her. She had enspelled him. Presumably removed the spell, but he loved her. So much the fear of her loss felt as if his heart had stopped. He could only stand there and maybe breathe.

"Harrel." Her voice came through the noise and pain, and he turned to see her drop the horse's reins and come running to him. Arms open. He embraced her, holding her against the entire length of his body. Yet, somehow, he managed a kiss and was rewarded

CatDragons

by its return.

It did not matter that his mouth was—by some standards—deformed by a cat's features. She accepted whiskers, fur and even a raspy tongue to return his welcoming passion. Her own arms were under his, holding him as tightly as she could.

"I thought...I was afraid I lost you."

"Takes more than a destroyed bridge to lose me, you...cat! What did you do? How...?"

"Your...CatDragons?" He eased back a little so he could look at her.

"Mine. All I could think of. Your rescuers had to fly into the castle. Then...What did you do?" Her words were almost a demand. A seemingly careless arm stayed around her shoulders as he nodded toward the horses. "Those CatDragons helped me escape from the Wizard's cage."

He offered that to her temper instead of informing her that her magical dragons had burned down the castle...the Wizard with it.

"Did he say anything?" she asked.

"Only that I could be traded for magic. Yours. But I didn't think he meant you could teach him. Could he have...stolen it?"

Instead of taking the horse's reins and mounting, she turned away to stare at the emptiness from the fallen bridge.

"Mayhap. Probably. There was magic in that bridge. Trolls built it and they use magic... There's an old saying: Trolls use magic instead of mortar.

"Steal that magic and bridges can fall apart."

"Castles as well. Stone bridges. Stone castles."

"He must have found a spell to steal magic...without knowing what else it would do. Whether he was alive or not."

Left to the Ranger now were ordinary chores. He caught up the reins of both horses and questioned Vallezza with a gesture—ride or no, as they continued on their way. The two CatDragons sat up and flapped their wings.

"Ah. Well? Stay dragons? Or change back?" she asked them.

"Maybe...overnight?" Slash replied.

Blacktail shook his head.

"Fine. I'll ask again this eve. Decide then."

Both pairs of wings flapped, and they jumped-flew into the air. Unnoticed, the people on the far side of the cliffs put even more distance between them and the supposedly non-existent dragons. It would be a while before the villagers knew what to believe about dragons. Did they listen to the Wizard who swore there was no such thing as dragons? Or to themselves and what they saw and heard?

The grasslands changed little as they walked, then rode. The Hafling's legs ached, and the CatDragons flew ahead, then rested their wings as they waited for the humans and horses to join them. It was a very welcome announcement by them that a hut was not far ahead. And before they arrived, Slash had caught two rabbits. For them. Both CatDragons had been successful in catching pigeons or mice for their meals.

It was not until Harrel was finished tending to the horses: unsaddling, watering and allowing the pair to graze since there was no hay available before Val noticed...something.

At first, she was busy, since she had the task of skinning the rabbits. She kept working, yet trying to see or sense what bothered her, when Harrel entered the small hut.

"What's that?" he asked, dumping packs and saddles on what he decided was their side of the room. The rest would have to house the horses since there were no stables or fenced paddocks. The Ranger did not trust even hobbled horses outside. There were laws about horses, but they could be hunted if the hunter was really hungry. There was no agreement on the meaning of hunger, and the Ranger did not trust what he did not know.

What he questioned was inside the hut.

A voice said, "Ah. Me." A spot of air quivered.

"Oh, my... You? Wraith? Is that you?"

"I've been waiting for you. The others told each other you were lost, but I didn't see why. You got away."

"We did."

"Twice," Harrel muttered. "Start your Tale from...from whatever that beast was. On the little bridge."

"I don't know what it was," he said. "Ne'er saw its like. It made noise, but I don't think it wanted anything from you. It turned away. Different way than all of you went. I watched for a while. I even tried to talk to it, but...I don't think it heard me. Most animals don't, you know. 'Cept dogs. They know, but just bark." He sighed at this. "I followed them along the Road."

Vallezza asked, "Through the village?" Both she and Harrel were preparing their meal, listening while they worked.

"I didn't stay. There was...a darkness. I mean, it was night and mostly empty. But it *felt* dark. Especially under the bridge."

"Under?" Harrel thought he had glimpsed houses, or ruined walls, under the bridge.

"Those old places were empty. No one has lived there for...oh, a long time. Not like here. This place is old, but others besides those two have been here. No dragons, though. I don't remember...dragons."

"CatDragons," Vallezza said. "And this other two?"

"The Lady and the Guardsman. They raced ahead of you. Fast. Got to that village. Bridge...something? They stayed the night in the inn."

"Together?"

"Aye. Quarreling. They've been quarreling since they've had breath to speak. He wanted to stay. There in the inn and here, as well. Wanted to wait for you when they were out of the village. The inn. She didn't. Said she'd go alone. Tried. When they woke up. He followed. They'd be...oh, a day or two ahead of you. I can't tell one rainy day from another sometimes."

CHAPTER 9

Once again, Harrel and Vallezza were riding through grassy meadows and forests. At first, Harrel had been happy to look over the Sorceress's head to follow the flights of the CatDragons. But it also annoyed him that his larger horse made talking to her impossible.

Only when they walked together could they talk and laugh enough to erase all but a fading memory of the castle and the Wizard's cage.

They talked mainly about the future of the CatDragons. How to introduce them to the Kingdom or how to raise kittens. The latter, as usual, was the answer to the CatDragons future. Kittens— if there could be kittens—would be irresistible.

"Big ones," the CatDragons shrieked. Slash came back first, with Blacktail arrowing in as fast as he could. Harrel's horse snorted, but he was becoming used to a CatDragon flying circles around him or landing in front of his nose. Harrel was too.

"Big. Big," both were yelling. Slash shrugged before closing her wings, while Blacktail landed behind Harrel. The basket was gone, but the CatDragon thought of the empty space as 'his.' "Big," he added.

"Big...what?" Harrel demanded.

"Ah...animals. Very big. Lots of 'em." Slash was more embarrassed by the inadequate report to the Ranger than her lack of knowledge. "Ne'er seen 'em afore."

"Where?"

"Over there." She pointed to the view to the side of the Road.

"We're on a hill. There's a valley. Deep. Grass. Can't see it from here."

"Then we'll go where we can," Val said. "We can't catch up to the others unless they stop, so we may as well go see." She turned her horse.

Harrel followed.

Slash jumped into the air, but Blacktail stayed where he was.

As the Hafling often said, cats had little stamina and the CatDragon needed a mid-morning nap. He had already caught two mice, eaten them and followed Slash to discover the 'big ones.' And he was also too little to have anything to do with them.

The two carefully walked their horses forward, watching Slash's circles and the growing view of the distant hills and mountains. As she had said, there was a sloping hill leading down to a wide valley full of...

"What the...?"

Harrel had no words, but Slash did. "Big ones," she crowed.

"They're..." Val started only to lose words. "I know them. I know what they are. Sheep."

Harrel looked sideways at her, his disbelief clear.

"Sheep. Wool..." she continued. "No. Wooly mammoths. They're wooly mammoths. I saw pictures of them in one of the books in Elsewhere. Only they're all dead. Gone."

"They might be soon enough." Harrel pointed to a moving line behind the herd. "There are men after them."

"People made them go extinct. Slash."

The CatDragon came closer.

"Go. Chase them away from the men," she ordered.

The CatDragon quickly obeyed. She flew down into the valley, straight at the line of men, banking just before getting close enough to terrorize them. One retained enough sense to throw something at her. Close too, she could see that they had sticks and bows. And now, she could see that most of them ran or ducked instead of using their weapons.

The mammoths trumpeted and, faster than she expected, ran forward. Some stood their ground until she screamed, then all of them ran deeper into the valley.

Satisfied they were safe, and the men unnerved, Slash returned, satisfied with her efforts and the results. "Noisy."

"The hunters are climbing up here." Harrel moved slightly so his horse was turned. Not blocking hers. Not protecting her. But available if needed.

They were waving their weapons while running uphill, at first, then walking. From the way they walked both could tell that they were too tired to run, almost too tired to walk up the steep, grassy hill. Yet they came forward, as if intent on these new people and their...pets.

The men came to a stop a spear's throw away. Most focused on the one who seemed their leader, while the rest appeared to be commenting on Slash. "Why are you Premontii rodents hunting our mammoths? Treaty says you'll leave 'em alone."

"We're the King's rodents. Ranger. Harrel." He tapped his badge. "Vallezza. Sorceress. And we thought *you* were hunting them."

"Slash," Val said quietly. "Go fly circles around the mammoths. Stop them from running."

The dragon jumped into the air, causing more excitement in the ranks of the hunters. At first, the equally excited mammoths tried to scatter instead of running as a herd. She circled them, low and well within their sight, and they became a herd once again. This time, defensive. The largest were in front of the others, and all of them were trumpeting and waving their trunks.

Satisfied with her efforts, Slash made wider circles, and the mammoths quieted. A few even pulled up clumps of grass with their trunks to eat. Slash eased into a low glide and returned to her place in front of the two riders.

She folded her wings and sat upright to watch the advancing men.

"What...? What is that beast?"

"CatDragon," Val replied.

Again, there was a hasty conference of the men in front, giving the pair ample time to observe them. They were big men, with Harrel's size and coloring. Unlike him, their features were just as big. Large noses, mouths and thick brows. Broad shoulders and long arms with well-formed and equally large hands grasping spears or cudgels. They wore furs and protective leather vests, wristbands, and boots. At the moment, all of them were breathing heavily, sweating and red-faced. It was impossible to know if they were exhausted by their heavy clothing or just by running. Their long legs gave them height, so they could run, yet most of the older men were bent.

Maybe, Val thought, maimed from mining or something similar. Something they spent too much time doing. The younger men stood straight and tall. Like the Ranger, they walked. And hunted.

"The people of the Hollow Valley spoke of...dragons. Large creatures. Dangerous."

"Slash can be."

Blacktail decided it was time to complain. Peeking around Harrel, he yelled, "You've scared away the mice." He joined Slash, but even upright, he barely reached her shoulder.

Once again, the men were talking, gesturing among themselves.

Harrel made a quiet noise. "They...look like Barbarians," he decided. "Only...clean. None of the red designs cut into their skin or hair."

"You sure?"

"No, but then I didn't think Captain was civilized either. Dangerous. And... I've lost another sword. I've only my knife."

Val smiled. "Well, there's only a handful of them."

"M'Lady." The one they thought was the Head Man correctly addressed the Sorceress as he stepped forward. "M'name's Ahgorh. Head Hunter."

Unfortunate Translation, both thought.

"Herder as well."

Since he had stepped forward, well within range of Harrel's knife, Harrel dismounted, and after handing Val his horse's reins, joined the two CatDragons. He decided to be honest about them. "Hillcat." Harrel gestured at Slash first, then Blacktail. "Cat. Magicals. Both of 'em. Fire breathing, as well."

"So. They said something truthful about dragons, did they? Those Premontii." The word was an insult.

"Something wrong with the Premontii?" Harrel asked.

"Near everything, you ask me. They talk about dragons as big as the sky. Burnin' whole villages. Mammoths too. If we don't stand with 'em, we'll lose the whole herd to dragons. Them Trolls ne'er said a word about small..."

"CatDragons," Harrel said flatly.

"What's a cat?" one of the others asked.

"A small, furry hunter. Of mice."

"Humph! Not sure we have any of those. Mice. Or cats."

"Wait! Trolls? You know where the Trolls are?"

He looked suspiciously at the Ranger, one brow cocked, as if he had heard that Rangers told unbelievable Tales about their journeys. "Y... Yes," he finally said. "Why?"

"The Lady Orwren said there was something wrong in Premontii, that the their Trolls were missing."

"Missing? Run away more like."

Now it was the Ranger's turn to be silent and thoughtful, then: "Could you take us to where they are? Or where they went?"

"Again, why?"

"It's what Rangers do. Find...whatever's missing." He tapped his badge again. "This sword stands for the King's justice. We go wherever we're needed. Do whatever we can to help. Without our swords."

"Good thing, too. Seein' how you don't have a sword."

"Lost it." He shrugged, smiling. "With a Sorceress and two fire-breathing CatDragons, I don't need it."

"Mice," Blacktail put in.

The Head Man started, as if he had forgotten that the little CatDragon could speak. "Have a bit more'n mice," he said. "By now, a deer be on a spit. If you and the ladies would join us?"

"Do you...ah, pass safely by Premontii?"

"Well past. And safely. Though there be times when they have guards out an' watching. But none be there when we came. No reason for 'em as we go back."

"Then we would be happy to join you for a meal." Harrel bowed, slightly.

"I. Am. Not. A. Lady," Blacktail muttered. "You neither," he added, seeing the shiver in the air. As usual, the others had forgotten the Wraith.

CHAPTER 10

The mammoths had created a wide path through the mountains. They ate everything or stomped it into the ground. Yet they were the same as the Kingdom's sheep or goats. They went southward, into the Valley's winter for grazing and calving, giving the new youngsters a start. Then they migrated back to their home pastures. There, it was summer, and the lakes and rivers thawed, making life for vegetation, mammoths and people easier.

Ahgorh left most of the herders with the mammoths to hunt and fish throughout the warm winter moon cycles. He took two with him, one to watch each of the two humans while he watched the CatDragons. Not that they did any more than hunt and fly ahead to nap until the humans joined them.

They did what all Rangers did—they walked. Since the mountains could be too much for horses, the mounts were left to graze near the mammoths and be ridden by anyone brave enough to try sitting on a horse instead of eating it.

The mountains themselves were like none in the Kingdom. They rose to the sky, as the Singers and Bards would say when they told of the wonders far to the north, and instead of being climbable by Roads and Rangers, they were sharp-edged, made of barren rock, and often clad in snow and ice. Only pines grew up their sides, and even they were twisted and struggling against the rocks and snow.

The Head Man assured his new companions that it was warm on the high cliffs, but even that could change with just one storm.

He also shared what Lady Orwren refused to disclose about Premontii.

In the Kingdom, the designs and desires of the Nobles were kept reasonable by the King, the Rangers, and other Nobles. Plus, a generous portion of the Magicals and FaerFolk. Most of the Nobles in Premontii were more than oathed to the ruling house or Hall. They were joined to them. By marriage, by strength, or by possessing something the Ruler and the Chosen Nobles needed.

What most of the Nobles needed wore collars. People. Trolls. Anyone. Anything.

The Different.

Of course, they called them by other names. But they were all different. Herders. Northmen. Magicals. Haflings.

Ahgorh admitted Harrel had surprised him. First that Lady Orwren had even ridden with an uncollared Hafling. Secondly, because he was both intelligent and human. Haflings, he had been told, were beasts. Nothing more than animals.

Clearly, Vallezza did not agree, but then, *she* was different. A Sorceress.

Ahgorh began talking again after walking and clambering between and over mountainous rocks for nearly an entire day. They were following a thin trail, if a traveler was of a generous nature about naming. Otherwise, the muddy notch in the rocks was only a hope instead of a pathway. The sun was often excessively warm, but there was also snow.

No sign of Trolls.

"I doubt the Trolls will let you in. Come to the end of this so-called trail, fine, but let you into one of the tunnels? I doubt it."

"Tunnels?" Harrel was probably the only one not out of breath or sweating.

"Trolls make tunnels in and out of the mountains. They're Masters of stone work. They build bridges...and not just little ones across a creek, but real bridges."

"We know. We saw one. Before it fell."

"Then no Troll built it. They build bridges to last."

"It could have. If a Wizard in Bridgedale hadn't stolen the magic in it."

"Impossible. Isn't it?" he asked Vallezza.

"Apparently not."

"But why? It makes no sense. If there's no bridge, people can't trade. At least close to. They'd have to go...moon cycles. To the Northmen. And there'd be no guarantee they'd have what you need. Or just want. The Northmen trade with the Riverenders. With boats. And too often, their boats get stopped. Anyone else's boats get sunk by the Northmen."

"We're all too aware. The boats they sink are built in our Kingdom."

There was silence again, except for the heavy breathing, when none of the Herders could think of anything to say about the connections they had not known. It was broken, first by Slash landing on the almost flat top of a standing stone, then Blacktail winging into a small clearing beyond a half circle of stones.

The first three entered, as well, and none of them said a word. Reaching toward what was left of the daylight, there were more sharp-edged mountains. On most, there was a layer of snow or outlines and new snowfalls on places where rivers of old snow and ice had crept down mountainsides or slid—very slowly—around the worn edges. The setting sun was coloring the cloudy skies a golden magenta. Beyond that, the skies and the mountains were deep blues and purples. A few bright stars twinkled in the approaching night.

But it was the mountain above them that provided the most drama. It was a straight cliff, shadowy and indomitable, while the path ended at the two standing stones that marked the exit or entrance to a small circle of flat rock. Nothing grew within the circle, and there was no snow. Therefore, there were no tracks, except where Blacktail was sitting in his best CatDragon pose.

"Where...?" Harrel began only to be interrupted by a grinding and Blacktail's hasty flight. He went straight into the Ranger's arms, and from that perch hissed at the cliff wall.

The cliff was slowly opening. Sliding to the side to reveal a dark hope of a tunnel and four short men. Trolls.

Few cared to admit that Trolls were human.

At best, they were homely, deformed and magical. Like wood sprites or dwarfs. Brownish for the most part. And if not for their faces and heads...they were ordinary. Small. Slim. Muscular as they aged and worked, usually with heavy tools and stones.

Very few thought of them as intelligent.

It was their features that named them Trolls.

Eyes, ears, mouths and noses were large. Made larger by small heads, which most others agreed was not conducive to brains, intelligence or abilities.

All reasoning said they could not possibly build bridges. Or a door that opened sideways in a mountain cliff.

None of this meant they were ugly; they were just Trolls.

And they carried swords or tools that had stone-breaking hammers on one side and sharp picks on the other. The shafts fit their big worn hands.

"Whadda you want?" The voice sounded like grinding rock.

A second voice asked, "What's that?"

"CatDragon," Vallezza answered because she had made them and sounded honest. "Hillcat. And a magical cat."

"Ne'er heard o' 'em." The first voice again, and one Troll came forward. "Wha' you be wantin'?"

"To see you," Ahgorh replied. "As head—"

"Heddar. Heddar," another Troll yelled. This time a young female came out of the darkness. She too had stone-crushing tools and looked as if she knew how to use them. She just did not have enough breath for tools or running. "The Premonts. They've found the tunnel. Accell wants you."

"Led 'em here, did you?" Heddar snarled and started to close the massive door. It was a slow closing. Ahgorh pushed forward, laying a hand on the stone, as if he could stop it.

"Front. To the front," the girl screeched. "They've their wizard. With a whole army of guards. Gonna take us back."

"Not our doing," the Herder yelled.

Harrel added his hand to the stone. "You'll need magic."

Trolls also had big, blunt teeth, and Heddar bared them. As if he needed proof that he needed their help, Slash came off the rock and arrowed through the door, flying over their heads and landing inside the dark tunnel. The Troll waved them all inside, and with their help, slammed the door shut.

Lights immediately came on. More like lanterns than torches, illuminating a tunnel made to Harrel and the Herder's size.

No one stopped to question or be awed by the tunnel's size or the lights. They ran, following Slash. She only needed a wingspan in order to fly. The tunnel branched off, and there were more Trolls. Blacktail left Harrel's shoulder, as well, to fly after Slash. Like her, he flew over everyone's heads, but few noticed.

CatDragons and people and Trolls erupted into an open space. The CatDragons flew up into the sky, while the Trolls, the Herders and Vallezza and Harrel stayed close to the cliffs surrounding the open space. None of the Trolls were interested in or concerned by the others running in all directions. Unlike the Hafling and the Sorceress, they knew the valley floor was covered with houses, roads and a multitude of green spaces now all filled with other Trolls. The visitors only glimpsed them, before following a multitude of Trolls—mostly armed men—running into another new tunnel.

Once again, this tunnel was large, and for half its length, well-lit. Then there were torches being lit, and the Trolls were lined against the walls, leaving space for Heddar and the summoned Trolls.

The herders went after them. A few of the Trolls tried to stop the Hafling and the Sorceress, but they had CatDragons circling above and around them. To the Trolls, Slash was a large dragon and most of them cowered against the walls as she flew near.

If they noticed Blacktail, they noticed that he glowed in the dark, a small white dragon that might be just as dangerous as the larger golden dragon.

There were Trolls locking a matching slab of a side-sliding door, causing the two CatDragons to land on the floor near them. Some ran, others hung off the metal latches and bars, too terrified to move or more conscious of their duties.

"Open the hatch door," someone order two Trolls. They immediately unlatched what appeared to be a concealing stone. If there was an army outside, along with the Wizard, they would only see a stone being pushed away from a small dark hole instead of a tunnel where mounted riders could enter. And with a sure-footed horse, they could ride up the inclined floor, if they did not mind the warning noise of iron hooves on stone.

The stone rolled slowly, giving those inside time enough to adjust to what was left of the daylight. There was just a crack of light at first, then a sunset of gold. The Trolls came out slowly to form a guard for their leaders. Harrel carefully blocked the Sorceress, then the two CatDragons. He cautioned them not to fly out until they could see everyone.

Beyond the open door, there was a rockfall, but if the Trolls had made it, they had forgotten about horses. A handful of riders carefully walked their horses through the rocks to where more riders waited. All of these were in iron-chased armor. The slashes of sunlight through the mountains made the metal gleam, and even the horses looked impressive.

"Those down the way have better armor," Slash reported to the Ranger. "They're the real fighters. Wait. That's Captain and that Lady in front." She partially opened her wings and rose. Harrel was disappointed. He had finally thought better of Captain. Or had hoped for better, that he had spoken the truth about himself and was not one of the Cave Barbarians. He had expected the 'lady' to front an invading army. Not Captain.

He growled softly.

The riders in front of their troop moved forward, but only the length of their horses. Behind them was a row of archers. Ready, but not with arrows nocked on bowstrings.

The Trolls moved forward, as well. They had arrived with weapons and kept them. Ready to talk or to fight.

Harrel thought they would be wiser to turn and slam the open door—small though it was—shut. Unless they knew something he did not, and he had only lessons on warfare, there was no way even a small army could get through the small door. The larger had to be open. Or breached.

The door was like a stone wall and needed battering rams the size of grown trees.

Harrel saw the problem and the answer the moment he saw the white star flash in the lowering sunlight. "Slash, fly up, over the heads of the riders, but watch out for the archers."

The CatDragon took to the sky with a loud beat of wings, scaring the horses. They pranced and turned, worried and excited by what they did not know.

Slash's wings snapped open, and on a gliding down-stroke, she flew over the heads of the riders. Since she had no love for Lady Orwren, and knowing she had left the village before they had changed, she flew directly over the Lady's head, screaming.

Now the horses bucked. Turned in circles, yanking on reins.

Lady Orwren's horse matched the sound, rising on his hind legs to paw at the flyer. The Lady fell over his tail. Captain grabbed for either the horse or the Lady but missed, almost unseating himself.

Someone yelled an order, and most of the archers armed their bows. Some missed strings while they tried. Others ran.

"Dragon," someone else screamed, terrorizing the front rows of the guardsmen.

A volley of arrows flew into the air, arced, and came back down with a clatter of wood and metal. There was a hit and a yell, a curse. The Trolls turned. Swords and hammers were of no use against arrows.

The first Troll hit the small door, and suddenly, the entire stone wall was full of dust and stones and slabs of rock.

Now, the guardsmen started yelling. The solitary guardsman in front of their ranks started yelling orders. For the most part—to wait for the dust to clear. There was barely a countdown of anticipation before they could see the Trolls rushing to defend the new opening. Some of them had bows, while others had armed crossbows. A bolt or two slid through the curtain of dust and rocks.

The horsemen were regaining their positions. Lady Orwren's horse had run off and she was shouting curses.

Which might have worked.

The man next to her—to where she had been—was in control of his horse. At least enough so the beast was just prancing. Excited by the noise of his own iron-shod hooves. His rider was about to raise at least one arm...

The magic hit the Hafling. A sharp pain instead of an itch under his leather belt. The door—full of itchy magic—had fallen because the man was another spell-casting Wizard. Stealing magic. Pulling it out of the door and the pile of rocks and rubble.

Harrel started to yell to catch Vallezza's attention.

A single arrow arched over the Wizard. Not his doing. It came from one of the well-trained archers behind him.

The arrow passed over his head. A single shaft with a deadly purpose.

"Blacktail," Slash screamed.

CHAPTER 11

The little CatDragon had been tired of bouncing or being squeezed in the Ranger's arms. He wiggled out of them when Harrel forgot about him and loosened his grip. He was almost trampled before getting enough of a wing-span and down-stroke to fly over everyone's heads.

Once again, he looked at the Trolls and men and knew he was too little to be of use. He was a small dragon. The best he could do was fly in high circles and watch Slash terrify horses.

The sudden fall of dust and sharp stones instead of snow or rain was dangerous. He shot into clear air and swooped a little higher...and was attacked by an impossibly sharp pain. It went through him, and his wings faltered, unable to maintain the rhythm of flight.

He heard Slash's scream but saw nothing.

Vallezza shot a Healing Spell into the air, knowing it was dispersing even as it flew upwards. She had only an instant to save the little CatDragon as he fell. It was already too late, and she could not...

The limp body and out-spread wings caught in the dust-thickened air and landed on the ground. Vallezza was there with a second Healing Spell. It kept the little dragon alive. Another spell, a StopSpell, would keep both the pain away and, when the arrow was removed, stop the blood from gushing out. Her hands flattened around the arrow.

"Pull it, Harrel," she cried. Even with the StopSpell there was blood, and her hands reddened

Yanking an arrow out of a wound was dangerous, and Harrel knew it, but he obeyed. He pulled it out. Blood squirted out of the little dragon. Vallezza slapped her hands against the wound.

There was one wound in and another one out. Blood was slowing leaking from both as the little CatDragon died. Vallezza tried another spell. A Closure Spell this time.

"Tired. Too tired," the forgotten Wraith said. The air around Blacktail thickened, enveloping him. It was like an unseen blanket that became a warmth, while the blanket itself was no longer needed. Inside the warmth, the CatDragon was motionless.

Slash screamed, startling everyone into looking up at her.

The hillcat-dragon was changing. Screaming in fury.

And perhaps in pain as her golden dragon hide became splattered with red. Her claws lengthened as did her lashing tail. Fins had replaced her fur's fighting ridge along her back, and now they became horns and spikes. Some were tipped with claws or thorns. If she were to run her back up against another dragon or anything else, the new sharpened tips would rip into even the strongest leather. Her face was still that of a hillcat, but with longer, dripping fangs.

And she glowed. Fire red.

She rose higher into the air, and her green-white underbelly glowed with hot coals.

Slash was a hillcat. A predator. A trained guard.

Yet she had always hated the unnecessary killing of innocents. Of small wonders. Faeries. Goldfish. Small helpless birds. Kittens.

Blacktail was only a kitten. He was a hungry kitten who enjoyed his revenge on fast flying pigeons. He had done his best to be a dragon in order to rescue a Ranger from an evil wizard.

Not fighting for gold. Or land. Or power over anyone or anything. Fighting for a Ranger he barely knew, but respected, even loved.

Without anyone noticing, she had watched over him as best she could because he was only a kitten.

It was *wrong* to kill kittens. Anyone's kittens.

Slash screamed, and a blast of red-black oily dragon-fire erupted, as well. More screams filled the air. The entire front line of horses and riders was on fire.

The archers and the guardsmen stared in horror before suddenly realizing they were flammable, too close to the screams and the fires. The horses bucked off riders or carried a few straight into the massed guards. They were faster than their noble leaders or officers. They got out of the horses' way, then they ran with the escaping horses. Downhill. All of them losing encumbering weapons. Packs. Pieces of armor. Whatever they were carrying because of their training or orders.

Even the Trolls moved away. Back into the tunnel. Leaving the two from the Kingdom and their dragons alone on the hillside.

If they could have, the Trolls would have shut and barred the doors.

Slash circled down, to land near the Ranger and the Sorceress. Slowly, she was losing her red coloring and the smoke from her flames. She even whined a little.

A kitten's lost cry for help.

Harrel moved closer. Not too close, for he could feel the heat she was shedding. "It's all right," he said, his voice soft and soothing. "He's hurt. But...alive. You...were just being a dragon."

She spoke. "It was different. The castle. It was different."

"I know," he said. He did not know yet he was not lying. He understood the hillcat had just been a very fearsome dragon and that he almost understood.

She stared at the Sorceress, before suddenly leaping into the air to fly down the hill as if she were chasing the guardsmen. Perhaps to destroy them, perhaps to apologize. In only a few wing beats, she was gone into the gathering darkness.

CatDragons

The Ranger glared at the smoking burn. At the blackened, oily lumps and small bumps under a slowly drying, hardening oily blackness. "What? Just. Happened? All of it."

"Slash was furious."

Harrel was not furious, but he snarled at the evasive answer.

"She's a very well-trained guard, but she's also a female hillcat. It's her nature to guard and protect... Kittens. Blacktail's no kitten, but he's young. Weighs almost nothing. To her, he's a kitten." She sighed. "I've read about hillcats. There are Tales about them that swear they can change. Because they are magical, after all. If they get angry enough, they can change. Slash, being half dragon, changed...into more of a dragon. Now, the question is...can *you* change? You are half hillcat. Can you change into some sort of monster if you get furious enough?"

They stared at each other, Harrel seeing what Slash had become, Vallezza looking at him carefully.

"Am I afraid you could?" she asked finally. "Yes. I think you could. But am I afraid? No. You've been very angry with me, but you did not hurt me, and I don't believe you would. Or could. Half of you is human, my love, Harrel."

Their entire relationship was an experiment. The first time he kissed her, she had giggled. He had been offended. Even when she apologized. "Cat fur. And whiskers."

He was still offended by the honesty of her words but wanted to kiss her again. And did. The third time, they both forgot about his mouth, which was not even designed for speaking, let alone kissing. She was in his arms. Holding her carefully because he was very strong and had claws that would have to be clipped if he held her as often as he wanted.

"Clothes," she had whispered and found ties. Then fur and skin.

Then, mouths no longer mattered. They simply wanted, and nothing was going to stop them from taking what they so urgently wanted.

And wanted again. No matter what the differences and dangers.

"You are not one of my dragons, Harrel. One of my mistakes."

"How so? A dragon rid us, all of us, of two thieving wizards. How was that a mistake?"

"A consequence, then. The aftereffect of magic. But if Slash is going home to the Wizard's Keep, she can get the spell reversed. It wasn't a Change Spell...not like...what Blacktail here, now has. He's been...infused by the Wraith's life force. He's now a CatDragon. Changed. For always."

"He'll...live? But not change back?"

"Can't. More importantly, he can't fly or even walk. He'll have to be carried. We can get something from the Trolls..."

The Trolls were coming cautiously out of the tunnel and, like Harrel, they were seeking answers and explanations.

CHAPTER 12

The Ranger stood in the ruins of the tunnel's destroyed door and watched the sun rise over the mountains. It was not as early in the day as it seemed because of those same mountaintops and the early winter. It had snowed—already—covering the hillside and the dragon burn with the false peace of snow. The snow covered anything the Premontii people had discarded in their rush to leave. Weapons primarily. But not those on the burn; they were like piles of ashes.

Near the oily black lumps that had been their leaders. Lady Orwren. Officers. Nobles. And one Wizard.

All the people necessary to lead the rest—or so the Trolls, the Herders, and one Sorceress had said. He had grown tired of listening to them and went to check on Blacktail.

At least, that was his excuse. He had convinced the Trolls to provide food and drink to Trolls and visitors alike, but none of them wanted to stop talking and go to sleep.

So, he left. Curled up beside the sleeping dragon and went to sleep himself.

Now he was awake...and they were still talking or had taken an unseen, unfelt break, because someone—probably Vallezza— had convinced them not to try going down the mountainside in the dark. To wait until morning.

Had Vallezza joined him? Could he not know? Sense her presence? Or had the comfort of her nearness lulled him into a deeper sleep?

Blacktail's stirring had awakened him. The little CatDragon

was almost slept out and recovered, just not ready to even walk, let alone fly.

Vallezza was gone, if she had even been with them.

The sun shone, briefly illuminating the tunnel. Harrel could hear wings flapping—Blacktail—then footsteps, Vallezza's.

She too appreciated the brief sunlight, being less of the Sorceress she had been most of the night and more the woman. She slid an arm about his waist and leaned against his shoulder. Harrel pulled her closer and kissed her forehead. Since he was in the mood to make her laugh, he twitched his long whiskers forward and tickled her. She was too tired and sober to laugh. But he felt her relaxing smile.

"Blacktail?" he asked.

"Happy to learn that the Trolls keep pigeons. Not that he'll be chasing them, or mice, for a time yet."

"But he's all right?"

"You'll have to carry him down to Premontii. No flying."

"Then the Trolls have finally decided? On what they want?"

"Took some doing, but yes. Absolutely no collars, of course. But swords. Sheathed.

"You've none."

"Lost it." He smiled. "If going down mountains is as difficult as coming up, it's just as well. Anyway, I prefer my knife."

She knew the large belt knife was his only real possession. She had seen him practice with it often enough, even examined it. Once she had seen it turn, magically, into just another piece of useless cutlery. Otherwise, the Wizard who had caged him would have taken it away. He had not because everyone wore a belt knife. And usually not too sharp or solidly made.

"Then finding enough swords is their problem. But..."

"There'll be women too. And some food. The Trolls keep goats and pigeons, but, of course, both think their cooking is better than the other's. Perhaps the presence of women will convince the townspeople that the Trolls aren't coming down for revenge."

"Aren't they?" he asked.

"Some would like to. But no drawn swords and definitely no collars. Or Badges. Or at least old ones. Most of those were ripped off when they first arrived up here. T'will have to be enough because the Herders agree. So..."

"So, it's time to leave." His tone said it was past time, but as a dutiful Ranger, he bowed to his betters, whether he thought them better or not. He also prepared himself for a wait. He could gather his belongings—a pack and a small CatDragon—in less time than it took to think on them, but the others—especially women carrying food—were going to be slow. Packing and traveling.

He did not mind too much, although he did scowl just enough to make a few hurry. He needed the time to exercise Blacktail's wings before settling him on his shoulders and pack, yet inside the hood of his cloak. It was going to snow again, and Harrel wanted to be warm. And to make a warm nest for the little dragon, who had claws. He would rather the claws made holes in the cloak, and then his pack, instead of himself.

Vallezza had also become used to quickly gathering her few belongs, but she had to walk carefully among the others and tactfully hurry them along. Even though the Trolls were more magical than she, they tended to move aside if she came near, instead of hurrying forward.

At least no one had to find the narrow back trail among the rocks.

The snow-covered hillside was a broad, clean-looking trail, twice used by men, horses and at least one wagon. It was now slippery, but with breathtaking views. There was a snowstorm some mountains away. Occasional flashes of sunlight illuminated gray clouds. And a waterfall that became an annoying distraction despite the sparkle and rainbows in the water. Sometimes, in the morning light, it looked as if something—frost faeries perhaps—

were sliding down the falls, but they were empty. Very little lived in the icy water.

Besides, the men and horses had churned the streams a muddy brown, making it difficult for this third band to discern the difference between muddy, flattened stream banks and the stream itself, until the brown streams joined the fast-running creeks. They were both clear and only ribboned with muddy brown.

Sometimes, the trail narrowed as it went around a fall or a stream, while at others, there were only a few rocks above an overflow of ice and water. These places had been crossovers before the snow melted, evidence that the attack on the Troll's tunnel had been planned for some time.

There were complaints and curses about this, suggestions that the Trolls were being too lenient with their former masters, and a few collars for some of them would not be amiss.

Then they came to the bridge.

While Lady Orwren had been traveling, seeking a Ranger and help from the Kingdom, the builders in Premontii had been building a wide bridge between the plateau and the high mountains.

It was not one of the Troll's permanent stone bridges, but a wide, swinging wooden bridge.

"Is it going to be safe?"

While the others asked the bridge building Trolls the same question, Harrel asked Vallezza. After seeing so much magic and too many wizards, he wanted to know about the magic the builders used rather than their craftsmanship. That, he thought, did not look promising.

But men and horses had gone over the bridge, twice.

"There's magic in its building," she said. "But it's in moving logs. Cutting. Getting those ropes across. It's common magic and solid enough. However..."

They were nearer the edge of the cliff than the others, who

were all talking about the bridge, save for the women. They were sitting with each other in a cheerful group. Talking. Eating. Vallezza leaned over and quickly leaned back, unnoticed, except by Harrel. He leaned over and saw what the others did not. A wagon lay partially in the water at the bottom of the bridged gorge.

"There aren't any horses, so someone might have just pushed it out of the way."

Blacktail chose this moment to stretch, reminding Harrel of Slash. She could have flown over, terrorizing the horses, forcing the driver to cut the traces and horses free of the wagon. He preferred to think they just pushed the wagon off the edge for whatever reason of their own. The less he thought of dragons and heights, the better.

He took a deep breath and, followed by Vallezza, pushed past the Herdsmen and Trolls to start across the bridge. The yells and cautions, he ignored.

A wind was blowing, and the bridge moved. It swayed. Harrel look down at the moving water. The bridge seemed to move in the opposite direction. The vertigo was unnerving. When he looked ahead, he stumbled. The logs, though they were cut, were rough and required him to watch his steps. The swift water could be seen through the cracks. To add to his angst, some of the knots in the ropes were frayed and loose. Harrel found he had to keep his attention firmly on the middle of the walkway. But he did ask, "Are you all right?"

"Fine," Vallezza replied. "But I never rode a dragon. So I've no fear of heights."

Harrel managed a growl, then he was off the bridge. There was solid mud and very little snow—at least on the path. It was in the air, falling in small flakes. High mountain 'dry' snow. Very soon, warned the distant, darkening clouds, that the thick wet flakes that piled onto everything would be arriving. By nightfall, when they reached Premontii.

More people were joining them on the far bank. Some with relief, the rest even unaware they had been high in the air on an unsafe bridge.

"The Trolls know bridges," Harrel said as he watched them manage to walk carefully across the bridge without being in lock-step, yet hurrying.

"Goes against everything we've heard about them." Vallezza rejoined the Herdsmen and Trolls at the front of the reforming line. Harrel followed, more to have a clear view of the oncoming storm than to be one of the leaders. He doubted the Trolls would be any more welcomed this night than the snow.

And they were not.

The snow was as heavy as the clouds warned. At first. Then, when the road was bounded by cleared fields and dry-stone walls, it began to rain. Everyone would have preferred the snow, but without complaints, or at least not too many, they slogged through the rain and mud. Many knew exactly where they were. They had built these stone walls, stone by heavy stone.

Walls and two pillars formed the defining entrance to what the inhabitants called a city. Just past these, there stood some of the inhabitants. A short line of very wet people. Those behind the line were just as wet, but they looked determined to greet whatever arrived. The ones in front looked resigned.

One young man had his cloak open, showing the light blue of a Healer's tunic while the rest kept their cloaks closed against the rain. None had visible weapons. Three were older women, while the remaining men were past the age when they held decorative swords. On either side there were two guards with lanterns rather than swords.

After a sigh, one of the women stepped forward. "We...We have been expecting you." She opened her hands with more of a resigned shrug than a welcome. "Your... Your dragon flew over us. Last night."

Harrel straightened at those words, and Blacktail made a noise. The Sorceress spoke before he could ask questions.

"We will speak of dragons later. Now, we all need shelter. Warm fires. Do you carry swords?"

"Carry them yes. Use them no. But if you want, they can be left at the door."

Vallezza nodded. She could see that a large portion of the followers, the Troll womenfolk especially, knew where they wanted to go. Which house they had lived in as servants. Left to Vallezza, the Herdsmen, and some of the younger Trolls stood the empty houses of the most noble, like Lady Orwren's house, palace, or whatever she had called her residence. There were few servants, but to a one, she and the others knew how to care for themselves.

No one could consider the small, despondent group welcoming, but they were even less welcoming of a Hafling. Ranger or no. They glanced at him, only to have their eyes skitter away. As if just looking at his face contaminated them. Harrel sighed and continued to look around the village. Mostly at the poles.

While the houses spoke of the Troll's handiwork, they were just suited to the climate. Stone work and mostly slate. With sharp edges and steep roofs. The defining stone walls enclosed gardens, with plants now drooping because of the heavy rain. Drips off the eves. Windowsills. Puddles below.

And poles. Tall thin poles, some formed on lathes, others young trees—pine most like—some brought up from the lower mountain reaches. Carved poles. His sharp, cat-enhanced eyes saw faces before he realized the carvings were faces. At the top of a pole—at a height above his own—there were round faces with smiles. Just below, the expressions changed to worry as eyebrows lifted and eyes looked downward, as if they were drowning. But not because the rainwater was sliding down their faces.

Below them, the faces were under...

Snow. The poles marked the amounts of snow. The lowest were buried in snow. The mid-level barely above the top of the drifts. While the smiling faces at the top were above the snow's usual limits.

Snow up to Harrel's shoulders. With drifts above his head, most like. The poles marked the paths to doors or cross-streets. Someone, Trolls undoubtedly, was—had been—tasked with digging out walkways, because all the rain that was now falling could easily turn into snow or ice. Hopefully, just snow.

It seemed a foolish time to begin a siege, a war. But perhaps snow and ice were the reasons to start one. The people of Premontii had no one to clear the streets and houses. No one to rebuild or clear their dangerous bridge before it collapsed from the weight of the snow and ice.

Trade would halt. Had halted. The Trolls had been gone for a long time, and if the others he had met or just seen were any indication, then the nobles were getting low on supplies. The Commoners were already hungry and not willing to welcome enemies who would want what little they had left.

Harrel and his thoughts followed Vallezza. The 'welcomers' had agreed, they said, that the Sorceress should be housed in Lady Orwren's dwelling since the Wizard had quarters there, as well. She could access, easily, anything magical she needed, and there was more than enough room for all the people who would want to speak to her. Or the Trolls. And Herders.

If there was a meeting Hall, a Great Hall, they were not offering it to anyone. Someone who would come to the forefront and do all the organizing and accept the necessary leadership. Whoever that person was, they all knew it was a position filled only by the agreement of a Wizard. Or a Sorceress. Badged or not.

And Badged or not, she would decide who lived with her. They might whisper among themselves, hoping her stay would be a short one, but they would not say a word about the Hafling.

Perhaps the little dragon he was carrying, but not the Hafling himself.

And they would never see that Hafling indulge in a small intimacy he truly enjoyed. Whenever, or at least out of everyone's sight, Harrel could touch, hold or kiss Vallezza. It was almost an unspeakable pleasure he enjoyed. He loved her. And she returned his affections. Even the briefest of touches gave him a sense of solidity. Love was real.

At the moment, however, the briefest of kisses was all he could share with Val. The Welcomers had given her time to choose a bedroom, an easy task since there was only one with an attached bathingroom where Blacktail was currently swimming. As a cat, he hated water, as a dragon, he enjoyed it, especially with warm water. But now, the Welcomers wanted to meet. With themselves and others.

"Good," Harrel said, kissing her again, lightly. "I heard one mention 'our' dragon, and that had to be Slash. I want to hear more."

"Be careful," Vallezza said. "If the rain turns to ice..."

"Best not or you'll have 'em all sleeping on the stairs," he added, then left. He no longer wanted extra people in the house than she, but if need be...

It was still raining as he strode through the puddles—the paving stones seemed Troll revenge, for they collected rainwater—before it went down the road. Along with more water. In ditches, however.

There were a few already soaked people out in the rain, but few had seen a dragon. They at least believed there were dragons about, but had yet to see one. That did not stop those willing to speak to a Hafling about the size of the dragon someone else swore they saw. They swore it was full-grown, covering the sky, or very small, about the size of a local lizard. That, a few agreed, finally told the local populace what happened to the summer influx of lizards in winter: they grew wings and fled to warmer places.

Harrel took that Tale with him into a tavern. The place smelled of beer, cooking, and now, wet wool. It identified itself primarily by these smells since it did not have an attached stable, but the sign for an inn was carved among a poles' faces.

The common room was small, crowded with a handful of tables, chairs and benches, and it was half-full of people, some eating what looked like watery stew with coarse bread. When Harrel asked, he learned there was no cider to be had. Few apple trees grew, even in the most protected of gardens, and because Harrel was a Ranger, the innkeeper said that no barrels were forth coming from Bridgedale. Rangers, he hinted, could fix such problems with a simple order.

And there was little he could offer a Ranger, despite a duty to do so. He did say that he heard—and the source was reliable—that a small dragon had flown toward the Easterly Mountains during the night. And another said it flew on, down the pass. To the southern mountains.

The rest who swore they saw a golden dragon, said she flew south. Or mayhap west. Toward Bridgedale. Or the woods, farther toward the river. Some of them said the dragon was headed toward the Wizard's Keep, more than in any other direction. He decided to agree. She would go home. To the Wizard who could break the spell that had turned her into a fire-breathing dragon. She could become a hillcat again. A guard.

But he doubted she would forget she had exploded into fire, killing so many people. At best, he could say that they deserved punishment for attacking the Trolls—their former slaves and servants—but did anyone deserve to be burned by a furious dragon?

When he had such questions, Harrel was grateful he was 'only' a Ranger. Questions like that were for Commanders, Lords, Wizards...and perhaps, a Sorceress.

He would ask for her thoughts and reasonings, but *after* he made love to her, he decided, letting his thoughts dwell on her instead of the missing CatDragon. Or on the snow. He was not used to having snow here in the mountains long before he thought it was due. Nor would it stop long after it should have begun to turn green once again.

Sighing, not even the thought of Val waiting for him lifted his mood. Besides, she was probably still meeting with the Trolls and anyone who thought they had the right to speak for the fallen nobles.

Apparently, they did. Almost every Premontii of fifteen and older had a say in who ruled them. Almost every person. No Trolls, of course. No one whose mind had been wiped. No one who could not understand what was being asked of them. And certainly no one who could not even make a mark in the correct place.

Or simply did not want to have an opinion.

Reasonable.

Then came the unreasonable objections. Lists of objections, and each one had to be discussed, reviewed and judged. There also had to be a list of those who could do the judging.

Once, perhaps, when even Halvarrarde was a small village, choosing Lords, High Lords and even a King—after choosing to have a Kingdom, of course—was simple and quick. This person or that one who actually wanted the position, and the duties, could try for it. Pay for a position.

That was acceptable, for a Lord or Lady knew how to get walls and castles built. Wooden balustrades at first, which cleared the fields for the crops. That was a necessity in order to feed the workers and get the stones for both walls and houses.

Slowly, castles and villages and farms were built.

Unlike the streets and alleyways Harrel now noticed that were empty. Premontii looked empty of people. The guards who had massed behind the nobles and officers were either at home or in the local taverns, deadening their worries about tomorrow.

And now, it was going to snow the fat, wet flakes that accumulated quickly. There was already an ankle-deep layer of snow on the roads and very few cleared paths. Footprints, like his were beginning to vanish.

And like a goad, Harrel noticed that he was now hungry. He couldn't remember when he had last had a meal—clearly before he began the hunt for Slash—but exactly when and what he had managed to find or even if he had found anything other than the tavern's meager offerings, he could not remember.

Nor could he remember the shortest way back to Lady Orwren's small palace. And the kitchen. There had been a bubbling kettle in the Lady's kitchen. Not a stew she would be served, but a thrown-together stew for servants and guards. Mayhap, even more importantly, for those cleaning paths through the snow. To the Lady's kitchen, not her front door.

He crossed alleys and roads, asked directions from the path shovelers, until he found a clear path to a door he remembered. And as he remembered, there was a kitchen maid serving a dipper full of mushy stew. The cook was chopping carrots, potatoes and onions that would soon be added. In the meantime, he and the workers had to subsist on bread, cheese and tea. And nuts, of course.

The Welcomers who had partaken of the richer meal, had already left. Perhaps because the cook said that Blacktail had become tired of the bathing room and flown down the stairs to fly in and out of the new rooms before settling next to the only fireplace with a fire. He was a very small dragon, but he was still a dragon. The cook insisted she was not afeared of such a small dragon and was glad to see all the extra mouths depart for their own homes and meals. She had enough to feed.

Harrel had just begun eating when Vallezza came through the kitchen door. She had been outside and was dressed for the weather in a wet cloak, which she hung on a peg. Boots went below and replaced by an ordinary pair of slip-ons. Gloves came off in one fluid movement, to be carelessly thrown on the kitchen table as she leaned over, kissed his forehead, and went to the fireplace. The cook and the maid stared as she took a bowl and dipper to help herself to stew. As she set the wooden bowl on the table next to Harrel, she wiggled her fingers, and the stew began to steam. Everything was now perfectly cooked, ready to eat, so she sat on the wooden bench and helped herself to a cup of water and a slice of bread.

Harrel was staring just like the two servants, but he always stared whenever he first saw her—marveling at the magic she used and the magic she was—to him, at least.

"Eat," she said.

Vallezza's welcome was much warmer than the wind that was now blowing. When Harrel left on the hunt for Slash's direction, he thought the additional cold would freeze the rain and puddles, but it was now snowing. There would be ice and slush, but with a covering of snow. For the most part, the rain had stopped, so the covering would not be ice.

"It's snowing." He was glad to be back, but cautious. The Sorceress was smiling and yet...

"Slash went both south and east. Probably east. Back to the Wizard's Keep." He took a deep breath. "Blacktail and I should be able to catch her..." He stopped moving. "Uh?" he managed, then added, "They finish?"

"Somewhat. The Trolls have gone home. Who becomes High Lord is not as important to them as knowing they will not be treated as servants. One or two will occupy the noble's house where they were not even servants. They were slaves, and *that* will not happen again. There will be no bridges built if the Trolls are not treated like the StoneMasters they are."

"Reasonable."

"They've yet to decide how the bridges will be built. If wood or stone."

She paused, and the fascinated cook and maid suddenly became very busy.

"They've elected a...Lord. The High Lord. Someone to lead them. Probably just during the Wintering. Mind, the people of Bridgedale will have little say until the Trolls build them a new bridge, but they all decided."

"So?" Harrel barely looked interested. But he had stopped eating.

"They want...you. Lord Ranger."

"No," he exclaimed without thinking.

"Yes. Sorry to say, but you're not human enough to be worrisome yet not fully a Magical. A Ranger. A Badged Ranger. Oathed to a faraway King. Oathed to give aid to whoever asks it of you. And a Dragon Master."

"I am not."

"Ah, but you are, my Lord Ranger. And you are the only one they all trust. The only one who has ever seen a King. You spent a year observing the last King. And you, personally, know King Gallen. You are the only one without ties to anyone here in all of the villages, if you include the Trolls Hollow Valley. And the only one with the backing of a Magical."

He was also a cat, and he growled, knowing she was right and would convince him before the snow stopped falling. Which might be next spring, long after this snowstorm trapped him here in Premontii.

Still, he tried to dissuade her. "No. Besides, I don't really know how to be a High Lord. A King, mayhap, but what's a High Lord do? Why aren't there more of them?"

"Because it's a temporary position. A title for life. Usually temporary when something catastrophic happens to Kings or Lords. Like now. The High Lord decides what the missing Lords should be doing. Something as simple as clearing snow. Until there's a new Lord. Usually for every castle or village. And, if possible, the High Lord has a Magical with him. To advise. Work whatever magic is required. You already have a Magical by your side." She smiled and then sighed. "There's another good reason to have you as High Lord. You have me...Hafling...so there's no reason for you to spawn lordlings."

Had another spoken such a hurtful truth, Harrel would have glared, or snarled, at least showing his fangs if not biting. Instead, he looked away.

She reached over and, touching his chin, turned his face to hers. "It will always be so, my dear Ranger. No matter how much gold you wear or the color of your tunic. Or how much you are loved." She caressed his cheek, then spat a very small cussword. "Whiskers. Damned cat."

He managed a smile at the too-familiar complaint.

"Some night, I swear I'm going to cut them off." She stood, gesturing for him to do the same. "Might as well...have a nice long bath. While we discuss your acceptance."

Yet she decided to discuss the reason he was so unwilling to acknowledge what was already decided.

"Harrel, Slash will be all right. She's a trained guard. Not a fighting guard, I'll admit, but trained. And a hillcat. She can fend for herself."

"She killed people."

"I know. And she wasn't trained for that, at all. One can't train to be a fire breathing dragon. It just happens. Mostly because she's also a female hillcat. Maternal. Born to care for kittens. And the helpless. Like Blacktail. And she'll have the entire Wintering to think on it. Spring comes, you can go after her. All of us can. You. Me. Blacktail."

She had a thought for a moment, then dismissed it. Following Slash would be easier if, like Songlest, she had the magic to see and use the transporting doors. She did not. Thinking about the doors made her think about the Faerie, then sigh and forget her. Songlest was probably on one of the Wizard's quests. Gone for the moment. Or mayhap off being one of those faeries who loved to dance in storms. Afterwards, they almost had to walk before gathering enough energy to fly. Most of them thought that an equal trade. Vallezza shrugged that thought away as well because she had enough to do and magic to do it.

Harrel believed the Sorceress. Trusted her. But he did not trust the fools who told him a handful of Tales about a large or small dragon that flew over their village and burned it to the ground.

Or mayhap being the cause of such an early snowstorm.

Whatever, he would do as they asked, as a Ranger. He would be Lord Ranger.

But he knew he would be The Hafling Lord. They would whisper that, to get rid of him as quickly as they could manage, not knowing—or mayhap not even caring—that he wanted to be gone as quickly as he could, as well.

She smiled again, and he knew the bath would indeed be long but filled with more than washing. And it would be very enjoyable. As would the rest of the evening. Time would have to be taken for another meal, something served before a fire, if he could find servants and firewood.

He could, he supposed, order those who wanted to be guests at his table to bring a log or two in trade.

While still saying 'no' Harrel strode through the palace and, looking for apprentices and houseguards, ordered the two tavern owners and the innkeeper's spouse to meet in one handful of days here in what was still called Lady Orwren's common room. And they were to be accompanied by one representative from what was now their district.

He did not expect obedience, for Rangers made suggestions,

sometimes backed by the King's Laws or even a sword. But now that he was a Ranger, he was surprised to discover that he had learned so much about villages and people just by spending so many years Wintering with them. The very next morning, he made lists of what he wanted to 'suggest' to everyone, no exceptions. By then, he had agreed to at least look the part.

However...

"Does a High Lord really require so much gold?" he grumbled. His green tunic was cleaned, repaired and looked like it was just a sensible color. Temporary. But there was a pile of gold on the neatened bed they had shared. "How did you come by so much gold?"

"Lady Orwren seems to have collected every piece of gold in the village. Chains. Gilded ribbons. Knots. It really isn't so much, but it will be impressive."

"Shouldn't it wait until I'm actually a Lord?"

"First impressions." She smoothed out the gilded ribbon and made it wiggle around the tunic hem. Then the sleeves. The neckline, which was cut simply to ease tying his shirt, acquired more ribbon and the accent of gold chain. A cut green stone sparkled in the center of the ribbons repeated design.

A second gold chain piled itself next to the tunic. It would go over his head and the Ranger Symbol of a gold tree, with more cut green stones that would hang just below the neck opening. Unnoticed, a gold design wiggled onto his leather armguards, which were polished and shone more now than they had when they were new.

"Dragons," he said, now seeing the entire design. "Why dragons? And where's Blacktail?"

He flung open the bedroom window, and the little CatDragon flew inside. Harrel expected complaints about the snow, but the CatDragon was dry. He circled the room, found a mirror frame as solid as a tree limb and settled there to wash.

"He's your answer. You've a CatDragon. And a sword." She gestured at the sword and leather sheath that hung on the back of a chair. "You can wear it or not."

"Swords are an obvious nuisance. I'd prefer my belt knife."

He took up his belt and found that it too was polished and free of nicks and scratches. The knife's leather sheath was also polished, but the knife looked common-made. Not a smith's best metal or work, because the magical runes were hidden.

He stomped into his boots, more to waste time than to see what snow, water and no cleaning had done to them. They were polished and fit perfectly.

"Oh, very well. I'll play High Lord." He offered his arm and left the chamber door open so Blacktail could follow.

There were fewer people crowding the common room and many of them were being 'softened' with generous helpings of tea, fresh breads and butter, and warm journey bread.

Ahgorh grinned at him and bowed with such flourish he alerted most of the others to their new Lord's arrival. They bowed with varying degrees of deference. Then, it seemed to Harrel that they attacked. Or intended to. Harrel was busy handing the Sorceress into the chair nearest what was certainly his. It was high-backed and elaborately carved with designs and what Harrel thought of as roses. He was more interested in the elaborately embroidered cushions and armrests. And if the chairback would hold Blacktail.

The CatDragon tried to balance there, decided he could not and fluttered down to the seat of the other empty chair. There, he folded his wings and sat like a royal housecat surveying the peasants.

The first of the peasants, a Troll with a goodly amount of gold on his tunic and a roll of papers to hand pushed forward. The accompanying Trolls blocked access by anyone else.

"M'Lord. The plans for the bridges. Repairs to the swinging

bridge." He sneered. No one liked the swing of the suspended bridge. "Then, near the same design for access to Bridgedale." A wooden footbridge while the stone bridge was being built. Not as grand as the old bridge but more than adequate.

"Magics will be necessary, M'Lady." He bowed to Vallezza. "For the stones."

She nodded.

Harrel understood his reasoning. There was wood for the first bridge and more than enough for the second, if the Sorceress enspelled them so no one could steal the magic ever again. An apprentice could even work the spells if she could find one during the winter, since a wooden bridge merely needed help with the stringing of the first ropes across the gorge. And a bit of lifting. One of the Trolls would cross on the ropes after they were firmly anchored.

"We would like..." A merchant, a high-ranking Commoner, began although it was clear what he wanted to say. "We want a stone bridge, M'Lord."

"They have wood, M'Lord."

"Means cutting down trees. The repairs. The rebuild he is suggesting... It will swing, M'Lord."

"I noticed," Harrel replied. "Can you lessen the swing, Sir?" The Trolls had a new home, but little access to gold, so it was difficult to know a Troll's rank.

"Yes, M'Lord."

"Then wood it is. Stone later. Probably *after* Bridgedale's new wooden, bridge."

"Yes, M'Lord," the pleased Troll said. Two new stone bridges would cost the villagers enough for a number of new tunics and jewelry.

"Then..." Harrel looked around the room, and an older man in a grey-black tunic with a dilapidated feather on his leather badge, waved papers at him. He was clearly Premontii's chief Scribe.

"Snow, M'Lord. I've lists. It looks to be near a half snowfall. Full needs...well, everyone, M'Lord."

"Then we shall have everyone," Harrel assured him although he did not know what a half or full snowfall was. The Scribe would tell him—he did think the colored poles on every street or near every gate had something to do with measuring—if the Scribe liked his rank. If not, there were more scribes since they were rarely drafted into the guards. Nor were they nobles. At least of high rank.

"M'Lord." Ahgorh claimed his attention again. "The snow's too heavy for traveling. Mind if I stay here for what you call the Snowfall Winter?" He managed to pronounce the latter in Common while being insulting. What he and the mammoths enjoyed, he did not consider worth calling a snowfall.

"Of course." Harrel nodded graciously. "Since you're a herder I'm certain we can find you a position you can trade for a room. Meals even."

He waved at the smaller secondary fireplace, which awaited a fire. There was kindling, logs, a box of strikers all handy, but the hearth held more than just a readiness for a warm fire—there were flat pillows on the hearth stones and the floor. Each one held a sleeping cat. They had spent the night meowing, eating in the kitchen that morning—some in exchange for a dead mouse—and were now asleep on the pillows, awaiting a warm fire. If someone came in with their dogs or birds, there would be a riot.

"Someone needs to herd the cats," Harrel said, smiling.

"I'll shovel snow, thank you. Straight to some kind lady's door." He bowed again, and this time Harrel stifled a laugh.

And before he thought being High Lord was going to be an easy task, he had to remember the men—and women—he had met since he was old enough to have memories. Some had wanted more, although he was sure they had more than enough. Like his long-dead master and others he had met afterwards. Yet there were generous men. Foremost was Welslin. A good man. A good Ranger. And others who wanted to help. Some for a fair share for themselves and for others. To be a High Lord, he simply had to remember both. To stop one and emulate the other.

And go out and shovel snow. He had done so often enough. Sometimes it was hard, cold work. Other times it had been play. Strapping boards onto his boots—later in his apprenticeship when he actually had boots—and stamping snow on the pathways and Roads until it became solid enough for a horse-drawn sleigh. The StableMaster usually came out to stop the nonsense: the snow fights, the extra patterns stamped in the fresh snow, the snow people and monsters.

When the innkeeper's spouse and the two tavern owners arrived, the populace discovered how unnerving a High Lord who growled orders could become.

All of them were to find at least one reliable, but unoccupied, guard who had a weapon at hand, and they were to go down the mountains to where it was raining, not snowing, and find any of the nut trees that grew in the warmer climes. They were to bring back sacks—on pack animals if they were available—or carried if not. The bounty was to be given to the three new lords. The two tavern owners and the innkeeper's spouse. They also had the task of searching the empty houses of the old lords for any supplies the people needed.

The people themselves were to clear the pathways to their houses and to clear the roads to the front and back.

To ensure compliance, he walked the streets, pounding on doors after wading through snow, to see why his orders were not obeyed. If there was a true reason, the new Lord was given the task of solving this problem, as well. And if this did not work, he walked the streets with the rapidly recovering and flying CatDragon. Blacktail was not capable of flaming houses or even pathways in the snow, but the idea was terrifying.

And if it was not, there was always a walk with the Sorceress. Vallezza was the only Magical in the High Reaches, and she had her own lists of things for people to do, and the means to enforce her orders.

Still, it was going to be a long winter, so Harrel gave them a hope they did not even know they longed for. Instead of exchanging the King's sword he wore on his Ranger's Badge for Vallezza's dragon, he left the sword and the red border. Both were his oath to them and that faraway King. He was High Lord for one Wintering. Come spring, they could decide who was to replace him.

Someone, he hoped, who could herd cats.

PART TWO

Elsewhere

JoAnn Parsley

CHAPTER 13

The rain became a downpour, drenching AJ. She swore a few unladylike words and hurried forward. It was perfect weather for trespassing, she thought. No one to see her. No one in the Victorian mansion. She passed a warning poster the demolition company had posted on a telephone pole. Tomorrow this area would be leveled in the name of progress.

Better, especially, than the fence. Damned fools, she called them. Fences made people think there was something valuable inside. So, they ripped open unauthorized holes. Big holes where someone could drive a small car through the missing plywood.

She squeezed through a smaller hole, because someone had strung wire across the biggest. This one was open, already full of mud from the morning's cold drizzle. Even the thought of the gray morning made her shiver.

Or so she told herself.

The old house was not haunted. AJ was modern. She did not believe in ghosts, monsters or demons.

Or the Albert Square Monster.

She glanced back. A few leafless tree branches leaned over the fence, scraping along the wood and metal. They were all that remained of the Victorian Square Park. The fancy, exclusive, little park for the Albert Square development.

Even over the rain, she could hear the highway traffic. The trucks and cars crowded the highway at all hours. But it only made noise when the traffic moved. During the rush hours, it did not.

Revenge, she thought, for dividing the square, tearing down

the old Victorian mansions to build a highway—above ground so there would be parking space under the highway for too many cars.

The Square with its dead trees and two mansions converted to offices were all that were left. And tomorrow morning, this one would be razed.

Already, the bulldozers and loaders were behind the fence, waiting. She ran past them.

AJ was here first. She had tried to get a permit to salvage anything of interest, if not of real value, but a student of Urban Archeology was not a person with any clout. It didn't help, and she knew that she still looked like a teenager.

An oddly dressed teenager.

Her work clothes were a Dickie's plain tan shirt and good, solid leather boots. She was grateful the boots were also waterproofed. The cargo pants were already wet at the hems. As wet as her long brown jacket. It was water resistant. As was the plain, industrial-strength backpack that made the rain drops sound like drumbeats.

The sound stopped as she squeezed down the crumbling basement stairs. Someone had locked the cellar door. Then forgot about it. Anyone with any business in the restored mansion used the front door. Even repairmen. She had been in the place, once, and knew the cellar door and steep stairs were off the modernized kitchen. That was now empty. Or was supposed to be.

These outside stairs were now full of mud, pieces of concrete, stones, bricks and dead tree limbs. Not forgetting garbage. Plastic bags. Newer extra-large coffee cups. Forever plastic.

And unmentionables.

The cellar door had once had a half-window—with broken glass—and a plywood cover. Also broken. AJ grabbed a corner and, saying something like a prayer, yanked. The wood cracked and most fell away. She could now reach through the broken glass panes—after putting on her leather gloves, of course—reach though and feel for latches and door knobs. There was one large latch and a doorknob, which fell off in her hand. Another yank and the door almost opened. She had to kick away garbage first, open the door, then after removing her pack squeezed through.

Frustrating, but she was a polite person, and she shut the door behind her.

She stood for a moment, breathing in the stale, damp air. It smelled of furnaces, storage and mice. Maybe rats.

To be honest, she did not know what rats or mice smelled like. Her apartment was small and cheap, but there were no mice. Just the occasional cockroach and the smell of bug spray.

This was what she thought of in the first cellar room while she dried off then pulled her miner's hardhat lamp out of her pack. Then put it on. The light, although old, brightened the darkness.

There were mostly thick stone and concrete walls. They were the reason this mansion had been renovated. The small-by-modern-standards mansion and its foundation were old-fashioned solid. Good workmanship. Now it was full of trash. Unwanted office furniture. A mattress. Everything of value had been removed long ago. This was unrepairable junk garnished in spider webs.

And two furnaces. A really old coal furnace that had provided steam heat, and a modern gas furnace. The AC came from useless units in the back windows. No one had wanted to install expensive AC in the front windows. They were too old and too big. But elegant. So the front rooms were hot in summer and cold in winter.

AJ edged around the junk to the bigger coal furnace, then behind it. There was a door in the wall.

It was an old wooden door with real iron hinges and a heavy-duty handle. Of moderate value, might fetch a few bucks from a second-hand shop. She grasped it and pulled. The door opened about an inch. The junk on the floor was door-stopping. AJ kicked it away.

The door opened to a coal cellar. And more spider webs.

Ancient. Black dust. Little else.

And a missing wall.

According to the architect's plans she had managed, finally, to find, there were four cellars. The one she had just been in. The coal cellar. One in the front. One to the side. A kitchen cellar, perhaps. A wine cellar. Who knew. Empty.

She moved her head so the light shone in the large room. As her lamp was more efficient in tunnels, most of the basement lay in darkness.

Suddenly, she felt a chill, as if someone, or something, was lurking in a dark shadow.

"I...know you're there," AJ breathed. Her heart started to pound, and her throat tightened. If she was lucky, it was just one of the demo guys, looking for something to sell.

"Who are you?" a man's muffled voice asked, his tone demanding but calm. "What're you doing down here?"

Instead of an answer, there was a crack of thunder. The storm had moved overhead. AJ flinched although it wasn't too loud and scary this deep in the cellars. Still, she hated thunderstorms.

The shadow moved closer.

"Oh, shit," she whispered, cursing. Very carefully, as quietly as she could, she began to unsnap her wet jacket. Then, the holster's snap. Her hand rested on the butt of her gun.

She hated the gun. It frightened her. Even hours on the range and safety lessons made her wish she had another choice besides a gun. She was just too small and defenseless, however, to go anywhere without it. "Stop. Please."

That sounded wrong. Too innocent. Naïve. "*Stop* and I mean it. I...I have a gun. I don't want to shoot you. But I know how."

"Gun?"

She didn't know if he questioned or sneered. She thought she sounded useless. Afraid. "A revolver. I'm a good shot. And I have...six bullets." Her gun was just an empty threat. True, she had taken lessons and practiced on the range, but only at paper targets. Not even paper people silhouettes.

A boom louder than any at the gun range made her flinch again. But this time, the crack of thunder was followed by a loud groan and then a crash as the ceiling fell. Beams and wooden planks crashed to the cement floor.

The shadow cried out.

"Are you hurt?" Her fear and the gun were forgotten.

There was dust in the beam of light and a pile of debris which had been an upstairs floor. A shape moved. Groaned.

Without thinking, AJ moved forward. And stopped. "What...? Are you okay?"

"Pinned," the voice growled. Then he groaned and she came forward, shining her light on him. His face was hidden behind a black respirator mask, and his head was shrouded in a hooded cape. The sight gave her a chill. A pile of debris had landed on his long winter coat, and a beam trapped his leg.

He was pushing off smaller pieces. "If it helps, my name's John." His tone was bitter and disparaging through the mask.

His name did not help because she intended to rescue him no matter how scary he looked. She stopped to see what she should do first. At a mere 5'4" and 100 pounds, there wasn't much. And she feared she did not have the strength to lift the beam, but she intended to try her best.

"Fine mess you're in here, John," she said, thinking that he was just calling himself 'John.' For his own reasons. Just as he was here, in the basement, for his own reasons. She'd bet that John wasn't his name, at all, and his reasons for being here were no more legal than her own.

"Damn," was all she said and rushed forward to the wooden beam, hoping his leg wasn't smashed. She grabbed on end of the beam and "One. Two. Three" lifted. With her legs as she had been taught. He did his best to help, then scrambled out before she dropped it. From somewhere above them there was an echoing sound. Both looked up in time to see the floor tremble.

"Run," AJ yelled and sprinted into the coal cellar. Heavy footsteps said he followed.

The upstairs floor creaked and crashed. Dust and smoke came off a debris pile, thickening the air. Creaks and groans came from the ceiling.

"Come on. If that goes... There's a door to the cellar stairs outside."

Suddenly, it wasn't there. The floor upstairs had fallen, and now AJ could hear—and worse—understand the crackling noise coming from above. The old house was on fire. The lightning wasn't just near, it had hit the roof.

"There's another door," she yelled. The old coal furnace was probably holding up this part of the failing upper floor, which gave her time to get into the coal cellar. "Here. Somewhere here. On this back wall."

She shined her light on the wall, moving her head back and forth until she saw indentations in the painted, plastered wall. "There." She yanked a large folding knife out of her pocket. After flipping it open, she started to dig the point into the wall. He followed with a bigger belt knife from a leather sheath.

"A secret door? In a cellar... How did you know?"

The paint was blackened grey, which only revealed the dents with direct light. Otherwise, there was just a paint-splattered wall.

"Journal. I...stole it." It was an insane time to talk, but the words insisted on flowing. "I volunteer for the Historical Society. They got...everything from here. Boxes. Trunks. Stuff for us volunteers to sort through. They took all...the antiques...and anything valuable...then discarded the junk in the basement."

She had dug down one side and started on the bottom indentation. There was another nerve-wracking crash on the ceiling above them. And perhaps a blast of heat. Or just sweat replacing the wet from the rain.

"I read the journal." The heat was coming down from the ceiling now sagging above their heads. "Said there was a door down here. To a tunnel."

Both worked desperately.

"Door!" It was a cry of triumph as the wood and plaster door sagged away from the knife-honed cracks.

"One. Two..." he said, gloved fingers digging into the opening and yanking at the door-sized wood. It fell away, revealing another door.

"Church door!" AJ shouted. "Wet?"

"Varnish," he said.

The shiny door was dark wood, with an arch carved into the top half. A wooden cross fit nicely inside. A sturdy beam crossed the mid-section, held firmly in place by two wrought-iron hooks. AJ reached for the beam, but he pushed her aside. The beam was solid wood and heavy.

He grunted, lifted it off and threw it aside. The door creaked open.

"Open?"

"Church doors. Open." She pulled on one hook, and the door groaned open. Both ducked inside. AJ first with the light. "I...I returned the journal."

"Why?"

"Tunnel." She could only breathe out one word. She spit out a spider web that had hung from an old log beam. There were more logs; some still had bark on them. "The journal said. A demon came out. Of the tunnel."

"Demon?" He snorted.

"I don't believe in demons, but The Albert Square Monster is a great urban legend. It's been called that for years and years. The earliest settlers called it a demon."

There was another crack. Distant. Either the upper floors fell, or the storm was moving away. By now, someone should have called the fire department.

Clearly, he did not believe in either the monster or the fire department. "Where...?" he demanded.

"Uh..." That was a question she did not want asked. "There are a lot of tunnels down here. Root cellars. Safe. Ah...the Underground Railroad. You know. If protesters had known the historic value here, they would have stopped the demolition."

"And you know this because?" He was growling.

"Oh. I'm AJ Walker. Alice Jane Walker." She said her entire, ridiculous name. "Urban Archeologist. Will be. Good Master's Thesis, these tunnels."

She tried her best to sound knowledgeable. Determined. Her friends agreed she was determined, but also cute when she lied. Or just said a partial truth.

This was a secret tunnel. Or a tunnel with a secret, but she had no idea where it went. She just walked forward.

Both eased down the dark tunnel. AJ went first because she had the light. She shucked her backpack, took out a spray paint can, and shot a splotch of red on the left wall.

"Why?" he asked.

"Red. Right. Returning." She quoted a sailor's saying. "I spray on the left so when I return, the marks are on my right. For boats and such. Never been on a sailboat, but..." She stopped.

He almost bumped into her.

"Listen."

Tap. Tap. Tap.

"Someone working on stone? Carving by chisel and hammer? Who's down here?"

"Turn off your light." He pointed to a light in the darkness. It was coming from a hole in the tunnel floor where someone had broken through.

A dainty, dirty hand suddenly appeared on the lip of the hole.

Then another hand, and a small green woman pulled herself out. Her purple hair was a fright, her filthy dress tattered, and she started crawling toward the darkness. How ever she had arrived at the hole, or created the hole, the effort had taken her strength. She collapsed, panting.

A nasty laugh followed her. Then another hand appeared in the hole—a clawed hand this time—also of a greenish tint. Then a dark green face appeared, long pointed teeth in a wide grin that was not a friendly smile. The green body followed. Easily. Beastly. And a smell so putrid...

The monster was huge, his massive shoulders covered with leather and metal-worked armor. And fur. Long strands of black fur. Or maybe hair, braided and twisted strands from his chin, yet he was bald. A rutted, warty bald skull. More of the same fur/hair hung from his beefy legs below a leather skirt, under which his huge, filthy hand disappeared to scratch his crotch.

The gesture was familiar to AJ, as was the smirk. She feared he intended to rape the small female.

The woman hissed at him, tried to pull herself to her feet to run, only to stop and stare at AJ for the first time. "Help," she muttered.

AJ turned on her miner's lamp and unsnapped the holster strap. "Don't you dare touch her."

The green monster turned his entire oversized body toward her. "Ah. More fun." He chortled and reached for her.

There was no talking to this creature. She pulled the gun but found herself suddenly slammed into the wall.

A fist flashed past her.

The green monster easily knocked the blow aside then flung John to the floor, easy as a ragdoll, laughing.

AJ's training snapped into defense mode. Gun up. Two hands. Elbows locked. Point. Shoot. The gun blast was far louder in the tunnel than at the firing range.

The green creature stopped his attack to look at the bullet hole in his armor and the black goo oozing out. But he did not collapse. Instead, he bared his teeth and lunged at her.

"Oh, no..." AJ held her breath. This guy was fully intent on murdering her. Fighting panic, she shot him a second time. Blood and brain matter sprayed from his bald head, and he collapsed.

"You killed him," the woman cried.

AJ stared. Astonished. Stunned. She *had* killed someone, something she had thought she'd never have to do.

With urgency, the woman waved the two of them forward. "Hurry. Others will come."

AJ holstered the gun, snapped the strap, then helped her hapless protector up off the floor and rushed him past the green body. The small woman kept waving at them while hurrying away from the body and the breach in the tunnel floor. Seemed rescue had given her energy.

As AJ ran forward, she glanced down into the opening. There was a dimly lit cavern below them. Torches. And movement. More green monsters were gesturing upwards. Their eyes were wide with surprise, but their pointed, blackened teeth were bared in anger. Then they were gone as she ran past the hole, her astonishment forgotten.

The three of them hurried forward to where light was beginning to grow at the end of the tunnel. And, AJ noticed, the green woman was beginning to get stronger. Running a little faster instead of collapsing.

The light did not become eye-scorching because the exit was covered with dimming brambles and roots. Then it splintered into spots of sunlight and greenery instead of just grey stone. The tunnel, as well, changed. The light revealed cracks in the ceiling, then rocky debris lay underfoot, and then the sun shone between the trees and bushes.

A whole new world suddenly opened.

The woman did not stop, but her followers did. Stopped and stared.

Brilliant blue sky had replaced the relentless rain. Sunshine illuminated a grassy hill below them, then a forest of trees, more distant mountains and even more forested mountains turning blue before they vanished into the clear sky.

"Hurry!" the frantic little woman ordered. "There should be a road that will take us to a hut."

Out of the tunnel's maw and half-way down a grassy hill, they came to a double-rutted path cutting across a meadowland of seemingly fresh-mowed grass and gorgeous flowers.

They call this a road? AJ thought although she obediently hurried.

There was no time, apparently, to ask where they were. If she started asking questions, she'd have to ask a dozen more. Like why was the small woman turning a lighter shade of green, her hair flowing long and clean, her dress mending?

AJ followed her into the shadows of the trees, not a forest it turned out, but just a stand, as they quickly emerged to another field of grass.

And a hut.

Four stone walls and a slate roof. Not much of a fence on the left side, a stone chimney in the back. In the front was a door made of wide wooden planks with black metal hinges. No windows. The woman ran to the door and shoved it open. Inside, there couldn't have been more than two rooms.

"Tonight," the little woman began immediately, "we'll build a fire to keep us safe from the ogres."

"Ogres?" AJ had so many questions. Just because she had seen a green monster—and killed it—didn't mean she could suddenly believe it was an ogre...that ogres even existed. Either she was dreaming, couldn't believe her own eyes, or in a place where she'd have to convince herself to believe anything was possible.

CHAPTER 14

T he green woman ordered them to go into the forest and collect all the firewood they could. "We'll need fires to fend off the ogres."

"Ogres are not real," AJ insisted.

"You just killed one," she countered. "They're very real Here, and come nightfall, they'll be hunting us. Lots of them. We need firewood."

"Okay. Firewood. But wait a minute." AJ had been right. Ask one question and there would come a dozen more. "Why are you speaking English?"

"I speak decent enough Common."

"But we understand you. Your lips move but don't match your words. Like some *foreign* horror flick." AJ waved an outstretched hand to John for conformation. "Right?"

He shrugged.

The woman looked red-faced and ready to swear. "It's a Translation Spell. The FaerFolk cast it so everyone can understand each other. All over the Kingdom. When you crossed from Elsewhere to Here, you came under the spell."

"I'm under a spell? You must be joking."

"Do I look like I'm joking?" The woman was losing patience. "The FaerFolk's magic is powerful. Perfect." She pointed to the door. "Firewood. Now."

When no one moved, little sparkles of light shot from her like a visible manifestation of her anger.

"Who are you?" AJ demanded, although she was becoming

worried. There was too much that was strange and unexplainable.

"Oh? The name trading you want then? I am Songlest. I am indebted to you. And who are you?"

"AJ."

"A-J." She nodded. "And you, sir?"

"John."

"Ja-hon." She mispronounced his name. "Now! Firewood. Dead limbs. All you both can carry. We'll need enough for all the night. Otherwise, the ogres can get in." She left to go out into the sunshine.

The other two watched.

"Ja-hon?" AJ asked him. "Why didn't you correct her?"

"I like it," he said in a calm, low voice. "Has a nice ring to it, don't you think?"

She shook her head. "We better get that firewood." Seemed shooting that ogre was not going to go without consequences.

"First..." He started stripping. Gloves, short hooded cape, winter coat...and huge shoulder pads. He shrank in size right before her eyes. In shirt and suspenders, he looked tall and slim. When he removed his respirator mask, there was but a shadow of a beard on a plain face. Dark eyes, crooked nose and mouth, and a mop of black hair, a bit disheveled by the hood. He adjusted the belt knife around his waist. "Too hot for all this garb."

He was used to living in a cold basement. There was sadness about his calm expression, embarrassment, and all together, he looked like...

"You," AJ exclaimed. "You're the Albert Square Monster. That's why you were in the basement. You've pretended to be the monster who's been scaring everyone."

He grunted.

She understood and felt the same embarrassment for exposing him as a fraud. "Your clothes...those shoulder pads...make you look gigantic, and scary. You disappeared because you went underground. Why?"

"I don't want to talk about it." His expression was harsh. He dumped the warm clothing on the floor and left, heading for the woods.

"I need to learn some manners..." AJ muttered to herself, "and when to shut my big mouth." She followed him outside.

After two armloads of firewood were stacked on either side of the fireplace, AJ handed Ja-hon one of her energy bars from the backpack. "Where's Songlest?" she asked.

"She is lying in the grass. Sunbathing. She's almost a pale yellow green now."

They both added armloads to the piles of wood, one of which almost blocked the door to the tiny closet on the other side of the fireplace. AJ thought of it as a very old-fashioned water-closet. Without a tub. But neither of them would have time to bathe, although they were dirty enough. Unless Songlest was wrong about the ogres coming. Then they would have all night. To bathe and to sleep before deciding where to go from here.

In the meantime, they both brought in another armload, and this time, Songlest followed them inside. "That's enough firewood." She bolted the door. "Can either of you make a fire?"

"Three years camp counselor," AJ said and proceeded to show off her expertise. As she dug into her backpack for matches, Songlest snapped her fingers, and a small flame appeared on her fingertip. AJ gasped. "How'd you do that?"

"Every apprentice learns the Fire Spell." She blew out the flame.

AJ snorted. "Every apprentice? Like wannabe...witches?"

"Faerie."

"What kind of place is this?"

"Here is our home. You came from Elsewhere."

"How do I get back?"

"You can't," she said.

"We came...Here...from Elsewhere?" Ja-hon pondered. "Is that the modern world?"

"Loosely translated," Songlest said.

AJ stared at her. "Crap."

"That translates too." She smiled.

"What do you have to eat around Here?"

"Look in the cupboard."

Since Ja-hon was in a more amiable mood, he stepped to a cabinet above the fireplace mantel and looked inside. "A bag of nuts. Chestnuts?" He took one out and examined it as if it were a fine jewel.

"Tastes better roasted," Songlest said. "Slice open the shells. Put them on the hearth and light—"

A thump under the floor stones stopped her.

AJ swallowed. "What was that?"

"Ogres. Start the fire."

AJ tossed logs in the fireplace.

"Two logs should be enough for now." Songlest finger-lit the dry grasses she had gathered for kindling. The fire sprang to full life, as if by magic. "When it's dark enough for them to come down the chimney, we'll need a bigger fire."

The thump sounded again. Louder.

"There. Take out that log." She pointed to a log that was ablaze, except on one end. "Put it on...this stone." She tapped her foot on the stone where the thump had come from. "It'll be hot enough to keep the ogres from getting in."

AJ gasped. "They're under the floor?"

"Ogres live underground. Dig tunnels, and they're fast about it."

AJ stepped closer to the wall while staring at the floor, expecting the stones to heave up and green monsters to climb out...like what happened in the tunnel. And she had only four bullets left.

Ja-hon placed the burning log on the stone, then put another log on the fire.

"You two," Songlest said. "The *chestnuts*. Slice and eat 'em while you still can."

AJ made a sour face.

Ja-hon took his knife out of its sheath. It sliced through the nut shells easily.

She did the same to one of her own, with her folding pocket knife, releasing a creamy aroma. It was crunchy with a bitter-sweet nutty flavor. "Not bad for being raw."

If there was anything else to be said, it was lost to a crash on the roof.

"More fire. Larger. Burn—"

"I got it." AJ tossed a handful of chestnuts on the hearth, then grabbed more wood that explosively enlarged the fire. Embers shot up the chimney, showing the ogres they were awake and ready to fight. She wished they had brought in just one more armful.

Ja-hon helped. He seemed to know what size log she wanted. "Good thing ogres are afraid of fire."

"Wait." AJ said. "They had fire. I saw torches. Through the hole."

"Bright light they avoid," Songlest explained. "Sunlight turns ogres into stone. Everyone knows that."

If that was all the explanation they were going to get, it would have to be enough. Judging from the ruckus on the roof, she was sure the ogres were breaking apart the chimney and throwing the stones onto the slate roof.

They only paused for breath, from then on, assessing the fires and keeping them high and burning for what seemed like hours and hours. The sounds below ceased, but the noises increased on the roof as they seemed to be dismantling the chimney. At times, they jumped up and down on the roof, trying to break through. The builders had not skimped on materials and expertise just because the structure was only a 'hut.'

They all flinched at the sounds above them, and all three stayed awake, although only one needed to stay up to keep the fires burning. The crashes and rumbles of sound grew louder as the piles of firewood grew smaller. The fire on the floor burned down, but the floor remained hot. Cooling, but hot.

When the wood was gone and the fire burned out, AJ shined her miner's light up the chimney. There was nothing but chimney to be seen. Not even one teeth-baring green face. Like the floor, the chimney was too hot for the ogres, although the sounds said they were still on the roof.

Then, finally, there was silence.

"The dawning," Songlest cried and bolted for the door.

AJ had to yank her away to stop her from opening it. "Just because it's quiet doesn't mean they couldn't be waiting for us to come out."

"I think the ogres below are still there." Ja-hon had his ear to a cold floor stone.

They waited, pacing, listening, until the chirping of birds gave life to a new day.

"The sun is up." Songlest pushed past AJ to the door.

She let her unlatch and open it. Sunshine gleamed in.

"Quickly. We must get as far away as we can." She hurried out the door, and the other two followed, Ja-hon in his winter coat and hooded cloak, leaving the mask, while AJ was in her cargos, Dickie's and jacket.

The air smelled of sewers and mold, the worst of city smells.

"The smell of ogres," Ja-hon said.

Loose stones lay scattered all around the hut, from the chimney. It would probably leak the next time it rained. Under a second night of attacks, the chimney would no longer stop spiders, let alone the ogres.

AJ followed Songlest, as she was already hurrying toward the woods.

Ja-hon stopped, looking up.

AJ turned around. "What's wrong?"

"Nothing. There's sunshine." He took a deep breath of air that smelled of wood smoke.

"Pretty soon you'll have to tell me why you lived in a hole in the ground." She hoped her words would pull him away from his fascination with the sunshine and back to the path before them.

"Basements," he said, just correcting her instead of being annoyed. He realized that his life had completely changed. There was no returning to the basement or pretending to be a monster. Besides, this world was occupied by real monsters.

AJ's life too had changed, but the full impact of having killed a living ogre had not fully hit her. She was on the move. On an adventure of a lifetime.

Sooner or later, there would be time to think about ordinary things that were seemingly gone forever. Her small apartment. The money she'd earned to pay next month's rent. A world both of them had left behind.

PART THREE

The Kingdom

JoAnn Parsley

CHAPTER 15

J a-hon woke before sunrise. He was used to awakening in some niche in a deep basement where there was not even a glimmer of sunlight. It was different in the hollow of a tree because the woman—the Faerie—glowed in the dark.

He did not think of Songlest as a woman. She looked like one, although her dress had now become an opaque pastel blue instead of translucent green. Her skin was a shimmering yellow-green and she stood barely four-foot tall. He thought her long purple hair was striking.

Woman or Faerie, she did not want him to touch her. She was friendly and accepting, but no touching. So, she was sleeping on the other side of AJ.

AJ was the one he wanted to talk to but, again, no touching. At least not with hands and intention. They had to touch since they all slept inside a hollow tree, but there was no 'touching.'

The Faerie woke suddenly and vanished outside. Even without wings, she seemed to float and dart.

Ja-hon tried not to wake AJ before realizing nothing would wake her. She just curled into a tight ball and continued to sleep. They all slept after working all night and walking all day.

Perhaps that was why the Faerie was a 'touch-me-not' last night. She had to have been overworked and terrorized by the Ogres.

That thought made him look around. There was now just enough dawning to see the tree trunks that surrounded him.

Trees. He knew little about trees. City trees had iron fences around them or were in a gathering. These trees were huge. He moved nearer one and patted its rough and unmoving surface. Bushes moved. At least here they did. Moved a little away from the hollow tree, then back again. For the Faerie.

He tried to tell a bush to move. It did not so he walked around it.

***

AJ woke at dawning in a hollow tree empty of company. The three of them had fit, though not comfortably, into the small space. The word 'guard' was mentioned, but no one could stay awake to stand guard. They had squeezed into the upright hollow and trusted a shield of bushes and young trees to hide them from the ogres.

Birds were singing somewhere, and a creek, which was almost a small river, burbled over rocks, but there were no other sounds. After rubbing her aching back, AJ pushed through more bushes and tall ferns to find the river.

Here, the rush of water funneled into a deep, inviting pool. She stripped and set her clothes and her backpack on a rock. She was filthy and did not care who noticed when she waded, naked, into the cool water. Whoever came along could make comments from the bank or join her.

She was surprised when a yellow fisherman's hat came up out of the water in front of her. The kind a small child would wear along with a yellow slicker because of the rain. Not because he was swimming.

Not because he was an otter.

The two of them blinked, eyes to eyes, until the otter paddled himself back a short distance. "Hello," he said, flipping his whiskers.

AJ managed to smile in spite of the trepidation stabbing her chest. *A talking otter?* She swallowed her angst in favor of staying calm. "Ah. Nice hat."

"Bit of a nuisance. Falls off. Whatcher doing?"

"Swimming. Watching the fish. There's a big one over there." She pointed to where the bank overhung the water, creating shadows. "I'll never catch it."

"Um. It's getting too big for this bit o' pond. Already too big for just one meal."

"There are three of us," AJ said, thinking she knew what he meant.

"Well then..." He offered the hat. "Hold this, will you?"

She took the hat and watched the otter double over himself without so much as a splash. At first, he was a dark shape in the water, then there was a silvery flash as a large trout was thrown onto the bank. It flapped but was too far from the shore to fling itself back into the water.

"Thank you." AJ handed him back his hat.

"Oh, good. Look upstream." He gazed past her and waved toward the rocks and waterfalls.

AJ followed his gaze. There in a pool of sunlight stood a white horse drinking from the creek...but this horse had a long straight horn on the center of its forehead, which, strangely, he dipped into the water and swished it around. "That...that's a unicorn."

"Aye."

"What is it doing?"

"Purifying the water. He hasn't been around for a time. Need him to keep the water clean in our piece of the Kingdom. See the gold rings? That's a new horn."

"New?"

"Course. Oh. Not from Here are you?"

"Elsewhere they say."

He nodded, happy to explain. "Unicorns get a new horn every spring. Like deer and such. Only more useful. Horn rings purify...oh, everything. Come across a horn he's shed, you take it to the Ranger. He'll let you keep some o' the rings, but he'll give most the rings to folks in need."

"Ranger?" AJ could not seem to say more than one word at a time.

"King's Ranger, miss. Heroes in this land."

"Where can I find one of these rangers?"

"Be a ways. That way." He waved a paw toward the sun. "Keeps a bit of a hut at the crossroads. And the bridge. I must go now. Good day to you." He dove into the water. The yellow hat floated along after him.

***

Where are you going? Ja-hon asked himself. *It's morning.* A shaft of sunlight made an appearance. No matter where he was, there were things to do, routines to follow as best he could.

He did so. Carefully, trying not to disturb anything. AJ or anyone who lived in a forest. Something, a bird perhaps, made a cheerful noise. Then a piece of a song.

The few birds he knew were silent. They grabbed crumbs and flew away. Pigeons were noisy. Their wings flapped.

A bird flew in front of him and landed on a bush. There were flowers on the bush, but not what the bird wanted. It flew away. He went to the bush and sniffed. It had a light smell.

Everything had a light, perfume smell. Trees. The leaves underfoot. The slight breeze. Maybe even the sunlight. He did not know if they smelled or if nothing stank. No garbage with its rats and feral cats. Or the pizza place down the block.

The thought of thrown-out pizzas and half-eaten dinners reminded him of breakfast. There was none and not much chance of finding one, apparently.

He looked around and realized that nothing was familiar. Not even the flowering bush was to be seen any more, and one tree looked like another.

He had not gone far. Past some big trees. A dribble of water. All were now lost. A path that he had followed, or so he thought, to a bit of grass and sunlight, was gone. There was only sunlight and grass and a rabbit. It bounded away into the shadow of the trees.

He. Was. Lost.

He was *not* going to call out. He was not going to be rescued by a green Faerie and...once again, by AJ. He was not. He turned around, but there were exactly the same trees and bushes in every direction. He stood in the sunlight for a while, grateful for it. He had not thought of sunlight as comforting in a long time. Danger lurked in sunlit places, not darkness. True, denizens of the darker world were dangerous—even to a pretend monster—but there were fewer of them. There were crowds in the sunlight.

Except Here. There were trees here.

He listened. Smelled the air. How long had he been gone from the hollow tree...had he been standing, looking at the flowering bush? How long had it taken him to wake up? Pay attention?

***

AJ shook herself and climbed out of the stream. The trout was only making half-hearted attempts to flip back into the water.

"Sorry," AJ said, hoping it could not talk. She would become a vegetarian before she ate something that could talk. Or worse, complain.

After she wrung out her sopping hair and dressed, she found her folding knife and efficiently prepared her much-needed breakfast. She had a small fire going and two large fillets on crossed sticks by the time Songlest returned.

"You caught a fish?" she asked, insultingly surprised.

"An otter did." AJ balanced the fillets and sticks on the rocks circling the fire. "And I'll be a bit slow today." She rubbed her cramped lower back and grimaced. "Cursed back pain...from sleeping in a hollow tree."

"Healing Spell then."

"What?"

"Stand up and get a Healing Spell," the Faerie ordered.

AJ stood. She did not believe the little yellow-green woman could cast spells, but she obeyed since she had little choice.

Songlest spread her hands. Whispering a stream of words, she ran both her palms up AJ and back down again without touching her. "There. The Spell will take care of that and anything else. Tomorrow, most like."

Once again, AJ stared, dumbfounded. Her back no longer ached. "What...what are you?"

"Faerie, remember?"

"Right...but you have no wings."

Songlest's yellow-green cheeks turned red. "Ogres," she hissed. "They...they caught me dancing in a storm, took great pleasure in plucking off my wings, and put me to work. They could have done worse to me, and since ogres usually kill those they...play with, I got off easy.

"You came along in the middle of my escape. They would not have put you to work, since you killed one of them. They would've eaten you alive, down to the bones. Ja-hon would have been digging tunnels until he was near dying. Fortunately, they don't dig extra tunnels just to go after people. Villagers. They might like to, but they don't. People fight back. You, however, killed one of them. Right in his own tunnel. They really wanted to find you. Us. They would dig a hundred extra tunnels to get their revenge.

"Now, we're far away and we'll have to find someone who can tell us where we are. Someone who lives here. On the ground. But not close to the ogres. What's needed is one of the King's Rangers. He'll know, because those green tunics have been all over the Kingdom."

"Ranger," AJ said. "The otter told me there's a Ranger

nearby. Toward the sun. East."

***

Ja-hon sniffed and smelled fire. Fire was dangerous. People crowded around garbage-can fires. The dangerous ones. The unfortunate built fires in the new garbage receptacles. Plastic. Or whatever it was. Not cans.

Not...wood smoke.

He knew that smell. He had smelled it all night.

If the wind kept blowing, and he made his way back to his companions—his bosses—he would do what the two of them ordered. Quietly. Obediently. Or pretty much.

Fish. Someone was cooking...breakfast?

He walked as quietly as he could while gathering more firewood. As if that was the reason he had left the hollow tree.

To AJ it seemed as if Ja-hon chose this moment to return. With an armful of firewood. "Fish?" He sniffed. "You caught a fish?"

AJ smiled. "The otter did. I held his hat while he caught this big fish."

"Otter?"

"It's a long story." With the backache gone and having Songlest, an actual Faerie, and Ja-hon as companions made this trip an adventure instead of a dangerous mistake. "Now we have breakfast, and then we can follow the yellow brick road."

Neither Ja-hon nor the Faerie understood. They did not have books, movies or TV. But they had fish for breakfast.

After walking all morning, the nourishment wore off. Finally, Songlest stopped at what looked like an unkempt hay mound. Grass and weeds sprouted from it in every direction. There was a door that faced the crossing of two roads. There were no signposts announcing who dwelt within. Or if anyone was welcome.

"Ranger?" Songlest called out.

There was no answer.

"I wonder if anyone is in there." Carefully, AJ went nearer, and after a brief rap on the wooden door, pushed it open. Darkness. She retrieved the miner's lamp from her backpack and switched on the light. The old batteries were losing power.

The mound was occupied by a bit of furniture. A small wooden table and matching bench, a small brick fireplace—no fire—and a cot on which lay a bundle of blankets.

Seeing a bit of green material under the mounded blankets, AJ stepped closer. "Ranger?"

Nothing stirred.

She moved to the bed, then shook the green material, thinking it was about the sleeper's shoulder. "Wake up."

The blankets shivered, and underneath the green material something disintegrated into dry, but smelly, bits and pieces. Like scraps of dry paper. Or dead leaves.

AJ scrambled back out of the door, hand over her nose and mouth. "He's gone. Into pieces."

Ja-hon leaned forward to see inside but did not go in. "Garbage," he said. "Very old garbage. With a touch of rot."

Both Ja-hon and Songlest eased through the door while AJ just shone her light inside. The blankets on the cot lay flattened. Songlest lifted a corner. "There's nothing under here."

It did not look as if there had been anyone here in a very long time.

"Humph." Songlest wrinkled her nose and, despite the smell, looked around. "That cloak." She pointed to a fall of greenish-black material hanging on a wall hook. "Take it. Needs be useful when it rains."

Ja-hon reluctantly took the cloak and tossed it out the door. His was too short for rain, as it had been a costume.

"And that tin box," Songlest added. "On the shelf above the hook. That should be food. Journey bread, most like. Never spoils."

Songlest thoughtfully hefted the Ranger's sword. It was leaning against the wall. She thought about the Rangers and the guardsmen she knew and their swords. They wore them, practiced with them and honed them. Then carefully sheathed them and put them away if they did not have an apprentice to do so for them. Rangers usually did not have apprentices, so when they carried a sword, they cared for them. They did not lean them casually against a wall. If this Ranger had left his sword, he was probably...dead.

"Can you use one of these?" she asked.

Ja-hon shook his head.

AJ patted her holster. "I prefer a gun."

Songlest snorted. Annoyed. She returned the sword, carefully, to the wall. Although it was valuable, the symbol of the King's justice, it was an inconvenience and none of them could carry or practice with it. "Leave the rest," she said. "We'll burn it."

"Burn?" AJ was back to one-word sentences, then: "Ah, shouldn't we tell someone?"

"He was the one to tell." Songlest walked back outside.

AJ moved aside to let her pass.

"We will tell the Wizard," Songlest said as she left. "If we can find him. For now, we need firewood."

AJ looked around as Ja-hon left to collect firewood. Considering where he had lived, she thought he must have seen a few dead bodies, but this place made her uneasy. On top of her shooting a live ogre made the unease stronger. And there were more threats than just ogres in *Fairy Tales*. She wondered if the Ranger had been murdered.

Her thoughts jumped to murder mysteries. She was familiar with murders because of all the books she had read. The TV shows she had watched. Murders happened when the victim had something valuable. She went back to the doorway and shined the light around the small room. If the otter was right, if that green-clad form had been a Ranger, he might have taken charge of a unicorn's valuable old horn.

There was nothing of value inside. No valuable unicorn horns.

Ignoring Songlest, AJ went outside and paced around the hay-mound. In back, there had been a wood pile, maybe an outhouse tacked to the hay mound, and a small square garden, still covered with winter mulch. And in one corner, a tall thin bird feeder with only a few shells in an empty seed cup. A circular cup. Lined with something like aluminum foil. Attached to the wide upper part of the stand, made from...*of course!*...a unicorn's discarded horn. Safely hidden in plain sight.

She pulled the pointy end out of the ground and removed the seed cup. She would have liked to shove the horn, with a dramatic flourish, under her belt, as if it were a sword, but just as she could not shove the gun into her waistband, she could not pretend the horn was a sword. It was a valuable horn. Disguised as a make-do birdfeeder. Besides, her belt was too tight.

She went around to the front, where Ja-hon and Songlest were building a fire, and picked up the tossed cloak. Since they were distracted, she wrapped the horn in the cloak and joined them to help with the fire.

The Wizard—if they found him—could tell her exactly how and why this valuable unicorn horn purified everything. Otherwise, she would have to guess.

CHAPTER 16

Whment Songlest said they were going to walk to the Wizard's Keep, neither AJ nor Ja-hon knew what she meant. AJ had walked, once, from one side of town to the other—when she was younger—but now she needed a ride. Paid for it with whatever was on hand. Cash. Credit card. Friend. Dates. Ja-hon, she figured, stayed in his own neighborhood—where basements and tunnels connected to one another. Why, she had yet to learn, but he was like others that way. Most people remained in their own neighborhoods.

There were no neighborhoods in Songlest's world. There were mountains. Roads. Trails. Paths through the grasses. Streams. Wet and dry streambeds. A few old bridges. Some stone. Some wood. All in a variety of conditions.

Once, however, there was a change. Just as they stepped into a wide meadow, a small herd of deer raced out of the woods and across the open expanse, their white tails flashing. First, there was one wolf, then a small pack of wolves followed them. The last deer was neither quick nor fortunate. First one wolf would race after it, then another. The deer was slowing, struggling, and the wolves were snapping at it, almost on it.

One caught a leg, and it was doomed.

The pack joined the hunt, and another wolf caught a leg and it went down. The rest attacked and their meal was assured, providing all the wolves obeyed their rules as to who ate first.

"Go ask them," Songlest said.

"What?"

"To share. Go ask them."

Both indoctrinated humans stared at her in disbelief.

"They won't harm you humans. It's a rule. Ask."

Neither moved, then Ja-hon threw off his cloak, and straightening to his full height, started across the meadow. The wolves were busily tearing at the deer. Only to stop snapping and growling to stare.

Ja-hon walked boldly closer. A wolf started growling at him and two more took up the chorus.

Ja-hon decided on what to take, if he dared speak. And if the knife he had so carefully honed was sharp enough.

"Good morning," he called, coming to a halt. "The...ah, Faerie suggested I... ask for a share. A small share."

When no one moved, he added, "We're very hungry travelers. From...Elsewhere. Another world. We're not hunters. Just hungry."

Silence. Even the growling ceased.

Ja-hon stepped closer. "Please?" He thought the wolf swore. Whatever, he backed away. The others followed his lead, although the growling resumed. Carefully, slowly, Ja-hon slinked forward, unsheathing the belt knife. He had never used it on a piece of raw meat, but decided, as he walked closer, to try to cut off the back leg. It looked like it would fit on AJ's fire-pit grill, and the leg was almost torn off, anyway. A few slices, a cut between the bones...

Cautiously, highly aware of the circle of intense stares—from golden-brown eyes, he sliced the leg free. A slow, careful movement and he had it in one hand. The other held the bloody knife. "Thank you."

"You and that Faerie are welcome, human," the wolf said, and Ja-hon almost dropped both knife and leg. He managed, barely, to back away, turned and breathed deeply, walked back to where Songlest and AJ waited.

"Into the woods," Songlest whispered. "Out of their sight."

"Gladly," he said, handing the haunch to AJ. By the time she had a fire and the venison cooking, he thought he would regain his appetite.

He did, but it took that long.

At least, as AJ pointed out to be positive and ordinarily conversational, there were no mosquitoes. There were bees aplenty, butterflies, and at least one large dragonfly, which had a rider...or so she would swear.

None of this convinced Ja-hon to stop shaking until she sliced off pieces of meat for their meal. He did not believe he had just *politely* asked wolves for a share of their kill; nor did he believe one said he was welcome to it, but he was hungry, and the venison smelled delicious.

There were now more stars than either had ever seen, and a sliver of a moon on the horizon just before the full moon rose—in the opposite direction. NorMoon, Songlest called it, dismissing it.

It wasn't until the full moon rose again that they saw a thin trail of smoke one early morning. It was two mountains away, and it was probably the smoke from a chimney. Out of a distant valley where the Road seemed to be leading.

After that, it began to rain.

Two days of rain and drizzle taught them two things: one, it was almost impossible for two different sized people to walk together under one cloak; Two, faeries did not get wet if they did not want to. The rain sheeted off Songlest whenever she chose, as if it no longer touched her skin. No more than the ground had touched her bare feet for day after day, mountain after mountain. Even without wings she floated.

AJ thought the accomplishment did nothing to improve her disposition.

Nor did the village.

Rain or not, there were only a few chimneys smoking, thin spirals of smoke that did not promise warmth or a hot meal. The village itself looked far from prosperous. The 'houses' were an assortment of small stone and wood buildings, and most could only be generously called square. A few might have been intentionally circular.

A rain-swollen creek ran between the houses, but it was clear that only one side was occupied. On the farther side, one or two buildings seemed solid enough for livestock, while the rest were beginning to collapse. As were the wood and stone bridges.

Besides the creek, the only things with energy were the dogs. A handful ran out of the stables, and while most crossed the bridges to stand in the road and bark, the rest remained on the far side. They did not look as if barking was worth the bother.

Then the men came out. Four of them walking carefully onto the Road, long bows nocked with arrows and drawn.

The fifth was just as ready, as he slipped around the houses until he was behind the visitors.

CHAPTER 17

AJ called out, "We have no weapons," although that was not the truth. They would not know her revolver was a weapon, and they certainly wouldn't recognize her folding knife.

A woman came out of the nearest house. "Odwin, put down that bow. They be travelers. Look to 'em."

AJ looked at her and decided this was the person in charge. She was tall for a woman, and stocky, as if she worked long and hard to build her muscles. But she was also shapely, winter-white skinned, light brown hair braided and covered with a scarf, loose brown pants and a goldish shirt, belted. Plus, an apron and gloves, which she was removing. "Good Morrow," she said.

"Good...morning," AJ replied.

"There be nobody to the east," the one called Odwin said. He had yet to lower his bow. The others had already done so.

"That's the truth." AJ agreed with him. "There's no one in those mountains. That's why we're hungry and wet." In case the Translating Spell wasn't working properly, she pointed to herself. "AJ Walker. Ja-hon. And Songlest."

"Elles," the woman replied. "Come in. Be welcome. Though another day an' yer be missin' us."

"Missing?"

The woman glared at the bowmen. "Aye. We be leaving. Yer be welcome to our homes this day. Such as they are." She waved them inside, yet she was still glowering at Odwin.

Inside the small stone house, there was evidence of her words. There were piles of boxes, barrels and trunks. On them, there were pieces of furniture, two carved wooden chairs with old pillows strapped to them, and a baby's cradle. Cloth bags sat in and on both chairs.

A table and bench sat alone by the stone fireplace with its empty mantle, save for a puddle of wax on the thick beam.

"There be 'nough for a bowl of stew. Iffin you don' mind a cracked bowl."

"Not at all. And we have nuts."

"That, we have. Journey cakes, as well. Sit. Sit."

The two humans sat at the table, watched closely by a handful of small children, an old lady, and a pair of tabby cats. The latter were caged in a strong wooden basket.

"True there be no one in the mountains?" Elles asked, serving them both generous portions of stew in cracked bowls with ill-made old spoons. The things to be left.

"None we ever saw," AJ answered.

She nodded, satisfied. "Know of the Wizard's Keep?"

"That's where we're headed. Off to see the Wizard." Once again AJ's reference went unnoticed. The people did not look as Medieval as their houses, but they were not modern either. "Some reason why you're leaving?"

"Mar'in said we were all going back. All of us. Though some of us didn't want to go." There were murmurs and AJ realized that the room had filled, mostly with women. Young and old. Or at least older. "The crones know what women did back there. Or didn' do! Not this or that. Little choice in who we be wed to. Less in when and how many of his *sons* we be having." She glared at the men again. "So them what want to stay here...can, since they who left have already done so. Gone, they all are. The whole village. Gone."

"Elles..." Odwin said.

"You and them others want to stay, Odwin Bowman, can stay. An' starve. There ain't 'nough of us to have a village. One of these.

One of that. No smith. No wheelwright. None knows herbs. You can barely make your own bows. Got the wrong kind o' wood 'round here. An' no one knowin' anymore 'bout what's best. We be leaving on the morrow. Taking the wagons and the horses whilst they can still travel. "An' don' you lot threaten me and them. You plan to shoot your own wife full of arrows?"

"No, mistress. I be with you."

There was a chorus of agreement.

"Be some sense in the lot of you, after all," she muttered. "So. Set out the dogs 'n' guards, Odwin. In case. The rest...Eat. Then off ta bed. We be gone early. Dawning. Rain or shine. No wastin' what be left of warm weather. We needs ta be in shelters come this winter."

Finished with her orders and words, she waved at all of them, including the three newcomers, to follow those orders. Some hurriedly obeyed, while the others made make-shift beds and either went to sleep or pretended.

Elles was as good as her ordering. She was up well before the sun, making tea and toast for those who staggered out of their beds. She even let most of them finish both before those with charges— children, pets and livestock—had to be gathering them in one central spot. Those who were not minders became leaders. Because it was an easier task to harness horses and lead them to the wagons.

Amid her orders, Elles stopped and stared upwards. Seeing her, AJ poked Ja-hon in the arm and pointed up.

Well above them soared a very large black bird. It flew in circles, rising...awkwardly, AJ thought, but enough of a flyer to vanish into a pinpoint of black.

"What is it?" Ja-hon asked.

"Only bird with that wingspan I know of is a California condor." She quit trying to see where it went. "But, I think, that one was bigger. And not soaring. Not as graceful. Hey. Elles. What was that bird?"

"Don' know. Don' care. You there," she yelled at someone. "Get back ta work. Bird comes over...two, three times. On sunny days. An' flies off. You heard me," she yelled again at the loaders. "Get workin' We're near leaving."

Since she sounded like she would leave behind anyone who was late, the bird was forgotten as the loading was finished, and the various riders were added to the wagon loads. A shepherd, two young children, and a handful of trained sheep dogs were herding a small flock of sheep and goats. They were to follow the wagons, so the wagon drivers yelled at their horses and snapped whips, making noise but not whipping the animals to start them moving. AJ appreciated the difference since she had signed numerous petitions against cruelty to animals. The drivers also seemed to know how far the horses would have to pull the wagons and how fast. The smallest wagon, with its team of two, had a lighter load than the four-horse wagons. So, they were going to be slower. AJ wondered if they were going to be like the covered wagons going west and be forced to drop off non-essential items along the way.

This first day, they made what AJ thought of as good time— or maybe fair time—for they were either in a valley with lower mountains on either side or something of a high plateau. Being a city girl, the only canyons she knew came from buildings and roads. This Road dogged a creek and occasionally crossed over old stone bridges just a little wider than a wagon.

There were more people somewhere in this wilderness than she had thought, but now they were all gone.

Except for the Wizard and his Keep.

They paused, briefly, to eat a mid-meal and rest the horses before reaching Elles's chosen spot for the night. Or at least she said to stop. AJ did not know if it was where the Head Woman wanted to stop or just did. But there was water, trees for some shelter and firewood, and pasture for all the tired animals. The people tried to pretend they were not tired. The children fell asleep.

Curiously, it became Ja-hon's task to hold, then lead the horses to water and pasture for the night. As far as he knew, he had never even seen a horse close up but was as fearless around the larger breed as he had been with the wolves. And he was quick to learn about halters and harnesses.

AJ was revising her opinion about him. He had been willing to do whatever was asked of him, but so far, it had been nothing more than grunt work. Carrying firewood for the most part.

Yet he faced wolves because they were hungry. Not starving, just hungry. Taking Songlest's word that these were not the wolves of old folklore. These wolves had rules. And they talked. Ja-hon had not known either, yet he faced them.

So, there was a bit more to him than the curiosity he had displayed in the far-off basement.

The next day was cloudy, but without the threatened rain, so they traveled what seemed to be farther before stopping. And it was easier. They now had a day's experience.

That morning, the black bird flew overhead.

"I don't know what that thing is, but I don't like it," AJ said, voicing everyone else's opinion.

"If we *borrowed* the riding horses," Ja-hon began, "we could follow it. See where it's going."

"There's a big difference in taking care of docile work horses and riding one of the others. They have minds of their own," AJ said, then added, "But we could...trot. We didn't have horses in camp. They were too expensive. But we had lessons in trotting. It's a sort of running. Faster than just walking. Not as tiring as running.

"We'd get ahead of everyone, but I don't think we'd get lost. There's nowhere to go, except this valley."

They found Songlest, put the plan to her, and when she agreed, they told Elles. She did not exactly agree, but she had no authority over them. They wanted to find Wizard's Keep as soon as possible. Or the remains of Mar'in's village. If they had gone home, as they wanted. Elles knew her small band would continue on to the Keep. Otherwise, they would stop and not move even one more day.

They began the walk/trot exercise AJ had learned, and before mid-meal even the following dogs were out of sight. Neither the village nor the black bird were in view. There were only ordinary animals grazing on the valley's grasses. And nothing that either of them could catch for a meal.

The next morning, the bird soared overhead again.

"Come on," AJ ordered. "I swear that thing is hunting this morning."

"There's enough to hunt." Ja-hon pointed out a herd of deer.

The valley had an incline, a grassy hill where the mountains began to turn aside, and as best they could, the pair trotted up the road, only to stop.

A larger valley spread out before them. The mountains still encircled it, but they were distant. Below them lay low hills, a naturally dammed river, and herds of animals. A variety of deer. Cattle of some sort.

And one large black bird circling over...a wooly mammoth?

"Impossible. There are no mammoths—"

"Dragon," Ja-hon yelled.

"What? Where?"

"There," he yelled. "Going after that bird."

Now both could see a reddish-tan speck arrowing toward the black bird.

The bird saw it coming and turned.

The dragon flamed but was too far away from the bird. It swept through flames and, with foreclaws extended, went for the bird's wing. It ripped off feathers, but at a cost. The bird slashed at the smaller dragon and caught its flank instead of an upraised wing. The dragon banked, flying out of reach. The bird circled unable to do the same maneuver. The dragon circled, but in a tighter turn. Still, it missed the bird.

By now, AJ and Ja-hon were running down the hillside.

The dragon swerved again, seeming to notice that the bird flew in wide circles. It came near to flying behind the bird, but the bird ducked, going after the mammoth again. A second turn, and the quicker dragon was banking into the falling bird. Too late, the dragon tried to attack and missed. Yet the bird flinched and instead of a killing blow, it sliced into fur and skin once again. The mammoth shrieked in pain and anger. The mammoth's baby cried out as well.

Now the dragon became less cautious, forcing the bird away from the animals and closer to AJ and Ja-hon. AJ stopped and unsnapped the holster strap. The pair were coming closer...

The bird managed a turn, straight at the dragon. It swerved, but the bird claws raked at it, drawing away skin and blood...as it flew closer, then almost over...

"Aim. Shoot," AJ ordered herself and fired two shots.

The bird disintegrated. Exploded as the bullets went through its weird feathers, into its chest, and the creature fell to the ground in a shower of black shreds.

The dragon wobbled, flailed. Held up by outspread wings.

Ja-hon ran to where the dragon was going to land.

It hit the ground in a roll, turning a summersault, wings still outspread, before lying still.

AJ was swearing. Racing after Ja-hon. Yelling orders. "First aid. Shirt. Stop the bleeding."

Ja-hon yanked off the borrowed villagers pack, then his outer shirt. Where the bird had clawed the dragon, there was a bleeding slash, but dragon skin was leathery and knobby. A slash that would have ripped open a fur-bearing animal, only cut through deep enough to bleed, profusely, but not to the bone.

Ja-hon dropped to his knees to wipe away enough blood to see the gash, then swore. Inside the cut, the red flesh was turning black. The same was the case for a second wound.

"The bird did something to it."

"Poison?" AJ stared, blank for a moment, then yelled. "Rocks. Get two. One flat. One round." She yanked off her backpack and began opening the side pocket. The gun was already holstered, freeing her hands. She pulled out two rings of the unicorn horn. Earlier, she had simply pulled all the horn-rings apart and stashed them in the backpack, until she knew what exactly to do with them. Now, if her thoughts were right, the results would be worth her assumptions.

Ja-hon looked around for rocks, leaving the shirt and the blood to her. He found what he hoped she would need and set them within her reach. She slapped a ring onto the flatter rock and smashed it with the other. When it was mostly powder, she lifted the rock and, as best she could, brushed the powder into the gash. She repeated the effort for the second wound. Hopefully, this unicorn powder would purify the wounds.

Ja-hon watched, understood, and grabbed one of the rings.

The mammoth was down. Her thick legs had buckled, and the baby was beside her, crying, touching her with its trunk.

Ja-hon was swearing. Heedlessly, he ran to the mother's side. He had to find rocks, then slam them together, crushing the ring over the mammoth's wound. It was dangerously black, and he swore as he worked, dumping the powder into the wound until it was gone.

Then he just stood, dwarfed by the mammoth's size and slowly started to realize what he had just done.

Something touched his shoulder.

CHAPTER 18

AJ looked up to see a second, smaller, dragon alight on the other side of the larger one. "Me-ow," it said. AJ stared.

Just as suddenly, a cat-man knelt next to it. "What have you done?"

A blink at the officious tone, and AJ realized he wore a lot of gold—real gold—on his green tunic. Whoever he was, he had the right to demand reports from underlings.

"Cleaned the wound as best I could. Sprinkled it with powdered unicorn horn."

"Whyever?"

"Ah...To purify it. Otter said it did, and that wound was turning black. It needed something."

"Healing Spell." When she stared at him, he ran his hands—his clawed hands—over the wound and spoke a mumble of incomprehensive words.

There were angry voices behind her, along with trumpeting from both the mother and the baby mammoths. AJ turned, and the cat-man looked down the hill.

Ja-hon had raised his hands, but the baby mammoth was head butting him, knocking him off balance. Whether this was with gratitude for helping its mother or defending her, it was impossible to tell. Baby or not, it was large and strong.

The men had arrows nocked in their bows and were pointing them at him.

"He's done the same," AJ cried. "Powdered horn rings."

The cat-man waved at the others. "Healers," he yelled, and

the bows dropped. The arrows stayed on the strings, however.

"Harrel. Ranger," a voice shouted, and both turned to see Songlest and Elles running down from the Road. Where there had been no one, there were now excited people. Many were yelling, pointing weapons and fingers. The riding horses were making noise and dancing, but the work horses were too tired. The dogs and cats were not, and they added to the din.

"What happened?"

"What was that noise?" The questions were simultaneous.

"Why'd she shoot?" Songlest demanded.

"Shoot?" Harrel turned back to AJ.

"Ah...that black thing. The fake bird. It was attacking the mammoth."

The Head Man and Ja-hon reached the Ranger and the dragons in time to hear the last words.

"The wound was turning black," Ja-hon managed.

Everyone started to explain or ask questions until Harrel stood and ordered, "Quiet."

There were glares and frowns, but more obedience.

"What black thing?" Harrel asked. "A fake bird?"

"Sort of," AJ answered. "It looked like a bird, but it wasn't flying right. Not like this...odd dragon?"

"Slash is a CatDragon. A Hillcat."

AJ thought that was no more an explanation than he was himself. "The dragon and the black sort-of bird were fighting. The bird only went in circles, while the dragon swooped in. Like an *eagle*. Only not that big. That black thing was big. Really big. It got the mammoth once, and him too."

"Her." Harrel absently corrected her.

"And when did she become a dragon?" Songlest muttered.

Harrel ignored her. "So, you shot it?"

"When they came close enough. Two shots. Hit both times and it...disintegrated. Like what we thought was a dead Ranger.

The black bird became that pile down there."

"What dead Ranger?" Harrel demanded. "No," he said when three of them started to talk again. "You." He pointed at AJ. "Who are you?"

"Ah...AJ Walker. From Elsewhere, so she says." AJ pointed to Songlest, then at Ja-hon. "And he's Ja-hon."

It was Elles's turn. For a change, she seemed awed and only answered with her name.

Harrel looked over the wagons, the horses, the supplies. "Where are you going?"

"To report to that Wizard," Songlest exclaimed. "There's too much wrong. Black things. Disintegrating things."

Harrel was thoughtfully silent.

"And you are a Ranger?" AJ asked.

The Herder answered with a laugh. "He's Lord Harrel. Won't answer to it, but he acts like M'Lord Hafling."

Harrel glared at him as Ahgorh bowed mockingly.

"Slash?" Harrel returned his attention to the CatDragon.

She merely groaned.

He asked Elles again. "Where are you people going?"

"To the Wizard's Keep," Elles managed.

"There was a village nearby, maybe gone," Songlest added.

"Gone," he said. "Since we're all going to the same place... You, Ja-hon. We'll take Slash to the wagons. Ahgorh?"

"Our cow needs proper healing." He nodded toward Ja-hon. "He did good, so there's no black in the wound. She and her little one'll need to be watched. Go to the summer pasture. Back home. But with the others. I want to see this Wizard."

"Then we'll care for her first, since she's getting up." The mammoth was struggling to her feet. "I can do a Healing Spell. Not the strongest, but good enough for traveling. You two. Back to the wagons. Make room for Slash." Harrel removed his cloak. "You two wrap her in this."

"Yes, sir." AJ was obedient, but sarcastic.

The Lord Ranger looked at her with what she realized were incredibly blue eyes. Like a Siamese cat. And if anyone asked, he acted like one. Imperious. Still, he seemed to know what needed to be done, so she gestured to Ja-hon for help with the cloak. Together, although they both glanced at what the herders were doing to the mammoth, they managed to wrap the CatDragon in the cloak, leaving just enough material to make a sling.

Harrel, the Herder, and the smaller dragon returned, the Healing Spell cast despite the annoyance of both mammoths. Harrel and Ja-hon took up Slash, leaving AJ and the Head Herder to walk together.

"Besides a Lord," AJ immediately started, "What is he?"

"Ranger," Ahgorh insisted, then relented. "Hafling. Half human and half hillcat. Same as Slash. Only she's a dragon now. Blacktail's a barn cat. And now a dragon."

It seemed to AJ there was both admiration and a certain amount of warning in his voice. As if being a Hafling was something dangerous.

She dismissed any prejudice against Haflings. This was a world with ogres, faeries, woolly mammoths, and CatDragons. All of them absolutely impossible. Why then be prejudiced against someone who was half a cat? Especially one with all the gold of a High Lord on his tunic.

And when she kept company with her own 'monster.'

She kept the herder in mind for more of this world's explanations and watched Ja-hon and this Hafling, Lord Ranger, carry the dragon to the wagons. Elles and the others—ordinary humans apparently—were carefully non-committal about dragons. One now to ride with them and one was to fly overhead. They looked at both, then looked away as if they saw dragons every day.

CHAPTER 19

The Wizard's chamber was filled. People were summoned. Some wanted to ask questions. Some to report. In addition, there were curious watchers, along with two CatDragons and an owl, which may have been stuffed for all the movement it made. That did not mean it was not watching.

"Where is the Sorceress?" Andruss asked first.

"Vallezza had to stay with the Trolls," Lord Harrel replied. He had nothing to replace his gold-embroidered tunic, so he had to endure being addressed as Lord Harrel. He was expected to act as such, as well. "The bridge between Bridgedale and Premontii has to be replaced."

"Why?"

"That's one of their questions. But no bridge, no trade. And would it be another stone bridge or just wood? The new one over the gorge between Premontii and the Trolls is wood. And suspended. Not grounded. It's being repaired now."

"The stone bridge. Why is it gone?"

"The evil wizard built his castle with the magic he'd stolen from the stone bridge. Along with some of the stones."

Andruss had not reacted to anything he heard before he began his questioning, but he flinched at the mention of the evil wizard. And his theft of magic.

"And the Trolls left because of this?"

"The Trolls left because they were being mistreated. Mostly by the nobility in Premontii. Otherwise, they would have known about the bridges. Both of them."

"Humm," was all the Wizard said. "And you two?"

AJ decided to be respectful. Mostly. "We came through an old door. As did a demon. Long ago. It was probably an ogre. I shot one. With my gun." She lay a protective hand on the holster. "You don't have any, but I'm not giving you mine."

"I don't want it."

"Good. Because it only has two *bullets* left. For those black things."

"Ahhh. Those black things. What are they?"

"I don't know. Not real birds. I know that much. It couldn't fly...properly. Like a bird. And it was big. Bigger than that dragon." She pointed to where Slash sat on the windowsill. Blacktail, being smaller, was on the top of the shelves with the owl. "It dissolved into a pile of black pieces of something when I shot it. Twice.

"The Ranger in his old hay mound home did the same. He disintegrated. I only thought he was a Ranger because of the green tunic. There was only a shoulder showing, but it was the same color as his." AJ waved at Harrel. "But no gold. None I could see."

"But...dead?"

"Before we arrived," she said, and Ja-hon nodded. "It was too dark inside to see much of anything. Except the shoulder of his green tunic." She stopped, frowning. "He was on his bed. Covered with blankets. Who did that? Covered him? Did someone or something think he was sleeping? Then cover him with a blanket. He was in his own *house*. Sleeping in bed. With a blanket. So, who covered him and why?" AJ almost demanded. The questions had been bothering her since they had found the Ranger.

"He did so himself?" Harrel asked. "But...he was in his tunic? Why would he be sleeping in what was probably his only tunic. I wouldn't."

"Because, maybe...it would disintegrate. Like that black bird. If anyone touched it. We can't know what we saw because it disintegrated, and then we burned it. She did not look at Songlest who had ordered the burning. She thought of it now as a crime scene. A very, very faraway crime scene. Something the Ranger who had lived there, who she expected to be there, would investigate.

"Umm," was all the Wizard said, then asked, "The wounds. On Slash, and the animal...what did you call it...wooly?"

"A wooly mammoth. Which is impossible. She can't be a wooly mammoth."

"And why not?"

"Because they went extinct thousands of years ago. Back when...sorry...the cavemen lived." She was looking at the mammoth herder, who did not look like a caveman, at all. It was the Ranger who reacted to her words and the insult. "Some say that those men killed them all. But others insist it was climate change. It got too hot for mammoths."

"They do go south for your winter," Ahgorh commented. "But no one kills them. I mean no one now. Maybe a long time ago, but not now. They are too valuable. Alive. For hair. Milk. Dung. They fertilize gardens. Plantings. Only when one dies, can a hunter take the tusks. Hides. Bones. Sometime even meat. Mostly for a special feast. So why kill them? Why was that black thing after the calf's mother?"

"It took a Healing Spell to cure Slash. Completely," Harrel added.

"Was her wound turning black?"

"It was. Around the edges," Ja-hon answered. "And I've seen wounds like that. Almost like that. *Gangrene*." Seeing that only AJ understood the word, he added, "Rot."

"I will think—"

Slash let out a screech as she fell/dived off the windowsill and out the open window. Blacktail followed, swooping over the heads of everyone in the room first and then out the window. As they flew out, black birds of various sizes—all smaller—flew in.

"Captain," Harrel yelled.

The newly appointed Captain of the Guard had been near the usually open door. He had nothing to report and was there only to watch and listen. Seeing the black things, he grabbed the nearest person—Elles—and threw her out the door. The second was Jahon. He caught up the wingless Faerie as well. A look back and he slammed the door shut. He had rescued those he could. Now he had a duty to protect them.

Harrel sliced through one of the black things with his belt knife, and the bird disintegrated into a flutter of black feathers. The Captain sliced a larger 'bird' with his sword, then again, when nothing happened, after a second sword-strike, it became pieces of black that made him gag.

AJ thought about drawing her gun but grabbed one of the candle holders with a burning, melted candle. Fire, she reasoned and lashed out. The metal hit one bird, as did the candle flame, and it burst into a dangerous flame. She ducked behind the Wizard. He picked up a candle from his table with two hands, rounded it into a ball, and threw it out the window. Another black thing burst into flames. He tried again with the same success.

Outside, Slash and Blacktail were diving between the flying things. Blacktail was using the same technique he used on pigeons while Slash lived up to her name. She clawed at the things, raking through feathers and bodies. Yet she was conscious of the damage some of them could do. The more dangerous were the larger birds, but there were flocks of smaller 'birds' that disintegrated as she flew at the clusters, scattering them. Some flew off, but others tumbled downward or smashed into stone walls or others of their kind. The rest hit the hard ground or stones and burst into fountains of black debris.

Here too there was fighting. The Keep's guardians had swords for the most part, but a few—those who could nock arrows the fastest—were aiming at the larger, higher flyers. Some had excellent aim and delivered a killing strike, while others would just wound their targets. Even these fluttered and fell to the earth, smashing into the ground and dissolving.

The mid-sized 'birds' were the most dangerous to the guards. They evaded arrows and swords to lash at a guard—or one of the Keep's unfortunate people—to rip open deep wounds that began to blacken immediately. The wounded screamed in pain, adding to the shouts and sounds of beating wings. The 'birds' themselves were silent.

Anything that managed to land safely, snapped at people and the guardian dogs with long hooked beaks. Intelligent creatures they were and well-trained, the dogs barked, avoiding claws and beaks. None would bite the foul creatures.

Still, as the defenders grew tired, the outcome of the surprise attack was in doubt. Everyone fought with all their training, already knowing, from whispers and outright tales, that even a small wound could bring illness or death. And as yet, the Keep's Healers did not know what they had to deal with. TaleTellers swore they spoke the truth—that a handful of Rangers were gone. No one had seen this horrific end to life except the attackers. And the skies had been black with them.

Then, slowly, the defenders realized the grounds were nearly covered with black pieces of 'birds,' and there were none in the air. Only their stench lingered. The defenders took deep breaths of relief and wished they had not.

"We need to burn everything," the Wizard said.

"Yes, sir," his Captain said and quickly left the tower room to issue the Wizard's orders and to find the Lady Keeper. Everyone who sheltered in the inner rooms now had to be put to work. Firewood had to be gathered, and the debris, whether wet or dry, had to be swept into piles.

Behind him, the Wizard cast a Cleansing Spell into the smoke of a handful of candles. "Those floor holders. And on the shelves.

More candles. They'll be needed in the courtyard."

Lord or no, there was more than enough work to be done, and Harrel would do his share. He caught up a cloth from a tray and tied it over his mouth and nose. A second cloth was ruined on the blade of his belt knife. The magical knife was more valuable than any fancifully embroidered cloth, and it needed a wipe. Later, he would clean it, although the magic in the runes probably would do so long before he found the spare time.

Any room where the creatures had died, had candles being lit. The Wizard would cast his spells, first on the inside of the Keep, then outside. In the courtyard and the walkways and the stairs as the sweepers added to the layers already on the stones. Places where there was dirt or sand would have to be sifted, then cleaned.

The Healers, there were two badged and innumerable helpers, would tend to the human wounded, so Harrel went to the stables. For the most part, the animals had been covered or housed, but a few required attention. He was surprised to find Ja-hon already there.

The off-worlder was not a fighter—at least with swords or knives—and the Hafling knew from the journey to the Keep that Ja-hon knew little of even the most common of animals. Yet he had a gentle and sure touch as he cleaned the few wounds and quieted a house, or even a barn, cat. Harrel added his own ministrations with a Healing Spell, noting that few needed a Healer's more powerful and immediate spell. His was more a precaution than an immediate healing.

When the Wizard had his people doing all that was necessary now, he signaled for Harrel to join him back in the tower. The Lady Keeper would soon realize that kitchen help was needed there to provide everyone with a good hot meal.

Harrel decided that the Wizard now had enough information to know what had just happened and would want someone, that someone being himself, a Ranger, to do...something. As his companions in the task, in the journey, he chose the Herder, the two off-worlders, and the Faerie. She might not agree since she was still wingless and would be flightless until next spring, but he needed the Wizard's information and directions, and she was used to getting both from him. As they all entered the room, he saw that the two CatDragons were already in the tower, on the windowsill, and properly being cats, they were washing themselves.

"Will the Sorceress be joining you?" the Wizard asked.

Harrel found it annoying. He delayed his answer by taking a mug full of tea and a journey cake, as someone downstairs had decided that they were needed by the Wizard and his select companions. "No," he finally said.

"Why not?"

The other four ate and drank as quietly as possible.

Harrel took a deep breath of the cleaned air, then: "The Premontii have a wooden bridge. A suspension bridge, they call it, but the only suspense is when it's going to fall. There's already a wagon crashed below it, and the ropes are frayed. The boards break. They just want to have it repaired, but the Trolls want to construct a stone bridge.

"There's also the fact that the Premontii have forests full of wood, while the Trolls have stone. There's also the fallen bridge in Bridgedale, but they want stone, and the Trolls say wood is enough. Faster. Bridgedale has both wood and stone."

"And the Sorceress must make this decision?"

"She is impartial. And powerful. I dealt with the Trolls all winter, but I came looking for Slash. She needed to know that using fire...as a dragon...was just an extension of being an enraged hillcat. Apparently, that's a trait we share."

"Umph," the Wizard grumped.

Slash continued to wash her paws.

"Are these two...obedient?"

"They're cats. Not even dogs are obedient unless they're

thoroughly trained."

"Ah, yes. And that, my Lord Ranger is why we're here." He addressed the Herder. "You, sir. Are these mammoths of yours obedient?"

Ahgorh stifled a laugh. "No, M'Lord. They are wild animals. Somewhat docile, but still dangerous when riled."

"And that, sirs...and M'Lady...is why those creatures exist. Build them, so to speak, so they are docile and obedient."

"But..." the Herder said. "Why mammoths? Why try to kill them?"

"Not because someone has raised the dead. Though that might seem so. No. Someone, a minor wizard, I'm sure, though it could be a sorceress. Usually isn't. Anyway..." He waved his hands as if dismissing sorceresses and most females. "The minor wizard needs material. Like your Trolls and townspeople, the more material he can gather, the more of those black things he can build. How many birds do you think he could build from just one mammoth? Big ones. Dangerous ones."

"They're about the size of..." Harrel began thoughtfully. "A good-sized band of goats. More'n most herders have. Plus, handfuls of hawks and small birds. Rabbits. Wild things. Though I don't know if they'd be obedient. And rabbits aren't hunters. They're prey."

"I may never eat one again," the Herder muttered.

"And there was that...Ranger?" Harrel invited further comments from AJ or Ja-hon.

"Ah...I've said...I don't know exactly what I saw. A bit of green material. Like yours." AJ shrugged. "I don't know if it was a person. Or not. It dissolved. Disintegrated. So, we burned everything. Inside the...ah, hay mound. Where the Ranger was supposed to live. We also took a cloak and a tin of Journey Bread. Those could have belonged to the Ranger. And he was covered because...whoever covered it, wanted us, or anyone, to think it was a Ranger. Maybe he had reached the end of his magic."

The others were silent.

"Not truly our problem," the Wizard muttered. "Very well. The lot of you must find whoever is doing this evil. There's supposed to be a rogue wizard in the High Reaches. You can start by finding him. Slash, you must remain a dragon. After you come back, you can decide if you want to remain one. Songlest, you stay here until your wings re-grow, then we'll see... Get whatever you need from...whoever has it." He waved them all away.

Slash and Blacktail dropped off the windowsill just before the Wizard cast a Blocking Spell on the open window.

"Should'a had that up before," Slash muttered as she swooped across the room and down the stairs ahead of the others. There was a small wall beside the outside stairs where the two dragons could be out of everyone's way and comfortable while they waited. The Ranger would remember them, but the Wizard had already forgotten all of them.

CHAPTER 20

Harrel decided to learn more about his new companions, besides learning that only AJ had even seen a horse up close. None of them could ride one, but they had a few days to learn by doing. The same way he had learned. A little questioning would distract them.

"When we began this journey," he started. They were close by, briefly walking the quietly obedient horses. The horses were docile and tired. A good time to be talking to each other. "We were in the woods. On the Road. There was a small bridge and this...animal blocked it. It was big. Good sized on all four paws, but it could stand up and wave its front paws." He lifted his hand and spread his fingers. "It had claws as long as my fingers. And it was covered with fur. Long fur. Brown. And a muzzle like..." he thought for a moment, "like a dog. Or a wolf. Teeth. Oh, mayhap half the size of its claws. And it growled. But just a warning. Perhaps."

AJ and Ja-hon looked at each other. Carefully. Both had already fallen off horses or at least slid sidewise off the thin saddles, which did not have a convenient knob for grabbing. They were loath to ask for a Western saddle instead of half an English saddle, as they had been repeatedly warned against speaking about 'modern' conveniences. Besides, everyone else rode horses with just the thin blanket and slightly padded leather. Or bareback.

"Ah? Maybe a bear?" AJ suggested. "A grizzly?"

Ja-hon shrugged. He'd never heard of such a beast, much less seen one, having lived in a basement.

"How big?"

"A grizzly is really big."

"The creature was twice my size."

"Brown. Kodiak. Polar." AJ listed the larger bears. "But a really, really big bear might be...considering the mammoths...a cave bear."

Harrel could barely breathe, remembering the Barbarians and their caves. The skulls they had stored there. The ones on the wall could have been *grizzlies*, but hopefully, the huge one was something else. Anything else.

"You'd best hope there was only the one you saw," AJ said thoughtfully. "And not pregnant with two or even three cubs."

Harrel sighed. He was becoming cautious. Or so he thought. Fearful and angry. Even after all this time, the sound of wings, even just the little CatDragon's, made him shiver. Look over his shoulder. Anger made him short-tempered with people.

It was possible the Trolls, Premontiians and Bridgefolk deserved a certain amount of determined decisions, but it was time to stop growling at them. Especially stop being fearfully worried because there were dangers in a Ranger's Adventurous Tales, and he now had more than a magical belt knife to lose.

He was not going to lose Vallezza. He was going to be parted from her, perhaps for some time, but was not going to lose her as he had lost so many possessions. And people. He had lost Welslin. The Ranger had died, and a piece of Harrel's heart had died with him. But his teachings and his love had not.

"Since we've a moment," AJ said, not wanting to get back on the horse. "There's a small bit of information I'd like. To trade." She gleefully remembered that lesson and the rules about trading. Harrel frowned but also nodded.

"It's just a difference we can hear, but don't understand. When you talk about the Wizard..." She waved in the general direction of the Keep. "He's that. A Wizard. But the one with the magic bridge is just a wizard. And you are too. You're a Ranger. And a High Lord. A M'Lord instead of just a lord. A nobleman."

"The honorific," Harrel said, hoping that was enough.

"Fine. How'd you get to be M'Lord?"

"Elected. Most of the nobles were gone and I, as a Ranger, was impartial. I didn't want the task. That should be the first consideration for electing someone."

"That's reasonable, but..."

He knew she would have something else to say.

"In Elsewhere, we elect just about everybody. Only they want the job. Well...most of the time."

"Not even the FaerFolk want most tasks," he said. "Like Prince Gallen. He didn't even want to be a prince, but he was born one. Fourth son of the King. And he kept acting like a prince. He rescued Lady Marrigin. Wed her. A Fair Lady. The most beautiful woman in all the Kingdom. And she'll be Queen Marrigin when he is crowned King. Whether he wants to be King or not."

He thought now it was not a fate that he—a Hafling—ever dreamed could be his. He was now thankful it was not because, back then, he was loved by Marrigin's companion, Vallezza.

Of course, AJ did not agree. "What if she, this Fair Lady, wants to be Queen? On her own."

"It's called The Kingdom for a reason. Besides, she will be a Queen. And Gallen will be a good King. He is, or was, a good Prince, and he knows how to be a King. His father is, or was, a good King. And that is enough of a trade." He became a teacher again. "Relax, AJ. The horses know how to walk with a rider on their backs. And they know we've a ways to go, so they probably won't run. Or even trot."

"Do they ever wonder where they're going?" Ja-hon asked, although he was ready to remount and try riding again.

"Only if they talk. Otherwise, all they want is to be with the herd."

AJ grumbled. "And if they talked, they'd laugh at us."

"We'll lose them soon enough," the Ranger said.

"Why?"

"Rangers lose everything. Horses. Swords. It's why we all learn how to survive with whatever's at hand. And learn to ignore people who think we should live by the sword. Since we're supposed to be the King's Justice. Mostly, we're his sworn help. And don't need our own possessions."

This made them thoughtful enough to be silent for a while. To concentrate on getting up onto a horse, to relax and yet bounce atop a horse. And to glimpse, occasionally, the surrounding countryside. The first day, there was only the same ground they had already covered, only backwards. The Ranger smiled at them and said it was a lesson. He had them look back now and again because the ground they knew looked different when viewed from another direction.

He also taught them to look for rabbit trails and nut trees. Since they already knew how to gather only dead limbs from live bushes and trees, he began to teach them—all three of them since the herders used little magic—how to light a magical flame on the end of a finger. The Faerie had tried to teach AJ and Ja-hon, but she was a less patient teacher than the Ranger. He taught them as if they were simply apprentices not other-worldly fools.

For AJ, the days past slowly. She had never traveled very widely but was used to taking only an hour or two to go what was now a day's travel. Modern travel left the rest of the day for classes or antique hunting. The thing she could learn most in these forests was the different names and types of trees and bushes.

Sometimes, because of where they were, she thought of the valley or the woods as enchanted. Now, she thought the long, narrow valley they were entering looked like some gigantic animal lying in wait. The sharper mountains above the grassy valley were like cartoon teeth, the monster's open mouthful of teeth.

Harrel thought the valley looked like a cave. There were dark clouds above the sharp, stony mountains for a roof, while the narrow stream was...

He couldn't decide what it was besides empty. He had three companions and two CatDragons, but ever since he left Vallezza...

And that was the trouble—he had left her, and it made him ridiculously uneasy.

He was a Ranger. And it was past time he acted like one.

"Incoming," AJ yelled, teasing.

The two CatDragons came flying out of the valley. Slash had a rabbit in her claws, proof that there was good hunting. At least for the dragons. The humans needed more than a rabbit to share between all of them.

"Thank you," he said anyway when she dropped the rabbit so he could catch it. "Now, we'll need shelter from that storm."

"Snow?" Ahgorh asked because he was used to snowstorms all year.

"Heavy rain. Thunder. Lightning. Good reason to find shelter."

They could now see the distant flashes of light, and when Harrel urged his horse into a trot, then a gallop, they followed while hanging onto whatever they could grasp. Nonetheless, the Herder fell sidewise, then off the horse as it jumped the creek. The other two hung on.

Harrel had spotted a cluster of large rocks that could be shelter or just a haphazard pile of rocks. He rode close enough to see that one of the slabs had fallen crossways to the others. It was not the best of shelters, but it looked like it was mostly dry and safe from lightning strikes.

The three dismounted and led their horses under the overhang. Ahgorh followed, limping.

"I thought about taking some horses home with me." With a shove on the horse's rump, he pushed the mare against the wall.

"But there's no reason to risk pain just to go a bit faster."

"You're supposed to stay on."

"It jumped that creek. What is it?" he asked Harrel.

"Stairs. Stone stairs cut in the rocks."

The thunder rolled down the valley while lightning illuminated the crevasse with brief flashes and shadows. Despite his experience and misgivings, Harrel felt drawn to the old stones. He still had a cat's curiosity, a desire to stick a paw into a dark hole. Carefully. Quickly.

"Unsaddle the horses," he said instead of acting on his curiosity. "We may as well stay here the night."

The others glanced at the stairs, then unsaddled the horses, using the minimal weight to secure the reins. A panicked horse could run, even drag the saddle with it, but despite the thunderous noise, the horses were content to stand with their tails to the light and the wet. It helped that they had the last of the horse pellets to eat.

There was debris on the stairs and although the CatDragons helpfully pawed it off, there was not enough for a fire large enough to cook the entire rabbit. Still, Harrel skinned and tried to cut small pieces. It would be a small meal for each of them. The fire shed more light on the stairs.

"Slash? Did the Wizard ever speak of a tunnel, perhaps, through the mountains?"

The sleepy dragon thought for a moment. "N-no. Not that I recall. There used to be a Keep around here. Somewhere. I remember a squiggle on one of the old maps, but he never spoke on it. That it was more than a mark. There was a road, however. Maybe an old one. But maybe not. The Wizard didn't answer *fool questions*. About much of anything. Besides, it's hard to read the Wizard's maps. They smell. And they're flat."

"Why?" AJ was as curious as any cat and thought the only way to understand anything was to ask. Otherwise, the people of the Kingdom never explained anything to her satisfaction. She still was uncertain why she and Ja-hon were included on this trip.

Harrel took a deep breath. "Magic. Those stairs have a lot of magic in them. Don't you feel it?"

"No, I don't think so. What does magic feel like?"

"Maybe something of a pulling," Ja-hon replied. "Curiosity."

"Which kills cats," AJ muttered. "So?"

"I want to see why," he answered, looking at Ja-hon.

"Me too. Sort of. Cautious curiosity. But I think I'd be better off if we just left. Left the stairs alone. And what's up there. Half a vote if we have such a thing."

"No," AJ said. "We've gone well past what we...I...intended."

He looked at the Herder for his opinion.

"Is this more of those Ranger Tales?" the Herder asked.

"Probably."

The Herder shrugged. "There's a pretty girl back home. Probably wed by now. So, it's yes, up the stairs."

Both dragons were standing, looking upwards. "Flyin' first," Slash said.

"Eat," the more practical Blacktail said.

Since there was a fire and food, mostly journey cakes heavily laden with chopped nuts, as well as the rabbit, they ate. Torches should have been next, but there was nothing to be had except candles and AJ's headlamp. She had used it sparingly, so few saw its light, and she had not wasted the batteries on demonstrations. Besides, she had heard—too often—that the FaerFolk did not like 'modern' equipment. She had to wonder what they would do if they discovered hers. But she did not want to find out.

She was not enthusiastic about leading their little party either. At least the two CatDragons went first. Growling. Blacktail flew up the stairs and into the darkness. Slash followed, but Blacktail was back immediately.

"S-dark," she hissed. "But little holes."

Harrel lit a candle anyway, and AJ turned on her lamp. Behind them, Ja-hon released the horses. They might run but might not. There was pasture and water just outside. Whichever, their riders could walk if necessary.

The beginning of the stone tunnel was large enough for the flyers, but soon, Slash had to walk. Her wings touched the roughly hewn rocks on either side. Blacktail decided to just stop flying and be carried by Harrel. He could see where he had to fly, and he was no coward, but he was just a small cat and liked comfort. Besides, he had learned how to be carried on Harrel's shoulders. Harrel simply handed off the candle to Ahgorh.

"*Damn!*"

He also recognized the word because Val used the useless English to swear. "What?"

"Oh, just spider webs." AJ spit. Her lamp showed a curtain of webs. Very old, dripping webs spun by long dead spiders that had crawled into the ceiling holes, made their webs and died waiting for flying bugs.

"Been some time since anyone's used this passage," Harrel said. He was listening for something other than the drip of water. The storm might have dripped into the ceiling holes, but he thought it more likely the water would come though the rocks. The small piles of debris on the floor might have come through the holes, but it probably came from melting snow. It would stopper the holes, one flake at a time, then melt, bringing in whatever grew or fell this high in the mountains.

They were climbing, slowly, as their legs were beginning to feel the gentle grade.

Then they heard the distant sound Harrel was waiting for and was afraid he heard it. Someone else or something else was in the tunnel. The sound was distant—just echoing in their be-webbed tunnel. Ahgorh was the first to recognize it.

"Mammoth," he said as if swearing. "Hurting. And angry. The

young ones go off and get themselves lost. Away from the herd. Most of the time we find 'em." His voice was a sad whisper. "Sounds like someone else found this one."

They were all quieter now, and the trumpeting louder sounded like the angry cow they had heard defending her calf.

And once again, the tunnel was getting lighter. AJ switched off her lamp. All the walkers crept forward.

The tunnel became a platform. The rocks that formed the floor spread out over nothing while the ceiling expanded into a large, well-lit cavern. Harrel put Blacktail on the floor and signaled for the others to stay back. The rock ledge could be unstable. Harrel crept as close to the edge as he dared, wanting to see the floor beneath the ledge and the furiously trumpeting mammoth.

As the herder expected, the mammoth was a young one, a number of years older than the calf, but it had still been with the small herd of females. Until a youthful curiosity or the females drove it away. Now, it was nearly as large as the cavern's opening and stuck to the floor. Because of magic, undoubtedly, for an animal that big, needed ropes or chains to keep it in place. He, most like, waved his trunk and mid-sized tusks wildly, furiously, trying to yank his feet off the floor. Some of his long fur was stuck to the shiny floor.

"Silence, you," a voice demanded, and a man in a long tunic came around from the rear. He waved his hands, and the youngling quieted, gurgling instead of trumpeting his anger and distress.

Wizard, Harrel thought. *And magic. Just enough to keep it quiet.* Instead of a Magicals' blue tunic, the Wizard's was brown and there was no Badge. Only the sparkle of cut stones—worth a small fortune to Magicals who couldn't fashion precious stones and either cut them or give them to a stone cutter. Some, like Val, could simply fashion stones and gold into designs. Hers was a sparking dragon.

The wizard walked behind the mammoth again and returned

with a sword.

Harrel swore and signaled the two CatDragons to fly around the cavern to distract the Wizard. Then he jumped.

It was higher them most men would dare, but he was also a cat. Neither Slash nor Blacktail would have hesitated to jump down.

Nor did Ahgorh.

He came down, landed next to the Hafling...and became stuck to the floor. Harrel was on his feet, balanced, but the Herder had landed feet first, then on knees and hands. Everything stuck to the floor. Feet. Knees. Hands.

"Ah-hah." The Wizard came out from behind the mammoth. The youngling was wild-eyed, it waved its trunk around but was ominously quiet. "A Hafling. Wondrously perfect. And what are you...M'Lord?" he mocked. "All that fancy gold. And green. You're that Ranger. The Hafling Ranger. And now what? Some kind of Hafling Lord?" He came a little closer. "A fool of a Hafling Lord is what you are. But not to worry. Fool or no, I'll use you."

"For what?" Ahgorh growled out, twisting to see the Wizard. "Let the mammoth go."

"Certainly not."

"Then...why?"

"Haven't either of you figured that out yet? He's material. There's enough in him to fashion a *real* dragon! Not that stone one you and that whore stuck on *my* mountain. I need a *real* dragon. As big as he is." He patted the mammoth's leg possessively. "Mine. Get away from here," he yelled at Slash. She had come close to the mammoth. Blacktail was circling higher.

On the stone ledge, AJ was carefully taking aim. Ja-hon held her in place with a grasping hand, careful not to disturb her balance, only to keep her safe on the ledge.

"Aim," she whispered, echoing her instructor.

She had been getting snippets of information and worries

about the revolver. About what was called Straight-Line Magic or Non-magic. Science said the bullet would curve, but here, in this world, it would go from here to there in a straight line—without any effort. Training, yes, but no effort. Anyone could shoot. Unlike a simpler weapon, which required training and the strength to string a bow or lift a sword. AJ had neither. She just had training.

"And squeeze the trigger."

The bang echoed in the chamber, a deadly sound on its own. The bullet went in its straight, nullifying, line. It cut through the spells in the chamber that surrounded the Wizard and his captives to plow another straight-line into flesh, blood and bone.

AJ fired again.

The first, coldly manufactured bullet did what it was designed to do, drilled into the Wizard's chest, then heart. The second was AJ's insurance. There was too much talking before shooting for her comfort.

And it was her last bullet. The gun was now useless.

The wizard clutched his chest and died.

His magic died with him.

Harrel had been drawing his knife and off-balance, nearly fell over. The Herder was positioned like a runner on a block. He sprinted toward the young mammoth. The animal raised his trunk and a foot, bellowing. The Herder had enough sense to stop and wave his arms.

"Out. Out," he yelled, and the mammoth's training made him hear and understand. He bellowed again and stomped on the wizard's body as he ran for the cavern's entrance, disappearing into the aftermath of the thunderstorm. Slash, being a youngster's minder, did the same.

Ahgorh sank to his knees again, touching the wet stone. It was just wet. "Magic's gone. With him." He gestured at the bloody carcass.

"Hey! Down there. Harrel." AJ still leaned over the edge of

the ledge with Ja-hon's help. "We'll go back for the horses. Saddles. Can you two go out and around?"

"Yes. Just stay in the tunnel. Or just outside. Blacktail. Go with them. Then go outside and find Slash." He waved the little dragon up to the other two and the tunnel's entrance. He knew Blacktail would go find Slash because he thought the dragon was more receptive to directions than AJ.

She nodded, waved her understanding, and leaned back.

"You shot him," Ja-hon said.

"Always have been a good shot. With just about anything. Huh. You suppose that's magic? Always hitting what I aim for?"

"Could be, I suppose," he said, following the little dragon into the tunnel. "There's more than enough magic around here for all of us."

CHAPTER 21

The walk back to where the other two and the horses waited took most of the day. The rock the tunnel was hewn from extended into the valley and had to be circled around. Slash could go over, see what was on the other side and report back. But then Harrel had to decide if going down to the stream or just going around the encroaching rock was the quicker path.

It did not help the decisions when the young mammoth made them. He wanted to wade in the stream, to shower himself with the cool water. It was warm, and he got hot just walking on the grassy banks. Ahgorh had to go with him. Or at least be nearby and risk a drowning when the animal's powerful trunk sprayed everything, including his herdsman.

It was Ja-hon who convinced the dragons to play in the water with the mammoth. They both like water and splashing in and out. Very quickly the mammoth realized he could—gently—try to squirt the pair in a game of tag, tiring him into some obedience to the Herder.

Ahgorh would have liked to keep at least one dragon with him, but the pair thought they belonged with others. Blacktail draped himself across Harrel's shoulders—thoroughly soaking his tunic—while Slash simply stopped playing and went to find the horses. She wanted to get to the Keep. And the Wizard. Home.

The mammoth then followed in the stream, not necessarily to the horses and the other two humans, but because the stream went in that direction, flowing past the rocks until it turned away. Now, he would go in that direction, which was what the Herdsman wanted. He joined the others, patted his horse in farewell and laughed. Rather grimly, knowing the task of getting the youngling back home was going to be difficult. He did not need the added responsibility of caring for a horse.

"Too bad you can't ride a mammoth like an *elephant*," AJ said with a smile and wished she had not.

"Ride?" he demanded. "Elle-font?"

AJ sighed. "In the East of Elsewhere, people train young elephants—animals kinda like your mammoth—to do all sorts of tasks. They ride them. Just behind their heads. Considering that all the animals around here can learn how to talk, you could start talking to this one. Get him to understand a word or two." She shrugged. "What else do you have to do on the way home?"

"Train him," Ja-hon added. "Gently. No sticks or anything like that."

"Of course not," the indignant herder said, as if insulted that he would even think a Herdsman would be cruel to one of his valuable animals.

"Friends," Ja-hon said. "You. Him."

This was something of a new concept, but the others could see from his expression that he considered it a good idea. Something he could try on the long walk home.

The mammoth wanted to try walking without a herder.

The others quickly shared what food they still carried. Harrel said that they would have time to learn how to hunt and trap rabbits. And Ahgorh was off, after his charge.

AJ and Ja-hon looked about as happy to learn about rabbits as they had about horses. Still, it was that or going very hungry. Neither of the two dragons could daily catch enough rabbits for even just three humans instead of four. Harrel did not wait until they had lost sight of the Herder and the mammoth to begin practice with the horses and lessons on rabbits. The valley, as usual, was crowded with rabbits, so the evening meal was assured.

What neither of the two other-worlders could envision was Harrel's interest in Ja-hon. He knew quite a bit about AJ, including the fact that her real name was Alice Jane, but he had learned no more than she about Ja-hon. "What is your real name?"

It took Ja-hon a while before he answered. "I don't have one."

AJ was silent although she really wanted to speak.

Harrel just nodded. He was familiar with the reasons people had no real name.

"The hospital gave me the name of John Wilkes instead of John Doe, until I remembered my own name. I was in an accident, they said. Had no *identification or insurance*."

This was for AJ's benefit since neither word was translatable to Common.

"So, now I'm Ja-hon. I like this name much better, than John, considering. I still don't remember much. Who I was. What happened. It took a while to remember how to speak. Sometimes, bits returned, but not what things were. Or how to pay my *hospital bills*. I learned to put on a shirt and tie a tie...and tie my shoes, but I didn't know what else to do. A nice woman, Gladis, got me a room in a group home. I lived there for about a year until the bullies drove me away. Then I went underground. I just couldn't adjust to not knowing much about anything."

He sighed.

"I felt different. And looked like...a monster. I had a smashed nose and cheekbones, and it took *surgery* to fix both. They did a good job, I guess. While it healed, people stared. At my face, wrapped in bandages, one eye hole, and a slit for my mouth.

"It was easier to live in the dark. Sometimes dangerous, but there are a lot of people around at night. And then there was the Albert Square Monster legend." He laughed. "It was easy to pretend I was him. Easier than being someone who was lost. I could scare the dangerous people. Keep them away from my basement, my sanctuary, my home." He shrugged. "But when you came along, AJ, I followed you because I was curious. Why were you there? What did you want? What were you looking for with that silly little light on your head? I thought...why not follow you? See what happens.

He groaned. "Then this...happened. Everything became impossible. All...this...that we found." He waved a hand around himself and his horse. He was already able to direct the walking animal with only one hand on the reins.

A tear burned in AJ's eye. "I'm so glad we met, Ja-hon."

His expression turned frightful. He gestured to the stream that ran along the Road. "Things like that bear and those wolves happened. That is a bear, isn't it?"

Now the horses became aware of the predators. Or of the blood smell of the deer the bear was guarding, or taking, from a circle of wolves.

"I have got to be more aware," Harrel muttered. He paused, then cautiously convinced his horse, and the one he was leading, to move forward. As long as they stayed on the Road, they could pass unharmed.

One of the wolves noticed them, said something to another, and slowly they moved backwards, away from the bear and his meal. A safe distance away from his paws, most turned tail and trotted away. Two of them, still watching the bear, came near the Road and the three riders.

"What is that thing, Ranger?" one wolf demanded.

"A baair," Harrel replied. He was used to talking animals, even wild ones like wolves. The horses snorted but stayed obedient mostly because they were horses and on the Road where they belonged.

"Grizzly. Bigger. Didn't know they were that big," AJ said.

Ja-hon was silent, as he did not remember seeing any bears.

"See that hump on his back? Sort of on his, maybe hers, shoulders. Grizzly Bear."

"Doesn't know any rules," the wolf said. "We chased that deer for two days. Got cubs, you know. Hungry alla time. Do something, Lord Ranger."

AJ scowled. "Bears are dangerous."

"Also newcomers," Harrel said. "They don't even know there are rules. And not any I can enforce."

Seeing the horses had stopped, the two dragons began to circle overhead.

"More of 'em," the wolf exclaimed. "What'er those?"

"CatDragons," Harrel replied. "And helpful. Did you cut that deer out of a herd?"

"Course. Lost 'em. Take days to find 'em again."

"Dragons fly overhead. So, while that baair is occupied... Slash! Blacktail! Can you find a herd of deer? Or just one or two?"

"Saw...deer. That way." Slash pointed a wing and banked afterwards. The two wolves followed.

One wolf let out a quick howl, and the others stopped. Seeing one running in a new direction, they followed at a ground-covering run.

Harrel unstrapped his bow. He had brought it with him because he always carried a bow if he could. If there was a new one available. There had not been deer or anything else that could be hunted with a bow since he left the Keep. Deer were wary of Roads. Too many four-legged predators used them along with human hunters. And Harrel had almost forgotten he wore it. Usually, he laid it down at night and forgot it the next morning instead of just strapping it on along with a pack and quiver.

Harrel followed the dragons and wolves after handing off the spare horse to Ja-hon. He was no better with two horses than AJ, just closer to the Ranger.

"Keep going. Find the hut. Slash," he yelled. "You go with 'em. Blacktail. With me."

Slash swerved to rejoin the pair. They all watched Harrel for a bit, then followed his orders after remounting their horses.

"He may not like being a High Lord..." AJ began, kicking her horse into movement. She found it impossible to understand the animal. At times, the horse wanted to follow the others. Usually when AJ did not. Otherwise, it just stood, then started grazing. Now and again, it wanted to run. Also, when AJ did not.

"But he gives orders like one," Ja-hon laughed, flanking her.

"You could have told me about your amnesia."

"Could have but got to the point where I didn't want to go back. You might have."

"From what I can see, we can't go back. Not just because of those ogres, but I doubt we could find the right Road. Or that ruined hut and the tunnel. From what some of them have said, I don't know if we'd go back to our own time. I think we could surprise the people who put in that church door. Go back a couple of hundred years. And they'd be a lot less welcoming than they are here. Don't know what we'll do here, however."

"Find the nearest hut. Make a fire and cook the rabbits," he said with all the practicality of the dragons. "Hey, Slash. See anything yet?"

"No," she said, flying higher. Sometime later she returned. "I found what's left of the huts down the next hill. Trees. Water."

"I remember that one," AJ said. "Just past the entrance to this valley. Barely enough stone works to call it a hut. Makes you wonder, though."

"What?"

"Who built them. Huts. Roads. Especially the Roads. Case you haven't noticed, the Road usually has two ruts or paths." Ja-hon nodded so she continued. "Where's the path for the horse? There are ruts for wagon wheels. And since the villager's wagons were pulled by two or four horses, they fit the Road. Smaller wagons. A small carriage. With only one horse wouldn't fit. The horse would be in the middle and always stopping to eat grass."

She kicked her horse again, lightly, just to stop it from grabbing a mouthful of grass. A solid kick would make the horse run. She'd be lucky if she stayed on.

"So. Who made these Roads and why? And why's the hut made to shelter someone who's been walking from morning to night. They weren't built for wagons. Wagons would be faster. And they have horses. They need stables. Hay. Straw. Grass or a horse trough."

"Ask the High Lord," Ja-hon replied, urging his horse into a trot.

AJ wanted to talk more, but her horse now wanted to trot alongside his, and she had to pay attention or walk, after she fell off.

Ja-hon yelled over his shoulder, "FaerFolk will be his answer and little else."

Yet she did not ask said High Lord when he rejoined them before nightfall. Harrel could gallop his horse and still stay in the saddle, so he was faster than they were. Plus, he had a dragon to find them, the smoke from their fire and a few birds yelling about dragons and people.

On the morrow, he would continue to treat them like apprentices and go on with their lessons in reading trails, setting snares, and cooking whatever they caught. At night, by firelight, they could fashion baskets. There was little else to do during the day besides riding back to the Wizard's Keep. And less to do at nightfall besides talk too much and sleep in a traveler's roadside hut.

The only thing he failed, repeatedly, was to teach them how to pull in enough magic to ignite a small flame on the end of a finger.

CHAPTER 22

There was noise all around the hut: horses whinnying. Thunder. "What the h..." AJ choked on a curse word.

Noises she had only heard on the TV. Mooing?

"Horses," Harrel yelled and dove for the stable door. He woke up faster than either of the other two, and even if he had no idea of what woke him, he knew he had to catch the horses or he and his charges would be walking the rest of the way to the Keep. Ja-hon was almost as awake and aware. Only AJ was wondering how sounds she had only heard in cowboy flicks could be crashing around the hut. A *stampede*?

It was almost silent when she raced through the back door to see the last cow running around the stone walls of what could barely have been called a stable yard. Harrel and Ja-hon held the skittering horses, either by their lead reins or halters. The thunder and lightning, which terrified both the horses and cows, was still lighting the sky on the wrong side of morning. In the west. The early sun was rising, as usual, in the east.

"That-that's no storm." AJ tried to be completely awake. To speak. To understand. Whatever she was staring at was no normal thunderstorm. Trees and mountains shielded the flashes of bright light, yet above them, the sky was colored yellow and orange. Solid light. Not the flashes that defined the distant hills and clouds in front of a storm, but glowing light that stayed in the sky longer than reflected lightning. And fire. The reflections of distant fires lit the sky before disappearing.

And there was noise. Continuous booms. More noise than

lightning. Impossible booms.

Fog covered the grassy valley on this side of the mountains. Plain, gray and white morning fog. Without any reflections or colors from the storm.

"Saddles," Harrel ordered. "Packs."

He handed off two horses to Ja-hon and shoved past AJ. She blinked, still understanding only his orders, not what had awakened them or was actually happening. Packs and saddles meant they were leaving—with no time for tea, a meal or the use of the small bathing room. No time for anything left by the fireplace.

They grabbed what they could, saddled only three horses and slid into their packs almost as they mounted their horses. Ja-hon had the fourth's lead rope.

The fog swirled over the hut, deadening all sound, and while Harrel wanted to gallop once they found the Road, he walked his horse. Half seeing the Road under the white mist; half trusting the horse to stay in a dirt rut.

"Halt! Who goes there?"

Not for the first time, AJ cursed the Translation Spell. She understood the words but needed to know the speaker; a sentry, she hoped. But whose?

"Ah...just us, sir." That seemed AJ's best reply. And in her most innocent feminine voice.

"Us?" a worried young voice came out of the fog. Then a step farther, she saw a man dressed in khaki, brimmed Brodie helmet, shoulder pack, and held his rifle at the ready. "Who's there with you?"

Rifle? Here? Soldier? Am I seeing things again?

She couldn't let the soldier see her bewilderment. "We're farmers, sir. Takin' our work horses home. Me 'n' Gran-pa." She hoped his army didn't need work horses. Or old men. If he could see enough to count horses and men, they could be in more trouble.

Harrel alone was enough to make him raise his rifle to a position where he could shoot it. "Who are you?"

The fog swirled. A horse snorted and stomped.

AJ had to wonder if Harrel had ever used the over-sized knife he wore on his belt for something besides skinning rabbits. And if Rangers had rules about who they filleted with knives or swords.

There was another, closer, boom that shivered the fog. And a whistle.

"Go another way," the soldier yelled and vanished into the fog.

Seeing his chance to chase down the soldier, Harrel kicked his horse into a trot, then a gallop, straight into the fog. The other two did the same. Galloping. Hoping to stay on the horses.

The fog lifted off the road. Harrel stopped to listen, as did the others. There were a few bird songs as the sun rose higher, burning off more of the fog. Here and there were patches of blue sky.

"What was that?" Ja-hon asked. "Who?"

"Soldier," AJ said, breathless.

"Why was he Here?" Harrel asked.

"Didn't that Wizard say a whole village...from somewhere around here, wanted to go home?"

"Yes, but—"

"Elles, the Head Woman, had an accent whenever she said a word in *English*. So, maybe she was from my world. Elsewhere?" When he nodded, she continued, "They'd left because there was so much fighting. Trouble is, there are places where the old *fairy tales* were written, where wars have been fought for years and years. The wars with Napoleon. World War One. And Two. If they went back home, they could have travelled right into a war. Maybe World War One."

"Why that one?" Ja-hon asked, remembering something, but not enough.

"Because that wasn't a thunderstorm that frightened those

cows," she answered. "I'm certain the noise and the flashes came from cannons and frightened those animals...cows. Some kind of cows. Cattle. But that wasn't thunder. That much I know. And that *soldier* was carrying a *rifle*. He wore a brimmed helmet, maybe from our World War One."

"Impossible," Ja-hon said.

"Any more than wooly mammoths?" she countered. "These valleys seem to have more time-holes than Swiss cheese. Who's in charge of the crossings?" she asked the High Lord.

Harrel shook his head. "The FaerFolk."

"Of course. Who else?" She snorted. "Well, they need to be told. We could be in a battlefield."

"Then we best get out," Ja-hon murmured.

Harrel was listening again. For wings this time. He was far more concerned about the CatDragons than about himself and the others. Taking a chance, he called out, "Slash?"

Within moments, the dragon cut through the fog. "The rabbits are all in their holes," she reported. "There was too much noise."

"We have more important worries than rabbits." That was Harrel's only comment on the lack of food for all of them. "What do you see? Off that way." He waved westward.

"Fog." She snarled. "Sunshine above the fog. Fog on the rabbits."

"No people? Nothing...making noise?"

"No people," she answered, hearing the worry in his demands. Until he told her why, she assumed—both of them being hillcats—that he was as hungry as she. "Oh. Those cow-things are off that way. Toward the sunrise. They've stopped running."

"But nothing else is there?"

"Fog," she repeated.

Blacktail floated through it, adjusted his wings, and flew to Harrel. He held up an arm and the small dragon landed on his shoulder. As best he could, he purred and head-bumped the Ranger as a sign of his affection. Harrel sighed, a bit ashamed of his temper.

"It'll lift," he said to Slash. "And we need to get to the Keep." Having said all he could at the moment, he urged his horse forward.

AJ, however, was not satisfied. "What's going on? How can we see a war?"

"We can't. Shouldn't. There's an opening somehow, a door between Here and Elsewhere."

"A time warp as well," she added.

Harrel didn't know the term but knew who would. "We need to see the FaerFolk."

"And we do that...how?"

"Talk to the Wizard."

"It's above our pay grade," AJ muttered and deliberately kicked her horse. It yanked on a tuft of grass, but started an equally deliberate, bone-jarring trot forward.

Ja-hon sighed and followed them, all through the foggy morning and well into the true sunrise. The CatDragons went after rabbits while the humans ate the fallen nuts from a lone tree. The horses used the time to graze, then, and when they stopped for the night. There were nut trees growing in the hut's 'front yard,' protected by the remains of a stone wall. But the mature, nut-baring trees were long gone. Time, and even the few fools who used the trees for firewood, destroyed the grove. Harrel managed to find a large shell-back, large enough for a taste instead of a filling meal.

On the next hillside, the CatDragons found a freshly killed deer near the Road, and Harrel sliced off a good-sized chunk of tooth-marred venison. AJ kept quiet, for a change, and ate her share. This did not mean she was adjusting to her new world and situation. She had never been truly hungry in all her life and was willing to adapt to her new circumstances. Once in a while.

"It's better than stale pizza." Ja-hon sympathized with her. "And better than rats."

"Nobody eats rats," she insisted.

Both the men were silent, but a quick look between them said they both had done so. And if there were any rats to be on hand, they both knew the CatDragons would consider them a feast.

None of them appreciated stopping—early—at the next hut, even though there was an abundance of rabbits and an overgrown plot of dandelions and onions. A stew usually contained all three items, but travelers did not carry the necessary kettle. The best they could carry was a small combination pot and cup for tea. Even then the cook had to be careful not to get scalded.

Still, this hut was only a two-day ride from the first of the Keep's fields. It only seemed farther away returning than it had been going. Now the Road began to fill with people going in both directions on a Road that was meant for wagons with only two or four horses.

"Perhaps..." AJ said, having little else to think on, "people are supposed to walk on the left path or right, depending on which direction they were headed."

Harrel ignored her. Besides, they were the only riders. And rode where they pleased. Where the horses pleased.

Both riders and horses agreed only when they hurried on the last afternoon, wanting to arrive before the evening meal. It would only be stew and fresh bread—or at least that morning's bread—but more than their usual fare.

The Keep, with its Wizard's tower could be seen, distantly, by mid-morning, for the Keep had been built on a high hill and could be seen from most of the land oathed to the King and the Wizard. The Road encircled a hilltop, but it was without walls or defenses, just an early welcome to travelers. Or a warning. The Keep had high stone walls, surrounding the towers and dwellings, which warned those on foot or horseback that they would have to climb a grassy hill, with few trees or stone walls for concealment. The defenses here were all pastures or gardens. Practical use for the land and a simple defense because attackers were clear targets in the open land. Then, they would have to surmount the walls.

As they all knew from the siege of the black birds, there was no defense against flyers except distance. Unless the flyers were the same hungry dragons that had fought those deadly birds. Then, there were pigeons for an unnecessary defense. There were flocks both inside and out, and as soon as the two dragons came near enough, they chased the real birds, alerting the guards. Slash quit first, but Blacktail enjoyed his revenge and relished the chase. Pigeons and dragons flew over the Keep's walls while sentries, guards, and a number of villagers watched and shouted encouragement or curses, depending on their attachment to the birds. Boys also forgot their tasks to stare upwards and yell.

There was even a trumpet salute.

It was a fitting welcome for a High Lord, and those villagers with an abundance of curiosity or those who could drop their work for a few moments and step outside their houses to line the Road and wave.

Harrel hated it. He did nothing but ride through the village, neither smiling nor throwing so much as a copper coin or an acknowledging wave.

"Fitting welcome for a High Lord." AJ snickered.

"Teach him to act like one," Ja-hon said.

"Somebody said he was a dragon-rider," AJ added.

Harrel growled, and the pair laughed. They were still smiling as they rode through the Keep's open gates. The usual hordes of boys raced across the courtyard to see to the horses as the riders dismounted and to offer anything else the newcomers wanted.

Harrel wanted nothing more than access to the Wizard's tower to report and then a meal, a bath, and a bed. All three alone. He handed the horse to the nearest stableboy, and straightening to his full height, strode to the tower stairs.

The lower door opened, and a woman in a blue gown rushed out.

Harrel stopped and stared, frozen in place. The woman laughed and ran down the stairs to fling herself at him. He managed to catch her and whisper one word, "Val," before she closed his mouth with her own and took away his senses.

His arms tightened, holding her close. Her arms were around his neck, holding her up since not even the tips of her toes were on the ground. To all the watchers—and everyone who paused to stare—they seemed alone. Only the two of them. Harrel managing to hold her close, gently, using little of his strength, while the Sorceress was merely welcoming her Lord. A woman who would make him even more welcome when she truly had him alone.

From behind them, AJ and Ja-hon watched, silent and unmoving until AJ was suddenly lifted into the air. Ja-hon had her up and in his arms. Startled, she stared at him and was kissed. Learning for the first time what was meant by 'being thoroughly' kissed. She was stiff with surprise at first, then relaxed. Returned the kiss.

"What?" she managed.

"Seemed like the right moment," Ja-hon answered.

CHAPTER 23

Harrel asked, "Where's the Wizard?" He did not actually care. He understood now why he had felt so annoyed and empty. He had been enspelled. He *was* enspelled. Maybe always and forever, and that thought made him understand that he had lost half of himself. He was sorry, but he did not intend to apologize. To anyone.

He was much more himself, a Ranger.

And a High Lord. At least in title.

The Wizard's Tower was empty. The owl was in its usual place on the top of the shelves, along with Blacktail, but the Wizard was not there.

The only others were Slash, on the windowsill, Ja-hon and AJ. And AJ kept glancing sidewise at her companion, with no interest in the Wizard either.

"The Wizard is gone," Vallezza said. "No sense asking where or why. I don't know."

Harrel looked thoughtful, but he no longer really cared about Wizards. He might, later, but not now. He only cared about the woman who rested her hand on his arm. "Then, how is it you are here?"

He tried to count all the days since he had left her, but he doubted that even on horseback could she have ridden here, to the Keep. Taken the same number of days. Without repaired bridges. Without the bridges, no one could have traveled between villages or anywhere else.

A door opened in the middle of the open room, and a woman

stepped inside the empty space, then carefully closed the door behind her.

All of them were getting used to 'the impossible' so a door opening without a wall was less of a surprise. The woman herself was what all of them would call beautiful, yet she was not. Harrel remembered his own words and thought her perfect. Well beyond beautiful. Perfect.

One of the FaerFolk.

"M'Lady." Val nodded in respect, as she was too familiar with the Lady to bow to the woman.

Harrel stiffened. He did not trust the FaerFolk anymore.

"Do you have a problem, Lord Ranger?" she asked, a chill in her voice.

"A war, M'Lady."

"War? Between...?"

"We don't know, M'Lady. Because it's not in our time. It's leaking from Elsewhere into our valleys. We could hear the *cannons*...The large *guns*..." He stopped. "AJ, please show her your *gun*."

AJ drew the revolver from its holster. "When it has *bullets*, M'Lady, it makes a very loud noise. *Cannons* are just enormously larger. They are also much louder. And can shoot farther. To knock down walls. And kill a lot more people. I... I've shot an ogre and one wizard. And one of those black things."

"Things?" she repeated, ignoring—for the most part—the English words.

Harrel went on: "The wizard she shot was making obedient servants from whatever he killed. He was going to kill a young *mammoth*. The Herders in the FarNorth keep a herd of them. They came through the doors, long ago, but in the same area. Since then, they've followed the mammoths into the Valley—in the winter— then back again. With no sign of the doors. But they leak in, M'Lady. Dangerously so."

"And you believe I—"

"Yes. You are the only ones who can seal the doors."

She turned slightly toward Vallezza. "You did say he speaks the truth. Not Ranger Tales. With no polished words."

"If he says something must be done, it must."

"Umm. Very well. We shall seal the doors and keep that *war* in Elsewhere."

"An entire village may have gone back to their homes. To Elsewhere. Or Elsewhen." Harrel shrugged, although it was considered impolite. Even annoying. Most people tried their best not to annoy—or even bother—the FaerFolk.

"And I am to bring the villagers back?" she asked, her voice warningly cold.

"Yes."

"I think not, Lord Ranger. There are those who object to..." She glanced at AJ and Ja-hon. "Even one or two humans crossing *into* the Kingdom. An entire village of people who do not want to be here?" She forbear to call the villagers fools. "They would be more than others could endure. So. The trade?"

"Yes, M'Lady," Vallezza said and felt Harrel manage to stiffen even more. But he did not growl.

"Lord Harrel, your Lady now owns a Traveling Spell. She can now travel like that." She snapped her fingers. "She will return to those people and the Trolls."

Harrel was not the only one who wanted to curse the stubborn villagers. If he really had a say, he would not build new bridges; he would leave all three villages on their own. He shivered, realizing he had just thought of the same answer to the problem most people had with new-born haflings—they would leave them on their own. To survive or not.

"For as many years as it takes to rebuild their bridges. And enable them to choose their *next* High Lord. Will you be joining her, Lord Harrel?"

"Yes, M'Lady," he said more ashamed of his own thoughts than subservient, so he dared ask, "The Wizard, M'Lady? Andruss is gone."

"And the Master Wizard," Vallezza added, backing Harrel. The Traveling Spell was too new for her to use of yet, to check in person with the Magicals' Hall, but even minor wizards had ways of speaking to each other, usually through magical fires.

The Lady smiled.

Harrel thought it was a smirk.

"I believe you, Lord Harrel, suggest we *do something* about the wizards."

When he looked dubious, distrustful, she continued. "No. Not Wiping. A Magical, even one whose mind has been wiped, is liable to become dangerous."

As both Ranger and High Lord, Harrel could propose Wiping a serious offender's—his or her—memories clean, but the actual Spell was worked by a senior magical. And so few times, he had never met the resulting person. Or creature. Someone or something with absolutely no memory, sometimes from day to day. At best, it was said, the person who had been wiped could be taught to speak and take care of him or herself. Little else.

"You suggested the punishment yourself," the Lady said.

But Harrel showed no reaction to her words. He had no memory of his words.

"A return to...an apprentice's schooling in Ethics." She smiled, then became serious. "All of them need a reminder that being a master requires *aiding* the rest of the world. Not destroying it for their own selfish reasons. Even their own selfish magic. They will return helpful, or they will not return. For a while. A long while, most like."

Both Harrel and Vallezza knew that 'for a while' could mean a day, moon cycles or even many, many years from that moment.

"Then..." She turned to leave.

There was a cough from the windowsill, and Slash dropped to the floor. "About myself," she said.

"A dragon? Or a hillcat?"

"Oh, a hillcat, M'Lady, because...I was a fire-breathing dragon. Burned people. And almost one of those black birds. I do not want to ever have that...anger in me again."

She smiled, but sadly. "But you do, Slash. Most of your kind lead quiet lives, but it's in you, a hillcat, to turn into something like a fire-breathing dragon. For the most part you remain a hillcat. With teeth and claws. More than enough to defend your kittens. But..." She looked now at the Hafling. "Hillcats have the magic to truly change into something very like a fire-breathing dragon."

"I think I'd rather be just a guard, M'Lady. An ordinary hillcat."

"You should only change yourself if you want to. Changing to make someone else happy...Or changing to be their idea of who and what you are is wrong, Slash. For you. And being a fire-breathing dragon is fearful. Something must be done about dangerous dragons."

"Yes, M'Lady."

"Do you want to return to being a hillcat?"

"Yes, M'Lady."

The Lady clapped her hands together as if squeezing Slash's wings and they folded into tan fur. Four scaled legs became furry and the paws had hidden claws. A long, furry tail fluffed out behind her and lashed. Free of restraints.

Only she was not. Once again she wore a blue leather harness.

"And, now? You, little cat?"

"Ah...I... I'm a CatDragon. I like being a dragon instead of a barncat. Can I stay a dragon?"

"Of course."

"Can I have a nice lady cat for company? For...ah, kittens?

CatDragons?"

She smiled at him, although she shook her head at his bad manners. Both knew he had nothing to trade. "Find her. If...*If* she wishes, she will change."

"Thank you, M'Lady."

"Now. You two. Come with me."

AJ and Ja-hon stumbled through the door after her.

"What do you suppose she wants with them?" Harrel asked, although most of his mind was not on his companions.

"Something which will benefit all of us, supposedly. Like keeping you as High Lord."

"I don't see how that benefits any of us. Was that spell so important?" Despite his thoughts and realizations about himself, his voice held a demand.

"It's convenient. But if you really did not want to *endure* being a High Lord, I would not have traded. Now, wherever you are, I can get there with a snap of my fingers."

"Like now? Were you that happy to see me?"

"I was that happy to know I missed you." She had honestly missed him. Her life had become empty because her companion was gone. Her bed had become empty because her lover was gone. Even her magic was gone, or at least dulled, because he was gone. Much too far away.

Having enspelled him had also enspelled her, as well. Worse, having him gone made her wonder if her astonishing memory of the Hafling Ranger, walking up the street from the docks, was her imagination. He said he had not been entranced by the morning and Halvarrarde. It was a good morning, he agreed, trying to avoid mentioning that he had forgotten even seeing her. Only when she was with him did she know her memory of him was true. He was a wonderfully young and confident Ranger. And Hafling.

The FaerFolk needed such men to force everyone else to remember what they were all supposed to be: Honest. Hopeful.

And well worth a simple Transport Spell.

"I thought you needed a surprise. You are a very sober cat, Lord" She rose up on tiptoe to kiss him again. "And with my new spell, I can follow you anywhere. Does that benefit you, my dear Lord?"

He was silent for a moment, then: "The three of you..." He indicated Slash and Blacktail and added the owl in the count. "Please leave us."

The owl made the most noise, but he and Blacktail flew out the open window while Slash cat-pranced out the door with the others.

Finally, Harrel and Vallezza were alone.

CHAPTER 24

Harrel was dressing in a new tunic when Vallezza said, "The first task for the High Lord is that Bahair. That is what she called it, isn't it?"

"Close to. Baair. But what am I to do about it?" He was wondering more about how Vallezza had come by a new tunic, not what wearing it would mean. He had already acquired the main chamber as their own, in another tower, with an adjoining bathing room. He and Vallezza had taken baths in the fragrant waters and made very satisfying use of the warm shower to do more than just rinse off soap. If that was one of the advantages of being a High Lord, then he was willing to endure the rest in trade.

Trade, he thought, meant enduring the queries about the missing Wizard, questions about everyone's new tasks and duties, and the inevitable complaints. Complaints were not usually about the Wizard, because he had kept to his tower room and his solitary magics. Complaints were more ordinary problems. The High Lord just had to listen, then give the problem over to the person who told him who could actually *do* something. Talking to a Lord made the complainants feel better. Or so Harrel supposed.

But baairs? What had he to do with baairs? Without AJ, he did not even know what to call the animal.

"There is also a wolf at the door," serious, but not unamused, Val repeated.

Harrel wondered how she could manage to be so inviting, yet proper. She was ready for the day, for her duties as the only magical in residence, yet she had been his willing, even enthusiastic, partner earlier this morning, and a goodly portion of the night.

And now as he added his belt, and found it free of dirt and scratches, he wondered, again, about the tunic. And all the gold embroidered on it. Everyone who could afford gold, found it, or had a magical who had access to it out of the air, wore gold. Gold fasteners. Gold embroidery. Gold designs in leather, as he now had on his belt and his belt knife's sheath. Mining gold kept miners, dwarfs, and even the ogres busy. A High Lord had to admit there were even thieves who stole from everyone, and when caught, had to be punished.

By him. By a Lord. A High Lord. Or the King.

Vallezza opened the chamber door, and Blacktail flew inside. Unless he was hunting pigeons or mice, he was always nearby and wanting to drape himself on Harrel's shoulders. Interrupting his thoughts.

The tunic now had an improvement to Blacktail's perch, as well. There was now green leather across the Hafling's shoulders because CatDragons had claws.

And he used them now, as he dropped onto Harrel's shoulders.

"Good morrow, to you too," Harrel said and offered his arm to the Sorceress, to escort her to the Dining Hall.

Yet Harrel stopped, partially reluctant to begin his duties as High Lord, partially for a brief bit of privacy. Words that had been on his mind had vanished when he saw Vallezza, were now squeezing back into his consciousness. He thought it was best to say them now, in the privacy of the stairwell, than later when there was more than just a small dragon to hear them

"That wizard said," he started, stopped and began again. "Before AJ shot that lesser wizard, he said that he could see Michael and the Dragon. On *his* mountainside. They're here? Nearby?"

"Yes."

"You've never said. Beyond that first look at them..."

"You haven't been ready to look," she answered simply. "Now?"

"Mayhap. The...words itch," he said, shrugging and disturbing Blacktail's nap. The little CatDragon purred.

The Sorceress looked around, then led him to a mirror designed to look for invaders farther down the curved stairs. Instead of those stairs, the mirror showed a snow-covered mountain. Snow was already deep on the sharp, rocky slopes, white against the blue morning sky, while below the summit, snow outlined Michael on the Dragon.

They seemed close, almost just outside the mirror-window.

Michael was delirious. Beyond his joy at flying, he was—as only Michael could be—delirious. He was flying. There was snow piled on his head that a brisk wind was blowing a trail behind him and swirling around the dragon's tail and wings. Harrel could also see the dragon's eyes, as he was looking back at his rider. His forever companion.

It did not matter to them that they were stone—carved by Vallezza's magic—they were together. Flying.

Like he and Vallezza were together. Enspelled.

What remained of the guilt he had felt, the joy of being rescued from the dragon, at the cost of Michael's life, faded. They had all traded.

"And it's past time I accepted who and what I am," he said, this time, knowing his words were finally true.

"The Hafling Lord," agreed Vallezza.

"The High Lord. Ruler of...well, my own little backyard." He kissed her forehead and covered the slim hand on his arm with his other hand. "Small wonder the King resigned in Gallen's favor. This ruling business—"

The doors to the Dining or Great Hall opened to a burst of

trumpets that made Blacktail flap his wings. And dig his claws into the shoulder-leather for balance.

"That will have to stop," Harrel growled, wondering whose task it was to order silence. Fully half of the ruling seemed to be discovering who did what.

Everyone used the Dining or Great Hall for every occasion, which required more than room for a handful of people. And three wolves.

They were welcomed with a place before the fire, large bowls of water or stew and the removal of the dogs. The cats had removed themselves.

Beside the fireplace, there was also a small boy and an older girl, one with a kettle of hot water and the other with a large tray and a fancier tea service than had been outside the bedchamber's door earlier. Harrel did not know if these two were the same ones from this morning, he did not know them at all, yet they were there to serve him.

"Good morrow," he said to the wolves.

"It isn't," the wolf replied. *Him*, Harrel recognized. "That animal is back. He went after the big cows, but they ran too fast. So, he ate berries. Guess he doesn't like berries either."

AJ had said that Baairs ate almost anything they could catch or just find.

"He finds our kills," the wolf grumbled. "And our cubs. Almost. That's why we're here. Can't have something new trying to kill cubs. They've been running free since they be born. Nothin' around to really hurt 'em, so they don' know about danger. Come near to runnin' right up to that creature. Can't have that."

"No. I agree." And those few words, Harrel hoped, would be enough for now. He had no idea what to do about a baair.

The wolf looked at him as if he knew, made something of a bow and left. Two nervous guards—who had clearly never seen wolves this close—hurriedly opened the outer doors for them. The wolf just walked past and outside, where, presumably, the gates were already open. They must have been open either for the wolves to enter or before they arrived. That was something the new Captain of the Guard must know, Harrel thought. He had other things to think about.

"We can use your new spell," he said, taking a sip of his tea. It was barely warm. "Go to where I first saw the baair."

"Actually, no. I can't go where I've never been. The spell's not strong enough, and I've little practice. Impossible to say where we'd go. When." She wiggled a finger at his tea and her own. Steam immediately came up from the cups. The two apprentices, or just convenient servants, looked surprised and nervous by the simple magic.

Clearly, the Wizard rarely interacted with the people in the Keep. It was named for him, but only because he used the tower room for his magic. This was what included him in the gathering of Wizards by the FaerFolk. He used magic for himself and no others.

"Horses, then." He spotted an older man in a Magical's blue tunic. It was worn out and only had cloth embroidery instead of gold. "Have the StableMaster prepare horses. And pack horses. At least three. With two more available," he ordered. If he obeyed, he was some sort of steward. Master of this or that.

"M'Lord," the man said with a slight bow. He was a steward.

"Two. Three days travel," Harrel said. "These fine villagers first." He managed to say that with a smile.

He gestured to the fireside table with its place setting, bowls of fruit and porridge, and backed chairs. Harrel, as High Lord, took the one that looked more like a throne—after convincing Blacktail to stop being a lazy CatDragon and fly off his shoulder. Vallezza took the lesser chair beside him. Then, they began to listen to the complainants and questions while being served the rest of the morning meal.

Most of the time, someone in the crowd of blue-tunicked watchers came forward to claim the problem, so by the time the morning was over, and he and Vallezza had made a quick stop to the common bathingroom—once again making the servants and cleaners nervous—before they went outside.

There were four saddled horses, two more with packs and two more in reserve. A guard—with some gold on his tunic—and an older stiff lady occupied two of the saddled horses.

"Probably should be at least three guards," Harrel muttered. "As well as more ladies for you."

"The wolves, M'Lord," the guard said with what was becoming the usual bow." Are outside the gate. They've been fed. From the kitchen."

"Someone has a lot of curiosity and nerve," the Sorceress said as Harrel escorted her to a horse. The hoard of stablelads were there to help her mount. Harrel just took the reins from one and mounted by himself.

Without a word or a wave, he led the small party out of the gate. The wolves were lying in the grass. They yawned, stretched, and padded to whatever place suited their rank while traveling. Blacktail flew overhead, circling down the Road.

Harrel, being High Lord, waved at the villagers, and when he had enough attention, he dismissed the guard and the lady—as if handing them to the innkeeper for the rest of the day. Or until the lady was so offended, she left.

"Now you will have to cook your own meals," Vallezza stated.

"I can cook," Harrel growled. "I can even catch my own meals."

He proved his words that night, and the next two, although it was difficult to snare enough rabbits for three wolves.

Blacktail caught his own.

The next day reunited the pack, and with Blacktail being their eyes, the males went hunting. Vallezza and the females watched over the cubs by watching for the baair. The wolf pack was hunting deer and that often brought him near. That and the cubs. They were old enough to play, a game of run and chase now, leaving any safety without a thought about how quickly they could become a quick snack.

Harrel and the wolves brought back a deer, some for the fire, the rest of the kill for a feast.

The baair did not join them.

It was Blacktail on an easy rabbit hunt who saw him.

Harrel and Vallezza left the pack horses in the care of the wolves. Either they were extremely docile animals or did not know anything about wolves. The other two were more willing to leave the wolves, but not to face the baair. They had to be left at the head of yet another small valley with grass and a small stream. A perfect place for horses, but less for two humans walking without even a path through the deep grass and flowering weeds.

Blacktail led the pair to the pond that was the beginning of the small stream. Water flowed down a hill, which was now scoured rock, and into a shallow pool. A portion of a deer carcass lay on the bank along with the root ball of a tree that had fallen off the shelf. It had cracked into a number of logs and pieces.

The baair had one log, an arm's length taller than Harrel, and was lifting one end, throwing it upwards so it slid down the waterfall and back to the baair. He lifted it again and flung it to the top to slide down the waterfall to the basin and the baair again.

"He...he's playing," Vallezza exclaimed.

"That log must weigh a ton." Harrel decided it weighed far more than he could lift.

"He's just a youngling. Doesn't know any rules because there's no one to teach him. I doubt he even knows where he is."

They both watched the baair play with the log again, before he stopped, turned and sniffed the air. Suddenly, he reared onto his hind feet, standing to wave his massive paws in the air and roar. Harrel and Vallezza were still transfixed. Staring.

The baair dropped to all fours and charged at them, mouth open and fangs showing.

The Sorceress raised both hands over her head and then in a circle to her sides. The baair was closer and his growls were the sound of his rage.

"Scream," she shrieked, lifting her hands again.

Without a thought, the Hafling screamed. It had been a long time since he let loose that side of him or showed his own fangs. The sounds echoed in the valley as the two of them, Baair and Hafling, came closer. Harrel wanted to do more than scream. The beast was faster than he thought. Faster than a human and even a hillcat. He pulled in another breath although he was now shaking...

Vallezza's arms dropped.

The baair slowed, digging his paws into the earth to stop. He stared, growling, but turned and lumbered quickly back to the waterfall and his unguarded kill. He put two paws on it, but the fang-baring growl was a nervous warning.

Harrel kept growling, breathing, but he carefully turned and walked away, keeping the baair in sight. Vallezza just turned her back to the creature, and it hurried farther down the valley. Above them, Blacktail made tight circles and whimpering sounds before he decided to land on the Hafling's shoulder. Harrel was still growling but allowed the little dragon to land.

Finally, he asked Val, "What did you do?"

"Became far too interested in watching a young baair. I forgot what I was looking at." She breathed. "That thing was fast."

"Magic," he growled.

"A simple spell. Only it didn't work the first time." They continued walking back to the horses. "I had to repeat it before he believed we had suddenly grown into monsters. Something to leave alone. If I pull in enough magic," she thought aloud, "I should be able to protect the wolves. With the same spell. I'll need to get them together to see if it will work."

"In a day or two, the baair will probably want to eat again. The wolves certainly will. We can hunt down a deer or two."

The pack was used to hunting together and accepted that the Hafling and the CatDragon would be hunting deer with them. Blacktail went off first, to find a herd near to the baair's valley. When he found the deer, he made enough circles to find the baair, as well.

Then the wolves followed his directions and chased the herd close to where Harrel was waiting with his bow to guarantee a good shot and a kill.

It took time for him to skin the deer and slice off a piece of venison for himself and the Sorceress. All the while the wolves growled or snapped at one another. A deer was a very good meal, but there were adults and cubs now waiting for a large share.

And a baair also waiting for his share. Drawn by the smell of fresh blood.

"Don't run," Vallezza ordered when one or two whined.

The baair came closer, loudly sniffing the air.

When he stood, Vallezza began to pull in magic. There was a lot of magic in the valleys and mountains because there were few who used it. Faeries of various sizes. Nymphs in the trees. And a few of the WaterFolk.

Being magical, Harrel could feel the pull, but other than a few spells, he could not duplicate what she did so effortlessly. She pulled the magic in and swirled it around the watching wolves.

"There," she said, smiling. "Start growling at him."

They only looked confused, uncomfortable as the large animal came forward on all fours. He bared his impressive fangs and... stopped, as confused as the wolves. They used the moment to show their fangs.

The baair began to back away. Then ran. Away.

The wolves stared before returning to being wolves and eating. Like everyone in the mountains, they knew winter was coming.

"It worked," Harrel said. "But..."

Vallezza smiled. "Always use simple magic whenever possible."

"But..."

"The baair has the right to live. As a baair. So do the wolves. But from now on, whenever the baair sees a wolf, he will see a monster. About three times his size. One wolf will make him thoughtful. A pack, even if they're cubs, will make him run. And make him go hunt his own deer. Which as we've seen, he can do. And if you care to, my Lord Hafling, you can take all the acclaim for the solution."

"Only if you do something like that to the Trolls and the villagers.

"Unethical."

"I suppose then that we will have to winter with all of them." He grinned. "And surprise them with unexpected visits from the High Lord. Aught to get those *damned* bridges built in no time. "And..." he smiled at her, "the unexpected will make sure we are left alone. Occasionally. They'll do their best to avoid bringing themselves to our attention."

"My Lady." He extended his hand. "Can you move horses and a dragon as well as ourselves?"

"I'll have to make a large door. I can't ride in, though. Too large," she said thoughtfully. "But, yes. I should be able to transport all of us."

"And mayhap an announcing trumpet? Just a warning, of course."

"For the Hafling Lord?" She took his hand with a little bow and a smile. "Mayhap a handful of trumpets."

CHAPTER 25

AJ and Ja-hon stepped through the door in the chilly stone tower and into warm air and waterfalls. The FaerFolk woman had preceded them, but she was not there now. Beyond the falls there was either a smooth lake or a very lazy river. Almost no ripples disturbed the reflections of the columns of rock and greenery that touched the cloudless blue sky.

"Where are we?" Ja-hon asked, trying to see everything at once.

"Pandora," AJ replied.

"What?"

"Sorry. Movie reference. It's a science fiction world. Only there, those rocks would be floating up in the air. And be the place where the dragons, or whatever they call them, live." She stepped down a few steps. Looking down to see if she was on rocks or actual steps. Whichever, they seemed the best route for exploring.

There were plants and flowers on either side, and she touched a bright red flower. A bee flew away. Following its flight, she now saw a house—or something like a house—at the foot of the rock-stairs. A fanciful cottage on the lakeshore. Wooden and unlike anything she had seen so far.

All the huts and the Keep's stone houses had slate roofs or wood and what might be called 'thatch.' This roof had moss. Artistic moss. On unbelievably large, thin pieces of slate.

The house itself was stone-worked, with influences from Japan and Home and Gardens TV. A porch with garden furniture in wrought iron. Wide doorways, and inside, open floor plans. And more wood. Artistically, yet a comfortable table and chairs, a soft couch, and then a modern kitchen. Sort of. More modern than anything in the Kingdom that AJ had seen, but not even matching what was in her apartment. There was even a small cabinet under the glossy wood counters that looked like a refrigerator. When AJ opened the door, there was a glass pitcher with cold milk inside. This was for tea, since a tea kettle was making noise in the fireplace. But no frozen dinners. No motor needed for the cold. Just magic.

And astonishing beauty.

"Could this be ours, or are we trespassing?" Ja-hon asked. AJ was in the kitchen area while he opened doors off the common room. "Bathing room. One bedroom. Humm. One bed, as well."

"Good. We don't need two beds. Just why are we here... Wherever here is?"

"Dinner would be good," the more practical Ja-hon said.

AJ only groaned, dropped her pack on the table, and stepped out the back door. This side also had a deck or patio, but no furniture. The lake—or river—must have curved around because there were stairs leading down to a small dock. AJ took them down to the water.

Ja-hon followed.

There were fish in the water. Multi-colored white, orange, brown and black. Large Koi. Medium. And off to one side, the small fancier goldfish.

"The big ones are Koi," she told Ja-hon. "I've only seen them in tanks. Not...wild, I guess."

They watched the fish for a while. The water was so clear, they could see the green seaweed on the bottom, seeming to caress the fish. It waved back and forth as if to get free of its roots. Other fish swam... AJ stopped her observations. Whatever was swimming in the seaweed was enjoying the clear, inviting water.

She suddenly began stripping. Heavy boots. Socks. Cargo

pants. Belts and after a brief pause, she pulled off her shirt.

In only sports bra and panties, she dove off the dock.

Ja-hon was not fast enough to be in unison with her, but he was close.

The water was warm. Not warm bath water, just not cold. Chilly in spots. Fish hurried out of their way, only to swim back and inspect them.

"Where'd you learn to swim, Ja-hon?" she asked.

"River. During those long summer evenings."

"You could've caught something in those rivers."

"Didn't care. I was hot and wanted to swim. So, I did."

"In..." she teased.

"Same as now. In whatever I was wearing. Or not." He splashed her.

He had a decent crawl, better than hers and could avoid her return splashes—to swim around, catch her from behind...

There was a cough from the dock, and both stopped playing.

A man was on the dock. Someone too far beyond handsome, and while he was dressed for a summer night, the transparent long coat was as revealing as the skirt he wore.

"Trespassing," AJ breathed, hiding her whisper behind a wet hand.

"Definitely."

She wiped away the water on her face. "Hello."

"Lady Astellyn is here," the man said and turned away to stride up the dock. As he did, his coat and skirt turned opaque, covering his nudity.

"Hey, mister. You wouldn't have a *towel*, would you?" AJ shouted.

He kept walking away, but first one, then another towel drifted out of the sky and landed on their piled clothes.

"Magic." AJ climbed out of the water. She looked up, smiled, but the man was out of sight, so she stripped out of her wet undies.

Ja-hon did the same.

"He was naked," she said.

"Saw that." He toweled himself off. Dropped the towel in favor of his pants. They did not care if the new man was on the edge of fashion. Both wondered if they would find a time and place again to get naked themselves. Now that they knew they wanted to, they did not want to be stopped.

Now was not the time. It was again someone else's place and not very private. They finished getting dressed to walk up the stairs. There, they saw no one until they entered the kitchen.

Lady Astellyn was also someone new, but she sat at the kitchen table completely at ease as they entered. Two mugs of steaming tea were set in front of empty chairs. A tea service sat in the middle of the table.

"Did you enjoy the swim?" she asked. Unlike the man's, her voice was warm and friendly.

"Yes. The water's just warm enough." AJ sat and fiddled with the tea things. She liked tea, but *real* tea. Plain black. Not even Earl Grey.

A plate of cookies appeared where none had been. Ja-hon took one.

"Ja-hon." The Lady smiled. "We've been watching you. You're a welcome surprise. Calm. Gentle. Knowing, but unafraid. Or at least not showing fear. Yet you tended to one of the mammoths. The dragons. Horses. You even talked to the wolves. You saw none of these in your world?"

"No, ma'am."

"We thought not." She looked just as quiet and calm as Ja-hon, but on the verge of saying something important and difficult. "We need someone like you. To quietly do what can't be ordinary for you. And with an acceptable partner."

AJ's eyebrows went up, and she understood the meaning of 'looking askance.' She was the one who talked, led them into this curious world, and had no idea what she was doing. Yet she was his partner?"

"We need a person...a human, most of us agree, to train a dragon and her riders."

She let the statement sit flatly on the table. The two drank their tea, since there was little to say.

"We will trade, of course. This..." She waved a hand at the house. "Whatever you need, now and after you finish. I'd say that you can even go back to Elsewhere, but you've been gone so long, there's really nothing left of your world."

"Wait. You mean there's been a war or something?"

"No. Forgive me. Your...place in your world is gone. You've forgotten. And the longer you stay the more time will pass. And in your time, things and events tend to cover over your...prior presence. Papers fade. People get old. They forget."

"They die, you mean."

"Yes. That too." There was a touch of sadness in her voice.

"Train dragons," Ja-hon murmured. "Why me? Really?"

She paused long enough for them to know she was debating honesty. "The one to ask is the Ranger," she said finally. "And he would do his best for us. He and the Sorceress. He rode an untrained dragon, and it near killed him. He still cannot forget. Or completely forgive himself and Vallezza for having another person rescue him. You have no such fears. At least of dragons."

She looked calmly at him as if she knew far more of his past than AJ. Or even Ja-hon himself.

"You already have a partner. There needn't be anyone else in your life. That...That was a problem. Long ago."

Silence fell, and this time they both had a cookie and the tea in their magically refilled cups.

AJ spoke to him. "It's more your choice than mine." She lifted her hand and straightened a finger for each point she made. "We've nowhere to go. No way to support ourselves. Neither of us really have any reason to...to try going back. I've been in college long enough to know it's time to quit. I haven't much of a career or future because of what I've done. You have choices because of what's been done *to* you. So. Are you scared of a little dragon?"

"I expect it's a big one."

"At the moment it's little," the Lady put in.

"Against..." AJ raised her thumb. "We're not one hundred percent welcome in Here... or in the Kingdom. Same reasons as above." She spread her fingers. "So...?"

He took a deep breath, and nodding, finally said, "I'm in."

"Good." The Lady clapped her hands. "Then now you can go meet the young dragon, Saysslith."

"Now?" they asked as one.

"Now. Before you think about it...or eat something she won't tolerate. Like steak and French fries."

"I knew this was going to mean *lettuce*. Green stuff," AJ muttered.

The woman laughed. "Just for now. Until she gets used to your smell and won't get confused. She's quite young, you realize. Almost just hatched."

"Dragons hatch?"

"Like lizards," Ja-hon said. "Almost."

"You ever see a lizard?" AJ demanded.

"Not that long ago. In a pet store," he said, with a cold edge which reminded her that she knew little of his life; that he was really not the Albert Square Monster.

"Once," she countered.

He nodded.

"Fine. Let's go meet her. Where ever she is."

"Actually, she's right outside your back door." The woman rose and with that same knowing smile, led them to the back deck and a gate AJ swore had not been there before.

They had not wanted a surprise meeting, AJ thought, and

knew she was right. There was a curved wooden bridge over the lake or inlet, but now there was another valley, more mountains and a cooler temperature. At the top of the bridge, they could now see another building, something of a barn or a large stable. With a white- painted fence in front of it. There was a rooster on the fence and hens below, pecking at the dirt and grass.

"Saysslith," the woman called in a voice anyone would answer.

A dragon, as big as a horse, poked her head out the open door. It was younger than the two CatDragons. A smooth blue-green dragon without the sharp frills and 'beard' of her elders. A lizard's head but with long leathery ears folded back, round golden eyes, and a forked tongue that flicked in and out between sharp, but babyish looking teeth, tasting the air. A kitten's teeth. The long fangs would—presumably-grow out later. A long, thin neck. Kitten claws on three-toed feet. Front and back. A fat-bellied body, strong haunches and a fat, short tail ending in the flare of a dragon's triangle.

A pretty animal, just another reptile, it seemed, until she burped a puff of smoke, reminding her visitors that she would grow into a fire-breathing dragon.

Still, Ja-hon reached over the fence, his arm stretched out, fingers curled under as he controlled the desire to wiggle those fingers in front of the dragon's nose. She came nearer, but not close enough to touch.

The Lady set a hand on his shoulder. "We wondered, we discussed what to do with her when we found her. There are now so few dragons. A good thing, some say, but that is not for us to decide."

"She's alive and deserves our best?" AJ said without doubting, or contradicting, such powerful magic.

"Well..." The Lady shrugged. "The best all of us can do. Ja-hon. You."

"And what do I do?" AJ asked. "Besides muck out the stable?"

The Lady straightened. "You seem to know people. There are seven candidates for riders. She only needs one."

"And I get to choose...? No favorites? No pre-selection?"

"That you ask, says you see the problems. One rider from seven. Decided by you. Ja-hon. And the dragon. No one else. They're behind the stable." She sighed. "Waiting."

"Wonderful," AJ muttered. "Ja-hon. Get to know Saysslith. I've got work to do. See you later."

He wanted to ask questions, but he had his own tasks and problems. He could, he supposed, ask the Lady, but he was not sure he dared.

AJ walked around to the back of the stable. There were seven young people lounging on whatever could be considered a seat. Some chairs. Bales of hay and straw. All of them were about college-age, dressed in excellent tunics and pants. Plus, new shiny boots. The rich kids' versions of peasant wear. And all slightly bored. Tired of waiting. All entitled to much better treatment.

"Okay, gang, time to get to work. You two. Find shovels. Start indoors and clean up the stable. No old straw. Nothing from the dragon." She pointed at two more, without worrying if there were two of the three boys or two girls left. Everyone was going to do everything regardless of who or what they were. "You and you. Undo the straw bales. It'll go in the stable. You get the water and food detail."

Some moved. Most did not.

"Tomorrow. Working uniforms. Seven pairs of sturdy boots." She lifted her own booted foot. "Blue, I think. Blue-green shirts. Dark blue pants. With pockets. Well? Move."

Six reluctantly stood. One did not.

"There should be a StableMaster here somewhere. Go find him. Or her. Shovels. Gloves. You're going to be taking care of a dragon. Get to know her. Move." She sounded like a drill sergeant.

Again, the six moved and one did not. AJ waited until the six were a little distance away. "Okay. No *grunt* work for you? You're just going to be a rider."

The young man lifted his head. "Yes. I am."

"No, you're not. You're out. Go home."

"But..."

"Leave. Now."

"You can't tell me—"

"I just did. Get outta here. Complain all you want but go."

He stood, bracing to do something.

AJ's hand dropped to her holster. The revolver was empty, but he did not know that. Just the way she touched it told him it was a dangerous weapon.

He left.

AJ breathed, glared at the others, then set out to find Ja-hon. He was now inside the fence, brushing the small dragon. AJ thought perhaps she was purring.

"You're doing better than me," she growled, but softly, as she leaned on the fence.

"I could hear. She needs company."

"There's six of 'em. Working. There were seven."

"A dragon needs dragons for company. Needs to learn how to be a dragon. Not a horse." He'd said this as if he hadn't just learned about brushing horses. "Humph. Big dragons are too dangerous. Slash would have been good company, but... Like racehorses have...not dogs, but cats for companions. Bigger cats than Blacktail. Bigger CatDragons."

"Ummm. There's six of those riders. One of them should know how to contact Vallezza. She'll know how to get or create more CatDragons."

Saysslith lost interest in Ja-hon and watched AJ climb over the fence. The dragon trotted over and playfully sniffed AJ. She carefully patted the dragon on her nose then sidled past, into the stable. There were still six recruits inside, working. Awkwardly and laughing at each other and themselves.

Maybe we'll make it yet, AJ mused, then asked them how she could connect with the Sorceress.

Easy, they all agreed and, with a snap of fingers, popped her into far-off Premontii.

CHAPTER 26

AJ screeched and landed on a small rug. On her backside and skidded its length on a polished wooden floor. Even when the 'ride' stopped, she kept her eyes closed.

"Uh. Vallezza?" she asked when she remembered.

"It's AJ, isn't it?" a voice replied, tinged with laughter.

"AJ, the person who knows *kids*." She opened her eyes and turned toward the voice. "Sorry about the interruption."

She and the Sorceress were in a small office-looking room with a table, chairs, and a cabinet filled with books and scrolls. AJ sat on the only rug.

"I... We need a favor. CatDragons. Ja-hon's got this baby dragon from the FaerFolk. He's going to train her, and he says she needs dragon company. CatDragons would be best. But big ones. As big as cats come. Maine Coons. British Shorthairs." The words came out in a rush, not knowing if the Sorceress understood them.

And the Lady Astellyn suddenly appeared, having followed AJ. "Sorry. Problem with younglings. It won't happen again. "Please." She offered AJ a hand up. "Come back with me. Establish a path. And a time? For the CatDragons?"

"Harrel should be able to get two perfect cats," Vallezza replied with an amused smile. "I had no choice in the choosing of Blacktail or Slash, but he's met a number of them."

AJ stood, keeping the Lady's hand since she simply did not release her. Despite her perfection, AJ thought that the Lady looked a bit more human. Perhaps she was—or had been—once. The human problems—ruling an entire world and yet not ruling the children—had remained, despite the perfection.

Now, was not the time for her to wonder. The Lady held out her other hand to Vallezza and together the three of them walked through a shimmer hanging in the middle of the room...

***

They stepped together onto the back deck.

"Outside is usually best," the Lady said to the Sorceress. "You've seen enough? To come back?"

The Sorceress nodded, stepped forward into yet another shimmer...and disappeared. AJ took a deep, calming breath. She did not believe she would ever become used to stepping through non-existent doors to entirely different places.

"Then I shall leave you," the Lady said and stepped into another shimmer and left.

AJ stared at nothing for a moment, then wandered back into the house, wondering if there was a supply of something harder than cider in one of the cabinets. Ja-hon was at the kitchen table eating a cookie.

"Where..." he began, but there was a knock on the real back door.

Harrel and Vallezza, each with a cat in their arms, had already returned to the back deck.

"Tea," AJ said to herself, for she was getting more and more disoriented. "For them too," she ordered as Ja-hon went outside. "And probably for their talking cats," she muttered.

The cat Harrel held was kin to a Maine Coon. A very large, but not fat, grey tabby with distinctive black stripes. A very fluffy tail and white paws. Gold eyes and an ordinary supercilious expression.

The other was almost as large, a Tuxedo cat with shiny black fur, white paws and whiskers, and oval gold eyes.

"We thought it better, for them, to travel as cats." Vallezza allowed the Tuxedo to drop to the floor.

He...a big confident male...shivered, then stretched. "Hello."

"He talks."

"'Course I do. I'm a village cat. I live outside. Mostly. But I know people." He stopped and sniffed. "Burnt?"

"Dragon, most like," Ja-hon replied. "And me. We'll all smell like a dragon before too long."

"Hummm. It's not too bad." He sat and began to wash his paw. He looked up at Ja-hon. "She says you've got cat food?"

"Yes. Nibbles. But mostly mice. You'd think there'd be none. Here. But they're in the stable."

AJ came out with a tray, a tea pot and cups. She set the tray on the table, and smiling, the Sorceress and Harrel moved away from the cats to take their share.

"She said...a name?" the cat prompted. "Short. Easier than mine own."

He and the other cat looked expectantly at AJ. Ja-hon would, might, take care of them, but AJ looked like everything else was part of her new role.

"Ah...*Tux*, I suppose. And *Tabby*. Short. Sort of...exotic. Fit for a dragon's companions?"

"What does the word mean?" the tabby asked.

"Your coat..." AJ said. "Your coat. It's changing."

The cat's fur was becoming scales. Long, thin scales of mottled grey while the black stripes were more like shiny leather. His tail was a feather. An ostrich feather—if ostriches were still dinosaurs. His paws enlarged, as did the claws, becoming longer and red. Ears enlarged and became tipped with more 'feathers.'

Tux had a snake's scales, lying flat and shiny against his long, powerful body. Dexterous, long white paws—excellent for opening doors and boxes—had silver-white claws. His whiskers had elongated as had his ears, which could now flip back to lie flat against his head.

Then, with a rush that made Harrel start, they both grew wings. Dragon-leather wings both fragile and strong. Delicately made and lightweight for flying. Leathery to lift the heavy bodies and resistant to claws and swords.

Both lifted their wings, flapping them. Tux lifted off the deck. Harrel looked away, managing to breathe, while Vallezza moved closer to him. Tabby just sat, wings going up and down.

"Pigeons," Tux chortled and flew off the deck, narrowly missing the top rail.

Tabby managed a small lift, came down and lifted again. He made a thoughtful noise and headed toward the stairs. Up. Then down. Flying. But his version of flight. He looked capable of flight, if necessary, but the rhythmic lifts, barely with his tail off the ground, suited him.

Tux was doing circles, occasionally brushing the tops of trees and bushes, before he disappeared. Tabby did the same but followed, closer to the stairs and the open space.

"They'll find the dragon." Vallezza gave Harrel a cup of tea.

"Wings," he managed, drinking the tea. "Mayhap I'll meet your Saysslith...before she gets too big, as she's a growing dragon." He straightened, shivering. Yet he lifted his head and became the High Lord. "We're changing. No one really wants to, but those..." He almost swore. Aggravating a Ranger was understandable because all a Ranger could do was suggest. Forward a report to the King. The High Lord was in charge and present. People could not afford to aggravate him. *"My* three villages are going to have bridges built by the Trolls. Like that or not. They can complain all they want. And perhaps, have some things changed to their liking. But they are going to have to do without wizards, nobles, and servants."

"But not magic," Vallezza said. "Those two CatDragons are magic by themselves, but there will be more. Blacktail has found a lady cat who admires him and is willing to turn into a CatDragon.

So, there'll be kittens. Catdragon kittens."

She raised her cup and saluted Harrel. "Even you, M'Lord, will become used to changes. And wings."

Harrel tried, very hard, not to glare at her, or flinch. Of all the changes in his life, she was the most important, the one thing he would not change. But he knew from her smile she was going to gift him with her teasing laughter. The hillcat in him disliked teasing and laughter. Especially laughter. Unless it was hers.

"It would be interesting to see where that winged horse you *say* you saw came from. But..." She shrugged. Her look questioned even *one* horse with wings. "Where there's one horse with wings, there is an entire herd. All with wings. Fluttering."

He managed not to react to her teasing, but knew the old image of the white horse flying away into the snowstorm was now entrenched in his memory. As soon as he, as the High Lord got the new bridges built—and made certain the two CatDragons had convinced a fire-breathing dragon to be civil, he—the Ranger—would want to go find the flying horses.

The High Lord took a deep breath. "Perhaps we should follow the CatDragons and meet Saysslith." He almost added, *before she gets too big. Or worse—before she grows wings.*

"Get her used to meeting strangers," he said instead.

"Good idea, M'Lord." AJ waved at the stairs. "She'll outgrow her stable soon, I understand. When she gets wings she'll grow even faster."

And after I find out, she thought, *why a Hafling Lord, who doesn't fear wooly mammoths or dangerous 'black' birds and wizards, is nervous around dragons. Big dragons. Not CatDragons. She had a second—*

The very air erupted in a screech, followed by screams and shrill curses, before both CatDragons arrowed up the stairs, flat missiles aimed across the room.

The Sorceress opened her arms and grabbed...

CHAPTER 27

Two humans, one Hafling and two CatDragons in her arms, and she dumped them with enough flowing magic for the heavier, non-flying people to fall onto the stone floor of the High Lord's bed chamber.

The Sorceress raced forward to slam a window open to the snow and cold. The two CatDragons continued their wild flight out the window without stopping and into the snowstorm to vanish. The sudden cold would slow their flight, Vallezza thought correctly. They would be confused, maybe frightened, but they would probably return when called.

"What the hell?" One voice rose off the floor.

Now Blacktail arrived at the door, accompanied by a young and female housecat. Then there were more of them, all crowding in the doorway. Blacktail eased into the room, along with one very small cat who looked like a black and white kitten—but was a full-grown female; if a cat who only weighed as little as a full cup of tea could be said to be full-grown. Blacktail, then the little cat slinked, cautiously, farther into the room. Blacktail walked to Harrel, and the little cat, after looking at her lap choices, scampered to AJ and climbed onto her lap.

AJ absently petted her.

"Tabby?" The Sorceress called in a gentle, insistent voice and shortly, the CatDragon flew in through the window. Vallezza held out her arms, and the cat, more than the dragon part of her, swooped to her, landed and snuggled.

"Tabby," Vallezza said. "What happened?"

"Meow," Tabby replied, and Vallezza revised her belief that having cats who talked was convenient and helpful.

"Talk, Tabby."

"I don't know," he managed, cuddling closer. "I came down the stairs. That big dragon...Tux was flying. Around her, I think. Not too close," he added hurriedly. "Over the fence. Yes. Over the fence. I was almost there, as well. And she yelled. Screamed. Knocked me tail over head. And Tux was up. Over me. Flying fast. Up the stairs. I followed. Fast. The big dragon was still screaming. People were yelling too. From in the stable. Maybe. I... just went up the stairs. And came here. Inside. Outside." He squeezed his head under the Sorceress's arm and made what must have been a soothing purr, because the other cats left the doorway, and seeing Blacktail with Harrel, chose to run to Ja-hon and climb onto his lap. Some purred at him, while others talked or meowed.

"Val?" Harrel said over the din.

The Sorceress closed her eyes, and still holding Tabby, looked far away. Out of the room, but at nothing. She shook her head. "The *door* is closed," she said and pointing with the CatDragon at AJ, ordered, "You. Think of where we were."

AJ closed her eyes, but she could barely remember the back deck. "My pack," she said. "I left my pack on the kitchen table." That, she remembered.

"All the markings of a fine Ranger," Vallezza murmured and Harrel managed a laugh. It was common knowledge that Rangers lost almost everything they carried.

"But...?" He stood up, helping Blacktail to his shoulder. "Why? What happened?"

"I think, maybe..." Ja-hon began thoughtfully, petting one cat then another. All of them had tried to get as close and comfortable as they could. All of them looked asleep. "Saysslith might have been afraid of them."

"Cats?" Harrel asked.

"Dragons. When I went into the stable to get something of hers, there was nothing there for a dragon. There were harnesses and saddles. Brushes. Things belonging to horses. But nothing for a dragon. I don't think they even know how to raise a dragon. And they don't know how well she can hear. I whispered to her while I was in the stable, and she heard me. Clearly. I'd bet she could hear them when she was inside her shell."

"Inside, but...Inside? How would you know that?"

"I may have seen only one lizard, but that pet store I spoke of had lots of snakes. One laid her eggs, and they hatched. Snakes. Small, but ready to be snakes. Or dragons. I doubt that anyone knew, so they talked. I heard the prospective riders, and so did she. They talked about dragons. Fire breathing dragons. Fierce dragons. Dangerous." The others waited for him to finish his thoughts. "A dragon is something to be feared. And suddenly, there are two of them. Maybe attacking her."

"They're little," Harrel said, taking the other side of the argument.

Ja-hon pointed to the little cat asleep on AJ's lap. "She's little. Not much of a cat at all. Yet AJ's carefully nervous because there is a cat on her lap."

"She's got claws," AJ said, but carefully petted the cat. It was pressed against her, seeking warmth and comfort. AJ was providing both.

"She's not using her claws. Yet you're afraid of her. So, your movements are nervous. Jerky. You could scare her into clawing. Biting. Running."

AJ stopped petting the cat. It cuddled harder.

Harrel asked, "So, this dragon...is afraid of dragons. Will she get over it? And begin training again?"

"The FaerFolk have locked the door, so to speak," the Sorceress said. "Hard to say what they will want to do if we cannot talk to them. And she'll get bigger, maybe with wings, by the time we come back. *If* we're invited to come back. By then...maybe one of the six will have become... Well, close to her."

"She won't be big enough to ride for a while. Maybe a long while," Ja-hon said. "Does anyone really know about dragons?"

Vallezza and Harrel both shook their heads. But he added an explanation, "A dragon burned the library. Some time ago. A number of books and scrolls were lost. And the people who wrote them have died. Except," he added, remembering. "There's a book, a number of copybooks, said to be written by my namesake. Harrell, a King's Ranger. He killed a dragon. The one that burned... The Dragon's Keep." He had to close his eyes to remember. "I think. Not the big burn on the other side of the Grasslands. Just the Keep. The books may have been about that. Not the dragon's early years. Or training."

"Yet he was the last to train a dragon," Vallezza said, remembering what she had been told.

"And where are these books?" AJ asked. She carefully resumed petting the little cat.

Harrel looked at Vallezza.

"The Scribe's Hall?" she said. "Though most of the scribes are just copying the old records. There aren't enough scribes to copy all the books and scrolls." Her tone was clearly disapproving. She was one of the numbers who said, aloud, that girls could be apprentices and then Badged Scribes. She and the like-minded others were ignored by the Scribes.

"So where are these old books?" AJ asked.

"The new library. Under the mountain, most like," Harrel replied, thoughtfully, but without any concrete knowledge. "Never been there."

"I have," Vallezza exclaimed. "And it's a mess. Everything got dumped. To save everything from the dragons, they say." Clearly, this was another of her complaints against the Scribes. "There is, or was, a single Scribe trying to restore order to...to the boxes most like."

AJ ticked her tongue.

The others asked, "What?"

"That's what I do!" She stood, cradling the little cat in her arms. "Did. I searched for old books and letters. Read them. Made sense of them. I sold most of what I found. That's how I ended up here. Following directions in an old journal. And that's probably why I'll never be a scribe. I was supposed to give everything to the *college*, the Scribe's Hall, not sell it so I could keep going to...the Hall. To listen to the Masters. But that's what I do. Dig through old stuff. Old books."

"You can't read Common," Ja-hon said. "I can learn words. A few written words at first. In copy books, you said."

Harrel expressed his thoughts aloud. "There would be more writing in Ranger Harrell's books than in an apprentice's. The word Dragon. Mayhap even drawings. Other Rangers make drawings. As best we can."

"More than enough. To start. How do we get there? To this library under a mountain. More horses? More riding? Days and days on the road?"

"N-No, I can take you. Bring you back here," Vallezza said, and like Harrel, thinking aloud. "But better stay here at night. With us. As valued guests of the High Lord."

"Probably more comfortable than the library," Harrel said, "At least until a new Lord is elected. They'd be visiting scribes. Needing new packs. Whatever else you need. Courtesy of the High Lord." He actually smiled. "Knew there was a reason to be High Lord."

"Good. Because the High Lord has a small problem." Vallezza bowed, though she held a CatDragon. "What do you do about them?" She gestured at Ja-hon and his hoard of cats. "Do you need a cat herder? Or more CatDragons?"

"It's their choice. Which is your task, M'Lady. You get to ask all of them. I probably have a hall full of people. Waiting for me."

"Yes, M'Lord." She smiled, managing a curtsey instead of a bow.

Harrel only smiled at the teasing. "As High Lord, I am second to the King. Correct?"

"Yes, M'Lord." If not holding Tabby she would have put hands on hips and looked suspiciously at him.

"Then I will have the new High Lord report to King Gallen. That he, or mayhap, she has been elected, while I, the previous High Lord, have gone off hunting."

"Hunting, M'Lord?"

"Yes. Hunting flying horses. Where there was one, there should be a herd. As High Lord, I will have to find them myself since I am the only one who knows exactly where I first saw that white *flying* horse."

"Mayhap, you may come along," he said, trying to be nobly gracious.

"Thank you, M'Lord." Again, she curtsied, but as the door closed behind him, she smiled and warned, "Flying horses have wings, Lord Ranger. It's hard enough for you to be Dragon Master. Do you really think you can ride a flying horse, as well?"

He lifted his head and ordered the other two dragons to attend him, and as many cats or dragons who wished. He was deliberately being The High Lord. Even AJ and Ja-hon understood the royal gesture. He was inviting his guests into his small castle to work, since he had led them into a small room off the common area. Sooner or later, a servant or the Head Woman herself, would come to see what the High Lord wanted. And to find out who the new people were and why so many cats were running from room to room. The gossip would make serving all of them with bed chambers and meals, both people and cats, worth the trade.

The Sorceress watched, her smile fading. She thought about the dragon and the FaerFolk. The screams she had heard from them seemed more like fear and panic rather than pain. Not those of a panicked youngster flaming her captors. A terrified youngster who did not know what she was. Running away.

But she was Big. Larger now than a good-sized horse. With fangs and claws...to rip apart a stable and scatter humans.

But she was dealing with very powerful Magicals who had closed off all access to her, her stable—or what was left of it—and a 'simple' house by a lake.

Forever? She questioned herself.

In time—their time—the dragon would grow. Herself, her wings and her ability to blow bursts of dragon fire.

How much of a danger would she be then? To them? To the Kingdom?

The answer depended on who moved as quickly as she had, isolating the dragon. Moving the apprentice riders to safety.

From what she had seen, none of them, not even the Lady who closed the doors, could soothe a dragon. The riders were young and entitled, expertly trained, powerful Magicals.

They were not Dragon Riders.

Her thoughts listed what she really knew of dragons. Real dragons. Not CatDragons—who were honestly capable of destruction, small though they were. There were, or had been, only two real dragons. Michael's dragon, and now Ja-hon's dragon.

Neither of them was afraid. Michael was awed and thrilled. Ja-hon was cautious...but he was not afraid. Of wolves. Or small dragons. Or big ones. That's why the Lady had chosen him instead of Harrel. The Ranger was wonderfully brave, but he was now afraid of dragons.

What would the six apprentices feel toward a terrified, rampaging *big* dragon? One that could trample them without a thought. Rip through a wooden stable as it tried to flee two tiny dragons.

If they had any sense, all six riders would be afraid. It would no longer be an honor to become a Dragon Rider. A challenge, maybe. But not something wondrous and bonding.

They could not bond with something they were afraid of.

Michael and Ja-hon were not afraid. Both were unique and unafraid. Michael because he did not know about real dragons; Ja-hon because he did not remember how to be afraid.

Harrel had been afraid, but he was a trained Ranger and a dissembling hillcat. A dragon would not have sensed his deeply buried fear because he was simply too busy surviving.

But that was what kept Dragon Riders alive. They were trained, and they were not afraid.

Ja-hon could teach that, if he could find even one apprentice who was not afraid. And if the FaerFolk would allow him to return. The FaerFolk were divided. Some wanted interaction with the humans; some did not.

Did any of them really want to do the work of interacting with a baby dragon? Do so without being afraid of it?

She did not know. Perhaps she would never know, unless, in the future, a dragon entered the Kingdom to find the people it remembered because of their brief care.

Or burning the Kingdom into a black smear because of the terrorizing little dragons.

There would be a large number of CatDragons if these people and cats continued, rather heedlessly, to produce them.

Sighing, she set herself the task of watching over all of them. She would have to tell Harrel, whether he was High Lord or Dragon Master, because he was still My Lord Ranger and charged with protecting the Kingdom, even from dangers he could not foresee.

Yet, as she left the room, she smiled. Perhaps there would still be time to hunt for flying horses. Preferably just the two of them...and probably a CatDragon or two.

Flyers finding flyers.

JoAnn Parsley was born and raised in Binghamton, NY, met her husband of 56 years while serving in the Navy, and traveling the world sparked her interest in art and storytelling. Having studied art in New York City, Weber State College in Utah, and Pellissippi State Community College in Tennessee, she also has a degree in English from Chaminade University, and her oils and pastels have won awards in multiple exhibits around the country. Now a retired professional portrait and landscape artist living in Knoxville, she has found the time to pursue her love of writing fantasy stories. CatDragon is her third novel in "The Hafling" series about being different and gaining respect for what you *do*, rather than who you *are*.

Be sure to read JoAnn's first two novels...

The Hafling, half human—half hillcat, is a young slave, beaten, abused, and hated by all. A King's Ranger rescues him, treats him proper, and makes him his apprentice. The student Ranger chooses a name, Harrel, and he learns social skills as he struggles to overcome his anger toward humans. His journey through the Kingdom and into adulthood is fraught with dangers from Dwarfs, Barbarians, Ogres, and worse, Commoner boys. However, it's also a magical land of fairies, sprites, trolls, and a white-winged horse he saves along the way. Acting as the eyes and ears of the King, the Hafling Ranger discovers a dark plot against the humans, and soon, all their lives will depend on Harrel successfully reaching the castle to deliver a message to his King...a dire warning of impending doom, but he fears no one will believe a Hafling.

Harrel, a King's Ranger, duty-bound to help those in need, rescues two women from the notorious Red Lord; Marrigin: young, beautiful, and dainty, and her companion, Vallezza: a bit older, wiser, and touched by magic. Harrel is smitten with Marrigin, but during the treacherous flight from the Red Lord's guards, circumstances keep her and Harrel apart, but Vallezza is always at his side. In dreams, she takes him to Elsewhere, a modern world where they meet Michael, a young man tormented by bullies because, like the Hafling, he is different. He loves flying: flying kites, flying hawks, flying dragons, and for this odd behavior, he's to be sent to a mental institution. It'll take a Hero, a Sorceress, a Fair Lady, a Royal Prince, and a real dragon to save Michael from a life in captivity.

http://www.twbpress.com

Science Fiction – Horror – Supernatural – Thriller – Romance – and More